BACK TO YOU

LENNY'S BARTENDERS BOOK #3

KATY MICHELE

NOTE TO READERS

Back to You is the third and final installment of the Lenny's Bartenders series.

Characters and various plot elements from *Giving Me Butterflies* and *Crash & Burn* will also be found in *Back to You*. It is recommended but not necessary to read *Giving Me Butterflies* and *Crash & Burn* before reading this book.

Back to You contains topics that may be triggering to some readers. These topics include explicit sexual content, bullying, sexual assault, death (on-page), grief, and therapy. This book also has brief mentions of a school shooting, suicide, domestic violence, alcoholism, and death of loved ones.

If any of these topics are triggering to you,
please do what you need to protect your peace.

PLAYLIST

"I HONESTLY THINK I COULD
KILL YOU RIGHT NOW."

Never Really Over by Katy Perry
Cross My Heart by Marianas Trench
self sabotage by MVSSIE
Already Dead by Daisy Grenade
I Think I'm in Love by Taylor Acorn
Stay The Night by Zedd, Hayley Williams
One More Night by Definitely Maybe
MIRACLE by BOYS LIKE GIRLS
Distracted by Honey Revenge
Dazed & Confused by Broadside
Back To U by SLANDER, William Black
Staring At the Sun by Post Malone, SZA
Two Is... by BOYS LIKE GIRLS, Taylor Swift
Sweet Venom by ENHYPEN
Mess by Real Friends
Remember When by Chris Wallace
The Cure by Lady Gaga
Plus One by Lake Drive
Dangerous Night by Thirty Seconds To Mars
I Like It by Stray Kids

Underscore by Definitely Maybe
Yours by Sueco, Bea Miller

LENNY'S BARTENDERS: TIMELINE

Back to You flashback chapters
↓
Giving Me Butterflies and *Crash & Burn* part one
↓
Giving Me Butterflies epilogue, *Crash & Burn* part two, *Crash & Burn* epilogue/extended epilogue
↓
Back to You

PROLOGUE

ANNIE

WHEN YOU LOVE SOMEONE, you let them go. If they come back, they were always yours. If they don't, they never were.

That's what all good romance movies and books always say.

They remind you that love is always enough.

But what about when it isn't?

Is love enough when you come from two completely different worlds? Is love enough when you have two completely different ideas of what the future holds? Is love enough when your "friends" corner you in a room at a party the night before everyone leaves for college? Is love enough when those girls show you a recording of your boyfriend confirming every single internal worry you ever had about how you weren't good enough for him?

Because it isn't.

Love isn't enough when one of you comes from wealth and stability and the other comes from hardship and insecurity. When one of you comes from a family that knows you'll do great things and the other comes from one that told you that you would never make it out of the trailer park.

When one of you has their whole life planned: college, law school, a career at his dad's law firm. And the other is moving across town to bartend at some dive bar and enrolling in community college with no idea of what to do with her life.

We were never meant to make it past high school.

We were never meant for a happily ever after.

Luke was always meant to realize the shy, introverted girl he sat next to in first grade wasn't going to be part of his epic love story.

You think you know someone after 12 years of being their other half.

Turns out, the person closest to you is the one who holds all the power to hurt you the most.

CHAPTER 1
ANNIE

SEVEN YEARS AGO – AUGUST

WALKING into Lenny's feels more like walking into a home than my real one ever did—the familiar neon lights, the high-top tables, the big bar taking up most of the space, the rock music playing in the background. It hasn't changed a bit since the last time I was here a few years ago.

The only thing missing is my father slumped over at the bar barking for another drink.

"What are you doing here, Vivian?" Emmett's voice brings me back to the present, and the use of my full name jars me. Luke is the one who started calling me Annie when we first met, but the nickname didn't stick for everyone else until freshman year.

The only people who still call me Vivian are my mom and the four girls I used to call my friends.

"I need a job," I reply to Emmett, but there's no way he can hear me with how quiet my voice comes out. There's only one other guy in here besides us, being that it's just after eleven in the morning.

My family has known Emmett's since I was a kid. Emmett, being over a decade older, used to keep an eye on me here when his dad was the one running the place.

I haven't seen Emmett in a few years, not since his parents moved down to Florida and Emmett stayed here in Wisconsin to run the bar, renaming it to honor his late sister.

His huge stature and tattoos are meant to scare off anyone looking for something other than a drink, but he's never scared me. Not when I remember what he looked like before all the ink and muscles.

"What?" Emmett barks from behind the bar. His arms are crossed and his permanent scowl is in full effect.

I didn't expect Emmett and I to reunite after these past years with happy tears and hugs, but I have to resist rolling my eyes at how he thinks his "I'm big and tough" act works on me.

Lenny's has been more of a constant in my life than either of my parents. Coloring or doing homework in the booth in the far-right corner was how I spent most of my childhood. Until Dad went to rehab and ran off with his sponsor four years ago, right after my mom was diagnosed with schizophrenia, refusing any and all help I tried like hell to give her.

It was the only place I could think of running to after what happened last night.

I step closer to the bar, repeating myself a little louder. "I need a job, and I go by Annie now."

"No," is all he says, and I don't know how I forgot Emmett's famous one-word answers.

Silly me to think he would be anything other than a man of few words since I last saw him.

He uncrosses his arm to reach down under the bar in front of him, grabbing a glass and filling it with ice. He grabs the soda gun, no doubt to pour me a Sprite like he always used to, the first time being when he was learning to use it.

Vivian, as Emmett knew her, or the old Annie would have said "okay" and let it go—turned around and walked out of here with her tail tucked between her legs.

But I haven't seen her since leaving Grant's party last night.

Emmett grabs the towel slung over his shoulder to wipe down the bar with one hand, grabbing a cardboard coaster and throwing it onto the bar before setting down the glass of soda with the other, his way of inviting me to sit.

I exhale, frustration bubbling up to the surface, but I push it back down. I can't walk out of here with nothing.

I need a job.

I need to pay for classes and an apartment.

I need to get out of that damn trailer.

Sitting down in the high-top chair in front of Emmett, I meet his eyes again. "I graduated in June, and I turn 19 next month. I need a job."

Before Emmett can respond, a voice chimes in. "That ain't the way to ask for a job, darlin'."

I turn to see the guy I noticed when I walked in, an older man with a beer in his hand. He's alone, seated a couple of chairs down from me, and his eyes are glued to the TV screen hung up behind the bar.

The man laughs to himself, not seeming to give a shit that no one invited him into this conversation.

My skin prickles as he turns to look at me, dragging his gaze down and back up. "I mean, you can't even crack a smile?" he adds, and I feel a switch flip on in my brain.

It's like every bitchy comment and backhanded compliment I heard all throughout high school was echoing over and over again in my head. Every smug smile of those girls, their shrill giggles and laughter all at my expense. The sound of their whispers as they walked away, each one making me wish I could disappear from this world a little more.

They looked at me as their friend up until something shifted when we got into high school, and I became their prey.

My head is spinning as I remember the looks of accomplishment on their faces last night when the tears streamed down my face as they showed me the video of Luke kissing another girl.

A girl who was supposed to be my friend.

My vision goes red. "And you can't even mind your fucking business?"

The words leave my lips before I can stop them, and it's like a dam finally breaking. All the frustration, the anger, and the betrayal from last night—the past four *years*, my whole *life* —comes rushing out, and there's no stopping it.

"Do either of us look even remotely interested in what you have to say?" I add, gesturing between me and Emmett, who is looking at me like I just grew a second head.

I don't give the man time to respond as I slam my hand down on the bar. "The last thing I need from anyone right now—let lone some stranger at a bar—is their opinion on what they think *I* should be doing."

I turn back to Emmett while I still have the adrenaline pumping through my veins. "And you," I say, pointing to him, "don't you dare try this overprotective, misogynistic bullshit I know you're about to spout!" My voice keeps growing in volume, but I don't care. The words are coming out before I can even think about them. "I don't need you saying how you'll have to look out for me or that I can't handle a fucking *bar* by myself—especially one I basically grew up in. You are going to apologize for wasting all this time and energy, and you are going to give me this damn job."

The slap of a hand on the bar snaps me back to reality. I see the man, having left a couple bills on the bar, turning to leave, huffing something under his breath.

The warm August air rushes in as the front door of the bar closes behind him, further bringing me back to what just happened.

My ears heat, and I have the urge to apologize as I turn

back around in my chair. The bar is silent aside from whispers of music playing, and I want to crawl back into myself as the aftermath of my embarrassing outburst settles in the air around us.

When I look up, Emmett is staring at me, and I can't help but notice the small smirk on his lips. He's looking at me with something I don't recognize, but it makes pride bloom in my belly. Our eyes meet, and a shared understanding passes through us.

Maybe he's seeing all my confusion, or the words I don't know how to say. Or, maybe it's a look of knowing, like he knew that something like this—speaking up for myself—was a long time coming.

He motions for me to come behind the bar, and I get an overwhelming sense of confidence that I have never experienced before.

The feeling has me promising myself that I will hold onto this new version of me forever, regardless of whether people know what to do with it or not.

I'm done being the easy target.

I'm done being the girlfriend who boosts your ego.

I'm done making it *my* problem how other people feel about me.

I'm done letting people in just so they can wake up one day and decide I'm not worth the trouble.

I've done it my whole life.

Never again.

CHAPTER 2

LUKE

SEVEN YEARS AGO – DECEMBER

IF YOU ASKED me who you thought I'd find when I walked into a dive bar—one I'm supposed to be interviewing for a job at—Annie would've been the last on the list.

She always talked about a bar she used to go to when she was a kid, one that her dad knew the owner of, but I'm sure it was Larry's, not Lenny's. And I didn't think it would be across town from where we grew up.

She hasn't seen me yet, and it gives me a second to appreciate what I've been missing these last four months.

Her brown hair is longer than when I last saw her, tucked behind her ears and putting her high cheekbones on full display. Her big brown eyes are locked on the drink she's making in front of her, and I watch as she sets the glass down in front of an older gentleman, her lips curving into a small smirk that makes my heart skip a beat.

Annie left Grant's party without a trace back in August when we all got together before everyone left for college, and I haven't seen her since.

I was supposed to take her home, but she was nowhere to be found when the night was wrapping up.

She was supposed to help me move into my off-campus

apartment the next morning, but she didn't answer any of my calls or texts.

I went to her place, but no one answered.

I had planned on asking Annie to move in with me that night. But, I figured it was a conversation that could wait until the next morning, and it ended up being one we would never have.

These past four months at school, I've tried reaching out—but it's been radio silence—and it didn't take her long to block me on everything.

Everyone was downing drinks in celebration that night before we all headed to our respective colleges, but I decided to stick to water after a bit of a crazy night with the hockey guys the day before.

I tried to ask the girls I saw her with before she disappeared, some girlfriends of my buddies from the hockey team —old friends of Annie's—but I had a feeling they didn't give me the whole story.

According to them, Annie got drunk and admitted that she wanted to break-up with me. "A clean break before we go to college" is what they called it, and it caught me completely off-guard because it didn't sound anything like the Annie I knew.

She barely drinks, and the community college she's going to is walkable from my university.

When I asked them for a little more clarity, they avoided giving me an answer.

I know that Annie's friendship with that group of girls was always hot and cold. They were all close in elementary and middle school, but it's like something shifted in high school.

Since then, they've never been too nice to Annie, but I always chalked it up to jealousy.

Annie didn't care to blend in with what the "cool kids" were doing when we got to high school. While Devin, Eliza,

Bea, and Penelope went the cheerleading route, Annie joined theater. And I think her friends were jealous of her ability to be herself and not care what everyone else around her was doing.

Annie had always been quiet and shy, but you'd forget it the second you heard her voice or saw her on stage. I still remember the day she got the lead in the school's musical our freshman year. She was so surprised, and humble as ever, as if she wasn't the most talented person in that whole school and deserved the leading role more than anyone.

Annie always told me it was easier to feel confident when she wasn't playing herself, but I knew that confidence was inside her, begging to come out.

And by the looks of it, it finally has.

I have a few minutes before I'm meeting with the owner for my job interview. And instead of finding him, my eyes find Annie again, and it's at this moment that I realize how weird it is for her to be a bartender, especially at a place like this.

The Annie I knew didn't do too well in crowds that weren't there to watch her perform on stage. She always sat by herself when she came to watch my hockey games, and she stayed by my side at parties. Aside from the last one, when I let Devin convince me that she and the other girls wanted to spend some time with Annie before they all went their separate ways.

Looking around, I see a group of men who I can assume are regulars seated at the bar, and the booths and high top tables are filled with patrons a few years older than Annie and me, most likely enjoying their time off from classes for the holidays.

Annie just turned 19 in September, and it's hard to imagine someone as soft-spoken as her here.

"Bill, does it look like I want to sit here and listen to you?"

Or not.

Her voice has an edge to it that I've never heard, but it's one I could definitely get used to. I watch as she rolls her eyes and starts wiping down the bar, and my body moves on its own.

I don't know if because I want to protect her—not that she even seems to need it—or because I just want to be close to her, but I've seen Annie almost every day of my life since we were six, and these four months without her have been like I lost a part of myself.

The most important part.

I'm a few steps away from the bar when I hear the man respond, but I can't make out what he says with his back turned to me.

Annie tucks the towel she was using to wipe down the bar into her tight jeans. She puts her hands on her hips, making her Lenny's tank top tighten around her chest. "You really want me to tell Emmett you're pissed he mentioned switching hard seltzer brands? I'm sure he'll say the same thing as me."

Leaning forward on the bar, she rests her elbows down right in front of the man. She leans in just a few inches from his face. "Fuck off". I watch as her cherry red lips accentuate each word, and I freeze.

My mind is spinning because I see Annie in front of me but I don't recognize her in the slightest.

Annie doesn't swear.

Annie doesn't speak up for herself.

Annie most definitely does not say what's on her mind.

She turns around and grabs a liquor bottle from behind her, saying over her shoulder, "You don't even drink hard seltzers. So, drink *your* stupid whiskey and leave me the hell alone."

What the hell is she doing?

She shouldn't be talking to him like this. There's no way she knows how he'll react, especially if she pissed him off. I hate that it's the truth so many women have to face, but men have a track record of not taking too kindly to being told off by women.

I glance to the other side of the bar as my feet finally close the distance between her and me, and there's another bartender behind the bar, a tall, built guy with dark hair and tan skin, but he doesn't pay Annie any attention, which worries me even more.

Does Annie have anyone looking out for her here?

Right as I get up to the bar, I hear Bill and the guys he's with roar with laughter, one of them saying how he remembers when he first met Annie and how she treated him the same way.

What?

I have so many questions circling my brain.

He remembers *Annie* talking to him like this?

Who the hell is this girl?

And what did she do with the Annie I knew?

Before I can fully process, Annie turns and we make eye contact. Her face pales, and every ounce of confidence I saw from her a moment ago fizzles.

My heart sinks to my stomach at the thought that the sight of *me* made that happen.

Her brown eyes cloud, and my chest tightens, and so many emotions begin to flood my senses.

Happiness because I finally found her.

Anger because she left without telling me where she was going.

Sadness because *something* happened to her.

Frustration because I have no idea what that *something* is.

Someone clears their throat, drawing our attention to the other bartender. "Everything okay, Ann?" he asks, his harsh eyes giving me a once-over before looking at her with concern.

It occurs to me that Annie mouthing off to some guy at the

bar didn't faze her co-worker, but her looking at me with this look on her face did.

It takes her a second, but she shakes her head, relaxing her shoulders, before turning to him. "Yeah, all good, Eddie."

Annie sets down the drink she was making in front of one of Bill's friends. She looks at me again, this time her brown eyes swimming with confusion. The same confusion that I'm sure is reflected on my face.

I'm confused about what happened that night at Grant's.

I'm confused why she refuses to talk to me.

I'm confused how she ended up here.

And, most of all, I'm confused about what the fuck happened in these past four months that turned her into someone I recognize on the outside, but who I am convinced is a complete stranger on the inside.

"You guys know each other?" Eddie asks Annie.

"Not really," she says to him, but her eyes are locked with mine. "Not anymore."

CHAPTER 3
ANNIE

PRESENT DAY

"CHEERS TO OUR NEWLYWEDS!" I say as I clink my gin and tonic to the two other glasses. The smile on the face of one of my best friends is brighter than I've ever seen, aside from the smile of her husband as he looks down at her.

It was only fitting that we came to Lenny's to celebrate Eddie and Mia's marriage.

"Thank you for coming today," Mia says to me as Eddie kisses her temple. Mia and I are seated at the chairs at a high-top table a few feet from the bar, Eddie standing behind Mia's chair.

Mia's blonde hair is curled, falling in waves over her shoulders, her long-sleeved bodycon dress a stark white against Eddie's black dress shirt and dress pants.

"Having you all there meant the world to us." Mia and Eddie *finally* tied the knot an hour ago in the Milwaukee courthouse with our group of friends and her brother, Mateo, as witnesses, all of us in disbelief that it's been two and a half years since Eddie proposed to Mia on stage while his band, Cross My Heart, was performing.

Working at Lenny's brought me friendships that made me

realize the people I considered friends in high school were anything but. Next month marks seven years since I marched back in here and demanded Emmett give me a job, and so much has changed since then.

It almost makes all the shit that led up to coming here worth it.

It brought me Emmett and Eddie, who became the older brothers I always wanted as an only child, and it brought me their better halves—the two pieces of my makeshift heart— Mia and Emmett's wife, Drew.

"Another round for the bride and groom? Emmett just texted that he and Drew had to stop home, but they'll be here in a few minutes." A voice calls from behind the bar, a voice that makes my stomach drop every time I hear it, but I've gotten good at ignoring the feeling over these past seven years.

Luke.

Working at Lenny's also brought me back to Luke, the person I was desperately trying to run from when I came here in the first place.

Co-existing with Luke has been doable, a little easier since I quit my bartending job at Lenny's to start veterinarian school three years ago, but not much because we share the same group of friends who have pretty much become family at this point.

We all spend birthdays and holidays together, and it feels unnatural to go more than a week without seeing each other.

I decided from the moment Emmett told me Luke would be working at Lenny's that I wasn't going to let that stop me from being the new Annie.

"One more round, bartender," I declare as I hold my now-empty glass towards Luke. Even without facing him, I know his eyes are on me. They always are.

To be honest, I always have to tamp down the feelings I

have for Luke when he's around, but I've gotten good at it, only slipping up once or twice over the years.

Our friends know Luke and I went to school together, but how well we knew each other is one of the secrets I keep from Drew and Mia, my two closest friends.

And I told Luke I would cut his balls off if he ever told Emmett or Eddie.

The three of us girls don't keep much from each other. They know about the money I send to my mom now that she's in live-in treatment—it takes the place of actually ever seeing her again—and they know the only hard liquor I can drink is gin because it's the one my dad never touched.

They know I have a hard time asking for help when I need it, and they know I have no interest in a romantic partner—sticking to little flings here and there—before I finish school, thanks to an old boyfriend who ruined relationships for me.

But they have no idea that, in reality, that old boyfriend is Luke, and I gave my heart to him, thinking he would take care of it, only for him to stomp all over it.

"You guys too?" Luke asks Mia and Eddie as he rounds the bar and walks over to our table, his eyes finally shifting off me—allowing me the quick indulgence of looking at him. "Or do you want to get it yourself, Ed," he adds with a laugh.

"Hey, Annie worked here too, and I don't see you putting her to work," Eddie replies with a laugh of his own.

Luke turns to me. "He's right. Annie, want to come back behind the bar and show me how it's done?" The glint in his stupid grin makes me roll my eyes, ignoring the flip in my stomach.

Luke is handsome, there is no denying that, even if I tried —and I've tried, *hard*. No one is immune to his charm. His blonde hair is long, how I've always liked it, and he shakes it out as he leans on our high-top table. The sleeves of the dress shirt he's wearing are rolled up, revealing his corded forearms, his body still chiseled from his years as a hockey player in high school and now as a player on a recreational team with his law school friends.

"Absolutely not," I respond quickly and dryly, gaining a laugh from Mia and a chuckle from Eddie.

Luke's eyes slightly widen, the same way they always do when I say the opposite of what he wants me to, but his grin doesn't lessen one bit.

He leans in a little closer to me across the table, and I fight the urge to lean in, too, just to show him he isn't affecting me like he wants to, even though he totally is.

"It'll be just like old times," he says, and my eyes narrow on him. I know he isn't talking about the "old times" that play over and over in my head when I try to fall asleep, but him looking at me the way he is now reminds me of how easy it is to love him. "Come on, you know you want to."

His bright blue eyes, like an ocean with a strong undertow, pull me in further and further before I can even realize how far I am from shore.

"I'd rather have my foot run over by a car." I deadpan, looking down at my empty glass as I push it towards him, but Luke's eyes stay glued to me.

Over the years, he's gotten more overt with his flirting, which prompts me to get *much* more overt with shutting it down. I think it just provokes him more.

"I'll do another beer," Eddie says, putting an end to the back-and-forth, no stranger to this tension between Luke and me. He turns to his wife. "What about you, sunshine?"

Before Mia can respond, Luke turns from me to Mia, swiping her glass with that 100-watt smile and sparkling baby blue eyes. "Of course she wants another one of my amazing tequila sunrises. I mean, they've only gotten better with the years." His eyes shine a little brighter as Mia laughs and they share a memory from when Mia started hanging out at Lenny's more and Luke helped her find her "drink of choice."

Luke pushes himself from the high-top table, giving Mia a wink and pulling another little giggle from her, before he turns his attention to me, catching me staring, his grin widening.

No one is immune to Luke's charm.

Not even me.

I look away, shaking my head, both at him and at myself for letting him catch me looking.

"Gin and tonic again, Annie girl?" he asks me when he gets behind the bar, and his voice saying his nickname for me is like warm honey enveloping me in a familiarity that I always wish was never there.

The nickname reminds me of simpler times when my heart used to flutter, but my heart was broken beyond repair all those years ago—there's nothing left to make flutter.

Before I can tell him what a stupid question that is, seeing as though it's the only alcoholic drink he's ever made me—all other alcohol makes me want to vomit, aside from the occasional white wine or hard seltzer, favorites of my two best friends—the door to Lenny's opens.

Emmett's large frame further accentuates how small his wife is even as she wobbles towards us with her swollen belly looking about ready to burst. Drew's red wine hair is twisted in a bun on the nape of her neck, her black maternity pants and tank top looking much more comfortable than the dress she was wearing at the courthouse an hour ago.

"I'm so sorry we're late," she announces as she throws her arms around both Mia and Eddie, hugging them as best she can with her stomach in the way. "I couldn't stay in that dress any longer," she explains, sitting down in the chair Emmett pulled out for her between Mia and me.

Drew didn't go back to teaching this past school year, Emmett not wanting her out of his sight even more than ever since she got pregnant; I don't think I've seen her stand any longer than two minutes since they announced her pregnancy.

I was worried about Drew and Emmett becoming parents, selfishly because I was so worried it would change things between all of us. In reality, it's been a true blessing, and we can't wait to meet the boy or girl she is supposed to pop out any day now.

The Lenny's crew is ready to expand after these seven years together.

"Don't even give it a second thought," Mia says as Luke appears at our table, setting down a glass of water in front of Drew, a tequila sunrise in front of Mia, and another gin and tonic in front of me.

I ignore the flip in my stomach as his body steals the space around mine now that a table isn't between us. With Emmett standing behind Drew's chair, Eddie standing behind Mia's, Luke stands behind mine

It always happens like this, even more over the years with our four best friends being coupled off.

"How are you feeling?" I ask Drew. It comes out evenly even though my voice is a second away from cracking. I've learned that confidence is all about faking it until you make it.

"Tired," Drew answers, "and ready for this baby to come out, but tonight isn't about me," she says, turning to Mia. "It's about you! How does it feel to be married?" Drew's smile is wide as she rests her forearms on the table in front of her, her gaze moving from Eddie and Mia.

I don't get to hear the answer because I feel my phone vibrate on the table next to me. I glance down to see it's a number I don't recognize, feeling Luke lean in closer from where he's standing behind me to look too.

The Milwaukee area code could mean it's from my advisor. I wouldn't usually answer any calls for school when I'm on break, especially after how taxing the past three years of schooling have been, but I'm coming up on my final year of veterinary school which means my rotations will be starting next month.

Starting in September, my life will consist of long hours of unpaid labor at my vet school's teaching hospital, private practices, zoos, laboratories, government agencies—basically any place where veterinarians ply their trade—but *finally* being able to put all of my training these past three years to use.

My advisor is supposed to call me, so we can talk through some experiences I hope to get approval for once my required rotations are scheduled.

I'm so close to being finished with school—my next step being the North American Veterinary Licensing Examination and the Wisconsin State Exam once I finish my rotation year —and it's hard to believe all this hard work is so close to paying off.

I never knew what I wanted to be when I grew up, not until I was in my third—and my last—year of college, having worked my ass off to graduate in three years. I realized I didn't want to be a bartender forever and started Googling what jobs I could get with a biology degree.

Being a veterinarian was the only career option that stuck with me, and it was confirmed when I started volunteering at animal shelters and working with the on-site veterinarians that I realized it was what I wanted to do.

It also helped that I had such a huge support system throughout the whole process.

Not only did my friends let me vent to them when I wanted to give up and go out of their way to remind me that I was capable, they're also amazing role models.

There's something special about being friends like we are, being able to watch each other grow and cheer each other on along the way. I'm forever grateful to have friends who have followed me along on this journey and who have let be front row to theirs, even Luke—but I'd never admit it out loud.

Thinking how I don't want to miss my advisor's call, I quickly excuse myself from the group and head outside. Since Emmett closed Lenny's for the night, knowing we would all be going to the courthouse and coming here to celebrate, we're the only ones here.

Emmett is still looking for long-term employees since Eddie and I left. We both still help out every so often—Drew and Mia too—but with Luke leaving in a few weeks to become a partner at his father's law firm and Emmett becoming a new dad, Lenny's needs more employees to keep her running.

"Hello?" I say as I answer the call. The sun has just begun to set; the skin on my arms, exposed from my red jumpsuit, pebbles from the cool summer air.

"Annie Mitchell?" a gruff voice replies into my ear. "This is Lou Dominic calling."

It takes me a second to register the name of the manager of my apartment complex.

"Oh, hi," I answer, slightly annoyed with myself that I didn't just let the call go to voicemail.

What could Mr. Dominic possibly need from me on a Friday night?

I pace the sidewalk outside Lenny's, avoiding the few people who pass by.

"You live in apartment 112, correct?"

Worry begins to settle as I hear the door of Lenny's open behind me.

"Yes," I answer warily, impatiently waiting for him to tell me the reason for this call.

I've lived in my current complex since I started veterinarian school because it was in the center of where I spent my time: my school, the animal shelter, Mia and Eddie's apartment, Drew and Emmett's house, Lenny's.

I pay my rent on time, don't disrupt my neighbors, and never need any maintenance or assistance.

I am a stellar occupant.

I haven't talked to Mr. Dominic since he gave me a tour of the place two years ago.

"I hate to be calling about this," Mr. Dominic responds, "but your apartment has been broken into."

CHAPTER 4
LUKE

I WATCH as Annie's face drops.

The way her brows furrow and her mouth slightly opens tells me she wasn't expecting whatever news was just shared with her.

I step closer, placing my hand lightly on the small of her back. I know something is really wrong when she lets it stay there.

The heat of her skin meets my palm, even through her red jumpsuit, and the smell of jasmine and roses overwhelms my senses, the same way it does every time she lets me get close to her.

Annie and I have been in this limbo together these past seven years, ever since I walked into Lenny's and found a brand-new version of her.

She fights me on almost everything I do or say, and it seems like every conversation we have ends in an argument or her telling me I'm an idiot.

And I love it.

I love the fierceness of her, the confidence, the shield she puts around herself and the heart she thinks isn't there anymore.

But she forgets I know her better than I know myself.

And when she acts like a brat, it turns me on.

I've known Annie since I was six years old. As classmates, as friends, as lovers; I know each and every side of her, and I know that she's fighting me every chance she gets because she still cares. Even if she pretends she doesn't.

At the beginning, I tried to talk to her about what happened between us. I wanted to do whatever I could to make things right—I still do—but she wouldn't let me. She was gone by the time I came out of my meeting with Emmett the day of my interview and it was Eddie who started training me at the bar for the next few shifts.

I didn't get to see her again until my first shift with her a few weeks later, and she ignored me the whole time. Acting as if I didn't exist.

When we were closing that day, we finally had a moment alone and I tried to talk to her. I asked her what happened at Grant's party—why she left me, what happened with Devin and the other girls—but she would barely look at me.

I tried to find traces of my 1st grade table partner, my homecoming date, my best friend, but I couldn't. She wouldn't even look up from the floor when she said we were both better off forgetting everything that happened between us, and I still wonder if she could actually hear my heart shatter into more pieces than I thought possible.

Forget growing up together?

Forget our first hug, our first kiss, our first time?

Forget how it felt to hold her hand or make her laugh?

Forget the only person who saw *me*? Not who everyone else wanted me to be.

Asking me to forget her was like asking me to forget how to breathe.

Then it was like something shifted inside her. Her eyes finally met mine, and she stepped so close that I could almost taste the cherry-flavored lip gloss on her lips.

Then she told me she'd cut my balls off if I told anyone about our past.

Half of me wanted to get on my knees and beg her to listen to me, to give me another chance, but the other half of me recognized that the Annie I knew was gone.

She wasn't coming back.

So I decided that night that I was going to do whatever I could to make her fall in love with me all over again.

It would be different this time. We were adults. Different people. We weren't 15 anymore, and I still had to get to the bottom of what happened between us in the first place.

I told myself I would stop at nothing.

Yet, here we are, seven years later, and the closest she's let me get to her is the night of Drew and Emmett's wedding almost five years ago when she got drunk, ended up in my hotel room, and told me she was tired of pretending to hate me.

It was the first, and last, time I ever saw her more than a little tipsy.

I wanted to ask her what she meant, but by the time I registered what exactly she was saying, she was sprawled out, asleep in my bed.

I watched her sleep until the sun started to rise, and I couldn't keep my eyes open any longer. I dreamed about how beautiful she was and how I was almost over that wall she had put between us, but she was gone by the time I woke up.

It takes her a second to register my touch on her lower back. She promptly turns to give me a glare and steps out of my touch as she listens to whatever the person on the phone is telling her.

"Okay, I'll be right over there," she says before hanging up and turning to walk back into Lenny's, ignoring me.

"Who was that?" I ask, stopping her mid-step, and I know it was the wrong question to ask as she slowly turns to face me.

One thing I've learned about Annie over the years is there is very little I can say that won't piss her off, but acting in any way protective or worried about her is a sure way to ensure she doesn't talk to me for days.

"Why do you continue to act like my business is any of yours?" she answers, crossing her arms.

"You seemed upset. Is everything okay?" I try again, hoping she'll at least tell me what had her so taken aback.

She rolls her eyes before turning to the front door of Lenny's. "Someone broke into my apartment," she answers over her shoulder, as if she's telling me my shoe is untied. "I have to head over there."

My fists clench at the nonchalance of her voice and the severity of what she just said.

Before I can tell her I'm coming with her, she's back inside and the door to Lenny's shuts in my face. I let out a groan because this girl *will* be the death of me, either by killing me with the way she acts or with her actual hands.

"Is everything okay?" I hear Mia ask Annie when I get inside.

"Everything's fine," Annie answers as she grabs her purse, but she doesn't look Mia in the eyes. "My landlord called with a small issue and needs me to head over."

"What kind of issue?" Drew asks.

Before Annie can give some bullshit excuse, I answer for her knowing I will pay for it later. "Someone broke into her apartment." There isn't the usual lightness to my voice; I'm not here to make light of things or make a joke in an uncomfortable situation like I usually do.

What if Annie had been home during the break-in?

I can't even think about it without feeling like I might hyperventilate.

Annie's shoulders tighten and her eyes whip to mine. She's pissed, and I knew she would be, but so am I. Not only because this situation is serious and she could be in danger, but because even for how much Annie has changed and evolved into this new version of herself, she still believes that asking for help makes her a burden.

She may not be scared to speak her mind or tell you what you don't want to hear, seeing as though she refuses to take shit from anyone, but I still have yet to see her ask for help when she needs it.

Years of parents treating her like she is nothing more than background noise and people who were supposed to be her friends telling her she's paranoid or overreacting when they made a joke at her expense left scars on her that may have healed but have never gone away.

The atmosphere of the bar shifts, and a worried Drew and Mia and a pissed off Emmett and Eddie watch Annie and me as we stare at each other, a silent conversation passing through us, one that has happened many times before.

Her telling me to stop talking, and me not listening.

"You're not going alone," I say, staring into her eyes. We're all around the high-top table, but the world around Annie and me disappears. Annie's eyes soften for a moment, and she lets me see past that hard exterior.

She's worried, probably scared. Maybe she's grateful that I knew she didn't want to go alone but didn't want to say so.

But then she blinks, and that moment of vulnerability is gone as fast as it came.

My hands itch to touch her, my arms ache to be around her, my lips beg to tell her that she doesn't need to be so guarded all the time, that I am here to love her and protect her and show her that she doesn't have to do it all alone, but I resist every urge.

The same way I always do.

"We're coming with you," Drew finally says, bringing me back to the moment. Annie's attention swings to our friend, and she knows better than to argue with Drew when she puts her foot down. Emmett nods his head once in agreement as he helps his wife out of the high-top chair.

Annie has her own history with Emmett, and I know he sees her as a sister. When I started working for him, I learned quickly that he wasn't as scary as he pretended to be—Annie is much scarier—and there is no doubt that if Annie is in any kind of danger, he'll be right behind me in making sure she is okay.

"Us too," Mia and Eddie say at the same time, the two always being on the same page. The newlyweds are two of the most stubborn people I know, but they are also two of the most loyal, not just with each other but with all of us.

Plus, both of them throw punches when they're pissed, so they are the perfect people to have in your corner.

"No, absolutely not. This is your guys' night," Annie tells Mia and Eddie before turning to Drew, "and you're about to pop. I don't even know what I'm walking into, but an apartment that was just broken into is no place for someone who is nine months pregnant."

Annie's face is hard, her features tight as she looks at our friends.

She's scared, but that's when she fights the hardest.

Drew crosses her arms the best she can over her stomach. "You're not about to go there alone," Drew says, her voice softening. She steps forward and extends a hand that Annie grabs.

"We're coming," Mia adds, stepping next to Drew and reaching for Annie's other hand.

I must not be the only one who can tell Annie is scared.

Annie's face relaxes, and the three girls pull each other in for a group hug.

Emmett and Eddie watch the girls with soft smiles on their faces, but the smiles don't reach their eyes. They're pissed.

The Lenny's crew—as Mia's brother deemed us a few

years ago—was built on issues with our own families, some more than others, and the five of them having to deal with a lot of shitty cards being handed to them.

Between Annie's dad leaving and her mom's diagnosis, the shooting at Drew's school, Emmett losing his sister, Mia's boyfriend's suicide, and Eddie almost killing his abusive, alcoholic father, it's safe to say that all of my friends have had the universe *actively* working against them.

The worst I've had is a father who treats me like spare parts for my older brothers.

Either way, because we know what each other has been through, we are all protective to a fault.

"So it's settled," I announce. I look at Annie, and even as her eyes narrow in her signature death stare, I give her a smile I hope still makes that black heart of hers beat faster. "Lead the way, Annie girl."

CHAPTER 5
ANNIE

"YOU'RE LUCKY, Ms. Mitchell. I know a break-in can be scary, but it was good that you weren't here, and that we were able to catch the kid," the police officer in charge explains as if I'm incapable of understanding how the situation could've been *much* worse.

"I'm lucky?" I question the man, handing him the list he had me write of all the things I saw were taken: my laptop, my headphones, my TV, and some jewelry I kept on my nightstand.

Looking around the disaster of an apartment just reminded me how little I can afford; how little I have of what others could perceive as valuable.

The cop is old enough to be my grandfather with an annoying sense of superiority as if he just solved the world's biggest cold case, even though all he did was catch some 19-year-old who took advantage of a faulty window.

The kid was able to get in through my *locked* bedroom window, run off with my shit to just get caught, and leave me to deal with it.

And I'm lucky?

I asked my friends to wait in the hallway, so it's just me

and Officer Grandpa—or Collins, as he introduced himself. Mr. Dominic and a few other officers are looking at the window near my bed.

I'm mad and frustrated and tired, and my patience is on the floor with the way this man is acting like I won the lottery with this break-in.

"That's for sure," he answers with a smile that does nothing to make me comfortable, his hands tucking into the pockets of his uniform as he looks around my place.

It's a studio, so everything, from my unmade bed to my destroyed desk to my disheveled kitchen, can be seen from where he is standing.

It might not be much, but it's mine.

And someone broke in.

I can't even feel scared about all of this because of how furious I am that someone could be so violating.

This apartment is the one place I feel like I can relax and not have to worry about a million and one things.

I glance at my desk and see a mess—just not my mess. My mess was made up of my vet school textbooks opened to specific pages I was reading, my lecture notes, my planner, and my laptop with all my tabs open.

This mess is all my papers scattered on the floor, textbooks pushed off, and my laptop gone and in some evidence bag.

My eyes sting, and I blink away the tears of frustration as I turn to face my kitchen. The cabinets and drawers are opened as if the stupid kid was looking for what else he could take. The small appliances that were on my counter are now broken on the ground as if he had a tantrum when he couldn't find anything else.

My toaster, my blender, and my well-loved stand mixer, all no better than broken parts.

Just like me.

How fitting.

Officer Collins and Mr. Dominic are now chatting in

hushed tones in my living room, and my thoughts are interrupted as the door opens. My friends file in to see the damage, lingering near the opened door, their patience no better than mine apparently.

I see their shocked faces and anxious features, and my stomach knots. I don't want them to worry about me.

"Did they catch the guy?" Mia asks, her arms latching around Eddie's.

"Yeah, and he didn't take much. The officer said I'll be able to get my stuff back in a few days after they process everything."

"Are you okay?" The concern on her face makes me feel guilty that they had to come here on their wedding night of all nights.

Before I can tell her I'm fine—leaving out how pissed I am at the kid who thought it was okay and the complex for their shitty windows, and how much of a pain in the ass it's going to be to deal with—Officer Collins and Mr. Dominic walk over to where we're all standing.

"Do you have somewhere else you can stay?"

I whip around to face the two of them, confused by the officer's question. "What? Why would I need another place to stay?" I look to the manager of the complex standing next to him, but his head is down, his face hardened. He doesn't look at me as he moves through the group of us and leaves my apartment. I turn back to Officer Collins.

"You said you already caught the kid," I argue.

The police officer lets out an exhale. "We will be opening up an investigation with the complex, seeing as the assailant was able to get into the locked windows from the outside."

My mind begins to race with how I'm going to start vet school rotations in a few weeks, and this man is telling me I'm about to be homeless. It's the middle of July, and rotations start the first week of September.

"How long will that take?" I ask, trying to keep my voice neutral.

"A month or so, give or take," Officer Collins answers, and my stomach drops. "Possibly more, depending on our findings," he adds. *A month? Maybe more?* "You should pack for what you need tonight, and then you can stop by tomorrow to grab the rest."

The ground is ripped from under me, and I feel like I'm free-falling with no end in sight. This night just keeps getting worse.

I know my friends would offer to let me stay with them, but I can't agree to that. Not when Eddie and Mia just got married and Drew and Emmett will have a whole-ass baby to stress about in a few days.

I can feel everyone's eyes on me from the doorway behind me, can almost hear them telling me I have a place to stay with them, but I can't do that to them.

I can't make my problems their problems, not when they have their own lives to live.

A moment passes, and I feel a familiar presence appear behind me, my body instinctively relaxes before my mind can register it. "She can stay with me."

Officer Collins gives us a nod and heads over to the other officers. Luke turns to face me, our friends' eyes burning into the back of my head.

I've made it my goal in life ever since Luke Owens came back into my life to always do the opposite of what he tells me to do. I told myself that I would forget everything that happened between us, even if I knew it was an impossible task.

I spent my childhood wishing I had his light, his confidence, his happiness, and I spent my teenage years hanging on to every word he said about our love, our lives, our future, until all of it turned out to be a lie.

I want to yell and scream in his face and tell him to stop inserting himself into my life, but I can't find the words.

"You're staying with me," Luke says to me this time, as if he still has the right to swoop in and make everything better.

Where was he when Bea and Eliza snuck backstage during opening night of my freshmen year musical and hid my costume? Where was he when Devin and Penelope told everyone in our homeroom that I gave the musical director blowjobs to get the leads?

Where was he when legs would stick out in front of me so I would trip in the middle of the busy hallway or when people I thought were my friends would pretend I wasn't there when I sat down at the lunch table?

Where the hell was he when Devin showed me a video of the two of them making out the night before Grant's party when he told me he had plans with the guys from the hockey team?

I shake the thoughts away, embarrassed with myself that I let this high school bullshit still get to me in my twenties. "Like hell I am," I tell him, before turning to our friends. "It's late, you guys can go. I'm fine."

Mia and Drew look at me, and I can feel them looking past the guise I'm trying—and failing—to keep in place. Drew opens her mouth, and I stop her before she can say what I know she is about to say. "No. My future niece or nephew will be here any day now. I know I call you two 'Mom' and 'Dad'," I say, glancing up at Emmett and back to Drew, "but I am not letting you stress yourselves out by taking me in."

"Ann, don't talk about yourself like a stray dog," Emmett says, his arm hanging over Drew's shoulder. His huge body takes up most of the door frame, and the place where my heart used to beat comes alive for a moment.

Emmett doesn't say much, so the things he does say hold a lot of meaning to him.

Even if he's wrong.

I'm just like those strays we take in at the animal shelter. The ones that someone wanted when they were a cute puppy but got rid of the second they became too much work.

The kind that are good in theory but not worth all the time and energy in the end.

I clear my throat, shaking my head as I tell him, "I'm not staying with you guys."

"Yeah, 'cause she's staying with us," Mia says, looking up at Eddie who nods in agreement, making more tears build behind my eyes that I have to blink away. I turn to face them, but before I can say anything, Luke walks out of my bathroom with one of my tote bags over his shoulder.

I didn't even see him go anywhere when I turned to talk to Drew and Emmett.

"I think I got everything. You ready to go?" Luke says as he approaches us, the usual lightness in his step, his calm demeanor is an evident contrast to my own worry and frustration about this whole situation.

I snatch the bag from him, glancing to see clothes, my phone charger, toiletries, my textbook, notes, and planner from my desk, and my fucking *vibrator* in the bag he packed.

I look up at him, and I think I'm ready to make use of Mia's punching lessons and knock that smirk off his stupid face when he winks at me.

Moments like these further convince me that I am capable of killing someone.

Specifically *this* someone.

I'm too busy thinking of the different ways I'd do it to acknowledge my feelings about how he knew exactly what to pack for me and how now I have one *less* thing to worry about.

"Where do you get off on telling me what to do?" I ask him, the venom to my voice no stranger to Luke anymore.

"On the contrary, Annie. I get off on *you* telling *me* what to do," he answers, and my fists ball at my sides, one of them ready to swing. "So, please tell me what else I can grab for you before we go."

"How about you try to keep it in your pants when I tell you to get the fuck out so I can figure out what the hell I'm going to do?" I fume, and I don't care about our audience—they're used to it. "I am not staying with you."

"We'll leave you two to discuss this," Eddie says, and there is a hint of a smile in his voice that I want to slap away, but I don't give him any attention. I hear the amusement in the goodbyes as the four of them file out of my apartment, and I make a mental note to tell them all to be *less* obvious with it the next time I see them.

I expect Luke to hit me with his lazy smile, the one he gives to remind everyone around him of the golden boy he truly is.

And like clockwork, it comes to fruition, but there's an edge I've never seen before.

One that stops me in my tracks.

"My apologies, Annie girl," Luke says, leaning in so close his nose almost touches mine. "When I said you were staying with me, it wasn't a question."

I'm ready to fire back one of my usual, smart-ass comments, ready to go back-and-forth like we have been ever since he came back into my life, but I can't.

The words get caught in my throat when I see his baby blues drop to my lips for a fraction of a second, before he says just an inch away from my lips, "Let's go."

I'm speechless, my mind racing a hundred miles a minute as he grabs my overnight bag from me and walks out the door, expecting me to follow him.

And for some reason, still unbeknown to me, I do.

CHAPTER 6
LUKE

I THINK I BROKE ANNIE.

She has not said a word to me since we walked out of her apartment, and her not talking to me is scarier than her telling me to fuck off.

Annie is no stranger to my apartment—the apartment that I was going to ask her to move into with me, before she completely disappeared from my life—but she's never stayed the night, let alone a month.

I have two bedrooms—mine, and a guest room for when any of my friends or my brothers stay over, and it'll be Annie's for the foreseeable future.

With only a wall separating the two of us.

I have her tote bag over my shoulder, the hard-on I've had since I found her little blue vibrator in her underwear drawer when I was packing her stuff finally subsiding.

She follows behind me, still refusing to say a word as we get to the door to my apartment.

When I unlock the door to my place, I hear the familiar nails clicking the hardwood floor as I swing the door open. Rosie, my golden retriever I rescued from the shelter Annie works at, welcomes us home, her tail wagging.

"Hi, Ro-Ro," I say, petting her head as I walk into the kitchen, setting Annie's bag down on the counter and flipping on one of the kitchen lights. "Look who's here—your mama!"

Annie lets out an exhale as she walks into my place, shutting the door behind her. "How many times do I have to tell you that I am not her mom," she says through her teeth, bending down to pet Rosie, but at least she's talking to me now.

I bend down with Annie, letting Rosie be the perfect buffer for us. I won't be able to get Annie to talk about the break-in or the details of her staying here, but she'll talk about Ro.

"Of course you are." I lean in letting Rosie lick my cheek, not caring if I sound like a complete freak with my puppy voice. "Ro-Ro deserves a strong female role model in her life, don't you, sweetie pie?"

Annie rolls her eyes. "So you kidnapped me to be a dog mom? That's weird even for you, bartender," she deadpans, but I know Rosie is her soft spot.

For as much as Annie hates me, she loves Rosie, and is always making sure I'm taking her to the vet, getting her groomed, and that she is up-to-date on her shots. She refuses to accept the role as her mom even though Annie was there when I adopted Rosie.

I got Rosie from a fundraiser at the animal shelter Annie works at—she was just a volunteer there at the time—and Eddie and I went to support her and the cause. We ended up both leaving with a pup, me with Rosie, and Eddie with Rosie's sister, Daisy.

Rosie is one of the only things Annie and I can talk about without her ignoring me or telling me to stop talking to her.

"Thanks for letting me stay here, by the way," Annie adds in a whisper, and I have to will my facial expression not to change, or she'll take it back and get mad at me for bringing up how she's being nice to me.

We keep petting Rosie for a few moments in silence, and it registers for me that this is the first time we've been completely alone together in I don't know how long—years, maybe—but it would be a death wish for me to bring *that* up right now, especially after I just got a moment of softness from her.

Rosie, realizing she is tired of sitting, reels me from my own mind. She licks Annie's cheek before flopping down on the floor and rolling her on her back.

Annie lets out a little laugh, and my eyes follow the noise, finding her smiling as she scratches Rosie's belly.

It's small but still so blinding.

"She's happy to see you," I say to Annie, not being able to look away from her.

It wasn't even a question that Annie would be staying with me.

The second the cop said she needed a place to stay, I was already planning on bringing her here. My one and only priority was making sure she was safe.

And it took a lot less convincing than I thought it would, but I don't want to think too much about it.

As we sit here with Rosie, in this comfortable silence, a smile on Annie's face, I can't help but think that this month we have together may be my chance to finally figure out what the hell went wrong between us.

This might be my only chance to get her back.

"Of course she's happy to see me," Annie replies, "she likes me more than you."

I let out a laugh because I can't even deny it, but I watch as Annie's lips lose their shape, and I wish I could think of something to say that would bring her smile back, instantly regretting the words I didn't say.

The weight of tonight is no doubt heavy on her shoulders, on top of everything else she is constantly dealing with.

Annie is so tough and doesn't let a lot get to her these

days, and while I know the burglary probably freaked her out, she's going to be more angry than anything else. Having to deal with the aftermath is just one more stressor for her, and she is already preparing for such an important year for vet school with her rotations.

I knew taking the stress of finding a place to stay that wouldn't make her feel guilty or like she's a burden was one thing I could do to help her, even if she thinks spending more time with me than she has to is the equivalent to eating glass.

The things I would do to show her that she doesn't have to deal with everything alone are unmatched. I just wish she could see it.

"I know you're going to be mad at me for asking," I start, the both of us still knelt beside a very content Rosie, "but are you okay?"

Annie thinks about her answer for a moment, and I use this time to study her. I watch as her shoulders slump and her eyes briefly shut. She takes a deep inhale before letting it out, and this feels like one of those rare occurrences when Annie lets me see the part of her that she tries to hide.

The part of her she shields.

The part that is tired of shouldering every single shitty thing that has come her way.

The part that refuses to ask for or even accept help.

Her eyes open, but she doesn't look at me. "I'm fine," she finally says, giving Rosie a final pat before standing up.

I didn't get a chance to turn all my lights on in the apartment, so Annie's face is only slightly illuminated as she stands above me. I'm on my knees in front of her, still bent down from petting Rosie, and when she looks down at me, time stands still.

Her brown eyes are locked with mine, loaded silence stretching between us. Her arms are at her sides, but I can see her fists slightly clenched.

I don't say anything, just keep my eyes on her. I don't

want to scare away this moment. We're still in our clothes from the courthouse wedding, the straps of her red jumpsuit falling over her shoulders contrasting with the long brown waves around her face and down her back.

She tucks some hair behind her ear. "You look good on your knees for me, bartender." Her lips are in a pout as she bends down, bringing her face closer to mine. I'm a good foot taller than her, being just above six feet tall, so there isn't too much distance between me on my knees and her standing, but I watch her intently, waiting to see what she's about to do.

I ball my fists, resisting the urge to touch her. It would take the slightest movement from either of us to close the space between her lips and mine. Her jasmine and rose scent makes me dizzy, and I wonder if her lips still taste like cherries.

Her eyes flick down to my mouth, and I don't know if my dreams are coming true or if she finally killed me and this is my heaven. Her eyes find mine again as she says, "If you ever pull the shit you did tonight again," that familiar edge back in her voice, "I'll bury you in your own backyard."

She straightens back up to her full height, stepping around me and grabbing her bag off the counter.

I'm still on my knees, my eyes glued to where she was standing just a second ago, as she walks straight into the guest bedroom and slams the door behind her.

———

Annie was gone when I woke up this morning, which wasn't a surprise. I actually would have been more surprised if she *was* here.

The key I left for her on the kitchen counter is gone, and I'm sure she had Mia or Drew pick her up to get her other stuff and her car from her apartment.

She'll spend the majority of the day finding other things to do, so she doesn't have to be here.

This is what I get for the shit I pulled last night.

Not only was I the one to tell our friends about the break-in at her apartment, but I didn't give her a choice on whether or not she was staying with me—not to mention my choice in her *overnight essentials.*

I completely deserved going to bed with nothing but the memory of how it felt to be on my knees for Annie Mitchell while she was fast asleep a room away from me.

Today is Saturday, and I have the closing shift at the bar, so my morning and afternoon were spent making myself busy around my apartment and mentally kicking myself in the balls every time I glanced at the door hoping Annie was back or checked my phone thinking she'd text me.

It took almost a whole year when I first started working at Lenny's to get her to unblock my number, so it's a silly thought that she would suddenly be sending me her hourly whereabouts just because she's staying with me for a month.

The only texts I get from her are in group chats we have with our friends.

I also had to resist the nagging urge to peek into the guest room, especially when Rosie kept scratching at the closed door, further proving Annie's point that my own dog likes her more than me.

The masochistic side of me always wants to feel close to Annie, even if it's the literal version of playing with fire knowing that I'll get burned. I couldn't stop myself from peeking into the guest room, telling myself it was just to make sure she had everything she needed.

With the temptation subsided, it confirmed for me that Annie may be the love of my life, but she is *still* the biggest slob who never makes her bed and leaves messes everywhere she goes.

Messes that I would gladly clean for her if it wouldn't make her threaten to cut off my hands.

There's no guidebook on how to be roommates with your ex-girlfriend who hates your guts for reasons still unknown to you. The same ex-girlfriend who you have loved from afar for seven years and now will be under the same roof as you.

My feelings for Annie are already mind-fucking enough, and having her close yet so far is going to be my own personal hell.

She starts her last year of vet school in a month, and I'm supposed to be moving back home to fulfill my role as my brother's replacement with my dad and oldest brother in a few weeks. The position at the law firm has been my end goal ever since my senior year of high school, but I wish I had more time.

I don't know when—if ever—I'll get a chance like this again.

I'm about to head over to Lenny's when my phone rings.

I ignore the embarrassing flip in my stomach when I think for a millisecond that it's Annie, and I externally groan when I see who's actually calling.

It takes me a few seconds to decide if I want to deal with *him* now or later.

If I answer the phone now, it'll probably ruin the rest of my day.

If I wait to call him back another day, it will probably ruin multiple days.

I decide to go with the former, answering the call before it can go to voicemail.

"What's up, Dad?" I say into the phone, no longer having that sense of hope that he's calling to check up on me or ask how I'm doing.

The hope I used to have.

The hope that led me to disappointment every time my

father showed me I was nothing more than spare for the son who didn't meet Daniel Owens' expectations.

I realized that accepting I was only a subject of my dad's attention because my brother, Bennett, went against my father's wishes and dropped out of law school to become a firefighter was easier than trying to convince dear old Dad that being a replacement for Bennett isn't my only purpose in life.

There's no hope when I answer his calls. There's just anger —at him but also myself—that I ever believed he cared about me.

I know he's only calling because he needs something.

"When are you starting?" my dad barks out.

He's called me more in these past two months since I graduated law school than he has since my first year. At least when he used to call back then, he would say hello or ask how my classes were going.

Now, there is no trace of that doting, committed father.

It was all an act to begin with anyway.

"Soon," I answer, not wanting to give him an exact date. "I still have to talk to my boss at the bar."

I realize that I am lucky to have the means to become a lawyer, both the time and money, and I recognize that having a father with a law firm waiting for me is something I should be grateful for.

But it was never meant for me.

My father never gave me the same attention he gave to Bennett and Caleb because he never saw me as *his*. And technically, I'm not.

My last name is Owens, and we're still related, but it's only because my mother had an affair with Eric Owens, Daniel's brother.

The secret came out when I was nine, but, at that point, Eric died of a heart attack, and the man who I thought was my father told me and my brothers the truth: how he and my mom agreed to never tell Eric the truth about me.

Looking back, it makes sense why my mom took Eric's death so hard, but she couldn't do much about it after letting Daniel claim me as his own before I was even born. But just like my dad, my mom never treated me the same way as my brothers.

How could she when I was the reminder of what she couldn't have? A reminder of her mistake or her lost chance or whatever she tells herself so she can sleep at night.

"I need you to start September 1st," my dad replies, never wanting to hear about how one of his sons is a *bartender* of all things. In his mind, someone with the Owens last name is too good to work in the service industry, let alone *know* someone who does.

He wants to say he raised me better than that, but that would be a lie.

He didn't raise me at all.

My brothers—technically half-brothers, but we've never differentiated—were my parental figures. They were the ones who raised me, and they did a much better job than the man who claimed me as his just to avoid having to admit to anyone his wife slept with his brother.

Along with Annie, my brothers were the ones who were there for me.

They were my family.

The ones who drove me to hockey practice and cheered me on at my games. The ones who always reminded me that I was so much more than my dad's bastard son.

And it all paid off. I landed a full ride on a hockey scholarship all on my own. There was a real possibility I could play as a career one day. I never thought I'd become a big shot in the NHL, but it was at least a *possibility*, no matter how small.

But then Bennett told my dad he was dropping out of law

school, and my dad was forced to look at me for the first time. Even if it was because the son he had grand plans for was letting him down, it felt like the man I saw as my father finally saw *me*.

I know now that he just saw me as an opportunity to still get what he wanted.

Caleb, the oldest out of the three of us, has always been fine, even happy, with following my dad's footsteps, but Bennett wasn't. And now that he was off doing what he wanted, it left me to fill in the gaps.

And I did it.

I turned down my scholarship, said goodbye to my dreams of playing hockey in college, and prepared for the path of becoming a partner at Owens & Son's Law Firm because it was what Daniel wanted for Bennett but would tolerate for me.

I have filled the shoes Bennett left behind for *years* because the feeling of my dad's approval grew addicting in a way that I didn't even realize it was happening. Not until I walked across that stage in May and was handed a diploma I never wanted in the first place.

"I'll let my boss know," I answer, not having the energy to argue that a month and a half isn't enough time to prepare myself for a life of hating my job.

"Okay," is all he says before I hear the beep of the call ending, and I want to throw my phone across the room.

He's calling to know when he can finally make use of all the money and time he threw at me, rather than the love and affection I would have given it all up for, and I knew that answering the call.

I knew I would feel like this after talking to him.

But I always do this to myself.

CHAPTER 7
LUKE

"WHO PISSED IN YOUR CAMPFIRE?"

I look up from the glasses I'm drying off to find Annie with her arms crossed over her chest across the bar. She's wearing cut-off denim shorts and a red halter top that compliments the color of her lips.

The lips that were inches away from mine last night.

"That's not a saying," I say to her because telling her about the conversation with my dad will just open up a conversation we're in no shape to have.

Annie knows about my history with my parents, and she knows that it doesn't really affect me much. It's not something I talk about because it just isn't worth it. I learned at a young age that family isn't always just about blood.

But, there are about a dozen conversations she and I need to have before theorizing whether or not I have daddy issues and the *surprise-I-don't-want-to-be-a-lawyer-anymore* conversation.

"Yes, it is," she argues with me, her lips pouting as she sits into her hip. "Drew said one of her students used to say it."

"So we're trusting the judgment of sixth-graders now?"

"Lukey-poo, that's the same as trusting your judgment,"

she replies without missing a beat, the familiar nickname always soaked with condescension.

I exhale. "Whatever you say."

Annie sits down in front of me, the bar mostly empty.

Lenny's is unusually dead for a Saturday night, most likely because of all the summer festivities happening, and it's the worst night for it to be slow after that phone call with my dad.

I've been left to stir it around in my brain for hours while serving our regulars who keep asking me either when Annie is coming back or when we're going to hire a "cute one" to replace Annie.

I am one more comment away from banging my head against the bar.

"So," she starts, and I raise an eyebrow at her as I make her a gin and tonic. "Are you going to tell me why you look like someone kicked your puppy?"

I look up from putting a lime on the rim of her glass, pointing a finger at her. "Don't be bringing Rosie into this," I reply, holding back the smile threatening my lips.

She puts her hands up in mock-surrender. "Don't get all pissy with me. I'm just trying to be nice, *roomie*."

"Maybe I'm just mad that *someone* didn't make their bed this morning. If we're going to live together, you need to be less of a garbage can."

Her eyes widen. "We need some ground rules if you think it's okay to go into *my* bedroom."

"I was just testing the waters, seeing if you put any spells to keep me out," I explain, setting her drink down in front of her.

She shakes her head as she pulls the glass closer to her. "A witch joke? That's just lazy, bartender." She takes a sip, her lips wrapping around the straw as she waits for my retort, and I let out a laugh.

"Is that why you're here? To insult me and drink for free?

It must be my lucky night." I say it as a joke, but she can sit here and throw insults at me for the rest of my shift if it means I get to spend time with her.

"Hilarious," she deadpans.

My shoulders lighten the more we go back and forth, and I think for a second that maybe I can talk to her about how the last thing I want to do with my life is work at my dad's law firm. Maybe I can just say the words I'm afraid to admit aloud: that I wasted all this time trying to impress a man I used to idolize and now I don't give one single fuck about him.

But then I see the contentment on her face, so different from last night, and I take a page out of her book and decide not to make my problems hers.

Not when I'm trying to win her back.

"I assume you're waiting for one of the girls," I prompt.

"It's Movie Night," she answers, and then I remember that it's the second Saturday of the month, and this is one of the many long-standing dates the girls implemented once we all started getting busier over the years.

"Movie Night" is the second and fourth Saturday of every month, but the guys aren't invited to it. We get to go to the monthly dinners on the first Sunday of every month and the bi-weekly Thursday happy hours.

"Whose turn is it?" I ask, knowing that I'll be able to predict what movie she, Drew, and Mia will be watching by whose pick it is.

Annie smirks in response.

"So, *Twilight*?" I know that if it's Annie's choice, she's picking her favorite *Twilight* movie which is the first one of the franchise.

"It's the best one," she replies. "Plus, we haven't watched any of them since last month, so it's about time for a rewatch. Might as well start at the beginning."

"Of course," I agree, knowing that these movies mean

something to Annie, Drew, and Mia that I will never understand but can appreciate.

Annie nods before she changes the subject. "So, back to the topic of *ground rules*."

I rest my forearms on the bar, leaning forward but not too close. "Rule number one: make your bed when you wake up, you slob."

She sits back in her chair. "No. It's a waste of time. You just mess it up again when you get back in at night."

I shake my head, partly in disbelief that someone as smart as her thinks with that logic but also because I don't know a single topic of conversation between us that Annie *wouldn't* turn into an argument.

"Rule number two," I continue, saving us from at least one argument tonight, "we keep each other updated on whether we'll be home or not." I want to add that we'll also tell each other where we are, but I don't want to push my luck.

"Sounds like stalker behavior to me," she replies, taking another sip of her drink.

"It's common courtesy, *roomie*," I correct. "It takes two seconds to send a text that says you're leaving or that you're on your way back." I resist the urge to add that it also ensures I know she is safe.

"Fine, I can feed into your stalker-ish tendencies for a month," Annie concedes, placing an elbow on the bar and resting her chin on her hand. "But I have some rules of my own."

"I'm all ears, honey," I quip, the endearment falling so effortlessly off my lips, my sour mood from before she got here making me brave. There's nothing she can say to me that can make me feel shittier than how I felt after the phone call with my father.

"Don't call me that," she bites back, and I can't help but feel even braver.

"But you're just so sweet," I say, giving her a wink. She

doesn't realize that the more she pushes me away, the sweeter it'll be when she finally gives in to me.

She rolls her eyes and tucks her hair behind her ears, and I can see the smallest tinge of pink on the tops of her ears.

Her voice takes a more serious tone. "I'm not home much for meals during the week while working at the shelter until my rotations start next month, so we can just plan to fend for ourselves. I'll do my own grocery shopping, and I'll clean up after myself in the kitchen. The bathroom and living room too."

I can almost feel the force she's using to push me away, always making sure she can keep people at arm's length. "We are just coexisting in the same space. Again, I appreciate you letting me stay with you, but let's not pretend it'll be more than that," she adds.

There's a hint of vulnerability in her voice, like she's not only reminding me of the wall she put between us, but herself too.

"And here I was thinking we would have candle-lit dinners together every night," I tease, hoping it comes off as a joke rather than the wishful thinking it is.

In reality, a sense of disappointment washes over me as I realize that this plan of using the month to get closer to Annie is going to be even harder than I thought it would be—and I didn't think it was going to be remotely easy in the first place.

"You wish, bartender," she replies, taking advantage of how I'm leaning on the bar in front of her, bringing her palm to my cheek to pat it twice before finishing the last few sips of her drink.

I shake my head, not missing how she pats Rosie just like that.

"Emmett's hired three more bartenders with me leaving at the end of summer and the baby on the way. Two of them are coming from different bars, but one will need training, so I'll be here most nights for the next few weeks, especially if the baby comes when it's supposed to." I push off the bar, standing to my full height and grabbing her glass to make her a fresh drink. "We'll be on opposite schedules, so no candle-lit dinners even if I wanted to."

Something passes over Annie's face, but it's gone before I can realize what it is. She shrugs her shoulders. "Fine by me," she responds, but the nonchalance feels forced.

We don't say anything until I set her new drink down in front of her, and I can tell by the way she watches the ice as she stirs her drink with the straw that she's thinking about how we can sit and make rules for this arrangement of ours, but there's no way of knowing how it's *actually* going to go.

And if she's thinking the same thing as me, it's how she can try to avoid me all she wants, but it doesn't change the fact that we are living under the same roof.

It won't just be coexisting.

Not if I can help it.

I have a month to make her love me again.

And if I can't do it, at least I'll be strides closer than I was before.

Because I'm never giving up.

I break our silence. "One more thing," I start, wanting to prompt some sort of conversation about how if she needs to stay longer, she can.

It will take some time to get her to talk to me about how she feels about the break-in or if she'll even want to go back to her apartment when the investigation is over, and I know staying with me won't be her first choice for more than this month we agreed on, but I could talk to the leasing office at my complex to see if there's something available for her.

"What? You want to implement a chore chart?" she teases, looking up at me with feigning innocence as she takes a sip of her new gin and tonic.

She's being a total brat, and she doesn't know what that does to me.

"Funny. Actually, I wanted to ask when you plan on putting that little blue *friend* of yours to use. We do share a bathroom and a wall, just want to make sure I can give you your privacy."

As the last word leaves my mouth, Annie's lips part, and her eyes slightly widen before they narrow on me, and I realize these words about her using her vibrator may have been the last I ever speak.

And I think I'm okay with it.

I can't help but grin with all my teeth pulling this reaction from her. I raise an eyebrow, inviting her to answer my question, seeing if she takes the opportunity to put me back in my place.

"I honestly think I could kill you right now." Her voice is like ice shooting directly into my veins, but there's nothing that could put out the fire inside me that burns just for her.

"I'm fine dying if you're the last thing I see."

CHAPTER 8
ANNIE

THE FIRST WEEK living with Luke goes by in a bit of a blur. Working opposite schedules Monday through Friday helps keep the much-needed distance between us.

I leave for my veterinarian assistant job at the shelter in the morning while Luke is still sleeping, and he's already at Lenny's by the time I get home.

We've barely crossed paths except for the texts we send about when we're leaving or when we'll be home, and we fell into a comfortable routine fairly quickly.

I feed Rosie breakfast before I leave for work; Luke feeds her dinner before he leaves. I load and run the dishwasher; he unloads it. I put leftovers from making dinner for him in the fridge; he puts out my tin of matcha and water in the electric tea kettle before he goes to bed.

Just *normal* roommate things, all of it happening as the days passed.

I close the door behind me as I take my shoes off. Luke is at Lenny's now, so I go through my new nightly routine of throwing my stuff into the guest room, taking Rosie for a quick walk around the block, showering, getting in my pajamas, and making dinner.

I was able to pick up my laptop and other things from the police station yesterday. I picked up more of my stuff with Mia and Drew last weekend, and I'm not letting myself acknowledge how it only took a few days in this new routine for Luke's apartment to feel less like a place I'm staying and more like a *home*.

I blame my familiarity with Luke for the feelings, knowing that my comfort with him never completely faded away all those years ago.

I keep telling myself it is only natural for my body to feel comfortable in his space.

But, despite how much I told him—and myself—that we were better off forgetting everything that happened between us, it doesn't feel like we ever will.

The memories we shared have faded, thinking about them doesn't hurt as much as it used to, but they all feel so tainted. He is so intertwined in my childhood, my teenage years, and now my life as an adult, and I hope I'll be able to one day look back at my relationship with Luke and not feel so much betrayal, especially because he's not going anywhere.

Not only because of our friends, but because I truly think that he would follow me wherever I go.

And that's starting to not scare me as much as it used to

I finish cleaning the kitchen from making dinner, and I am about to head into my room to find something to do for the rest of the night when my phone rings.

I already heard from my advisor earlier this week about my rotations, and I was able to get my rotation schedule finalized, so I know she isn't the one calling. The number looks familiar though, and when I answer I understand why.

"Hi, Annie," the gruff voice greets, "Lou Daniels here. I have an update about your apartment."

Hope bubbles in my chest at the same time a sliver of disappointment makes its way into my stomach. If it's good news, it could mean that I can move back in.

If everything went well with the investigation, it could mean I don't have to stay with Luke for the rest of the month.

So why is part of me hoping it isn't good news?

Mr. Daniels continues, "It looks like the investigation is on track to finish by mid-August, but I noticed that you are due to renew your lease on September 1st."

My feet move on their own, pacing back and forth across the living room as I wait for him to continue. He clears his throat. "Due to your *unique* circumstance," he starts, alluding to the break-in that *his* complex may be at fault for if the police's findings prove the complex was negligent with the windows they installed, "I understand if you do not wish to renew your lease with us."

"Um," I start, my feet stopping me in the middle of the kitchen, "I haven't decided yet."

It's technically true—I haven't. But, before the break-in, it never would have been something *to* decide. I would've renewed my lease without a second thought.

My mind has been so focused on just getting through this next month living with Luke, I haven't thought about what I'll do after the time was up.

Do I really want to go back to a place where all of this bullshit happened?

The break-in definitely spooked me, but I can't deny that I *was* lucky. At the moment, it didn't feel like it, but I can understand why Officer Collins said so.

I was lucky I wasn't there, that the kid couldn't take much, and that they caught him. The hassle of dealing with it all is what has been weighing more heavily on me than anything else.

"If you could let me know your decision by the time the investigation is over, I would appreciate it," Mr. Daniels says, unaware of my inner spiraling.

"Yeah, definitely. I'll think about it, and I'll let you know. Thanks, Mr. Daniels," I rush out.

He mumbles off a goodbye before we end the call, and I start pacing again.

Do I want to move back there?

It's the easier option, and I did love the complex before this whole debacle put a sour taste in my mouth.

If I don't go back there, where the hell am I going to go?

I can't stay with Luke—not with our history and everything that resurfaces when we're alone together—and my two closest friends have lives of their own; they aren't at the point in their lives where they are looking for a roommate.

But I'm going to be 25 in a few weeks, and I've lived alone since I was 18. The thought of a roommate just doesn't sit well with me, and I don't have the kind of parents who would let me stay with them until I got back on my feet.

I don't even hear the door open and shut behind me until I see Rosie jump off the couch where she has been watching me pace back and forth for who knows how long.

"Anxiously awaiting my arrival, Annie girl?" Luke quips, his signature smile on his face. His long blonde hair looks like he just ran his fingers through it, and his blue eyes have an amused sparkle as he takes me in.

My pajama set suddenly feels entirely too revealing, and, even though the shorts and tank top cover everything, I don't need Luke, of all people, to see.

"You're home early," I say, putting my hands on my hips.

"I texted you," he replies as he walks into the kitchen.

I glance at my phone, and sure enough, a text from Luke—I must have not heard the notification when I was on the phone.

"But it's only 8 o'clock, who's at the bar?" I know Emmett has been opening all week, wanting to make sure he gets as much of the administrative stuff for the month done before the baby is born.

"I figured Ava could finish the shift on her own."

Ava

Another girl's name on his lips makes my skin prickle.

"Who's Ava?" I ask, wanting to slap my hand over my mouth the second the question leaves my lips.

Luke's eyebrows raise as he sets his backpack down on the kitchen counter, and I feel the tips of my ears heat. I untuck my hair from behind my ears before crossing my arms. "Jealous?" he coos, and I want to kick him in the shin.

I take a few steps into the kitchen, coming to stand in front of him across the counter. "I just feel sorry for any girl who has to spend her nights with you," I reply, hoping the confidence in my voice doesn't sound as fake as it is.

For the past seven years, Luke has never once talked about his dating life or if he has been seeing anyone. Not with me at least. I know he's had flings because one of our friends would always mention it.

He can do whatever he wants, I don't care.

I do whatever the hell I want.

But the prickly feeling on my skin only worsens when I think of Luke spending his time with another girl.

And that only proves that Luke and I should *not* be in the same space, alone, for extended periods of time. It brings up too many emotions, ones I have been able to bury for years. It's only been a week, but when he leaves me notes on the counter that say "I hope you have a good day" or "Thanks for making dinner again", I can't pretend that I don't wish things were different.

"I have one more week of training her, but she should be good to go by next week," Luke explains. "But don't worry, she'll never replace you." He's trying to get a rise out of me, and it's working.

One month is already way too long to be spending here— especially because it is *much* harder to ignore my feelings about Luke if our paths are going to start crossing much more with him having fewer shifts with the three new bartenders.

An idea pops into my head, when I remember that Luke is

supposed to be leaving Lenny's at the end of August. I know he has his plans of moving back home—back to our hometown—to start work with his dad.

I have my own opinions about that son of a bitch, but it's not my place anymore.

Regardless, Luke plans to move, so maybe I could take over his lease here when he does.

It's a win-win for both of us.

Kind of.

That sliver of disappointment is back when I think about what happens after this month of living together, but it's a stupid feeling to have. I don't even want to be here in the first place.

Right?

"So," I start, ready to broach the subject. "I just got off the phone with my apartment complex." I watch as Luke's playful expression takes a more serious one.

With someone as happy-go-lucky as him, *seriousness* always looks so foreign on him. "The manager wanted to know if I was going to be renewing my lease in September."

"Okay," Luke says warily, stretching out the word.

"But, I'm not sure if I want to."

He rolls his lips together as he keeps his eyes on me. I can't quite decipher what I see in his eyes—hope?—before he gives me a curt nod, urging me to continue.

"I was thinking, since I'm already staying here," I start, but, before I can say more, both of our phones go off.

We both check the message, and then look back up at each other.

"The baby's coming," we say at the same time, and then we're running out the door.

CHAPTER 9
LUKE

WE'RE SPEEDING to the hospital, and I don't even have time to wonder what Annie was about to say to me back at our—no, *my*—apartment. She's next to me in the passenger seat, on the phone with Mia.

Part of Drew's birth plan was to have both Annie and Mia in the delivery room with her and Emmett, and the message from Emmett in the group chat said Drew was going to be ready to push within the hour.

Leave it to Drew to wait until the last possible second to tell her husband, "Hey, these contractions are coming in fast and are really starting to hurt. Maybe we should go to the hospital."

I think that's why Drew and Annie get along so well— both always putting on a strong front, both hating to ask for help.

At least Drew learned after everything she and Emmett went through—Annie, not so much.

"Are you guys there?" Annie asks Mia over the phone, but I can't hear the response. We're stopped at a red light, no more than two minutes away.

Her slightly wet hair is falling over her shoulders and down her chest, and her exposed arms are pebbled with goosebumps. It's a warm July night, but I turn the heat in the car on a little bit anyway.

Annie didn't even think to change out of her *stupid* pajamas with those *stupid* little cherries on them. She just slipped on some sneakers in our rush to get out the door.

Now—not only do I have to worry about what Annie was going to say to me before we had to rush to the hospital, and that two of our best friends might have our niece or nephew before we even get there—-I *also* have to worry about how the fuck I'm going to go to sleep every night for the next three weeks picturing Annie in the room next to me wearing *those*.

She turns to look at me, and she catches my eyes fixed on her. She glares back at me as she tells Mia we're almost there before hitting me in the arm and pointing to the traffic light that is now green.

I turn back to the road and have to resist the urge to groan out loud at all the thoughts circling in my head.

We pull into the hospital parking lot and see Mia and Eddie walking up to the entrance. Annie is out of the car before I can even put it in park, and then the four of us are running through the halls of the place looking for where we can find Drew.

When we are finally all where we need to be —Annie and Mia in the room with Drew, Eddie and I in the hallway outside—I take the first breath I have since I got home tonight and ran into Annie for the first time since she moved in last week.

"Can you believe it?" I ask Eddie, grabbing his shoulder and giving him a little shake. "Drew and Emmett are about to be *parents*. We're about to be *uncles*."

Eddie shakes his head, looking down and letting out a chuckle. "I know, man. It's fucking nuts."

We both lean back on the wall across the door from Drew's room, staying out of the way of the doctors and nurses who keep going in and out. Emmett came out to tell us that it shouldn't be much longer, and I haven't seen the man with that much emotion on his face since his wedding day.

"So, Annie hasn't murdered you yet," Eddie says. "I assume the two of you living together is going well?"

I can't help the smile that forms on my face as I think about how *good* living with Annie has been. Even though we haven't seen much of each other, sharing a space with her is the closest I've felt to her in a long time.

"Being alive to tell the tale is answer enough," I tell my friend, wishing that I could say more. Out of all our friends, I think Eddie suspects something between me and Annie the most. All our other friends know that there's *something* between us, but I'm positive they think I have a harmless crush on her that she doesn't reciprocate.

"We'll see if you can say the same in a few weeks," he says before he laughs.

I let out a laugh of my own, remembering all the thoughts that ran through my brain when Annie and I were talking in the kitchen.

She said she might *not* want to go back to her old apartment.

Does that mean she wants to stay longer? I can't lie and say I wouldn't be surprised if that's the case.

Maybe she was going to tell me she was going to look for another place? If that's the case, my complex is an option. Of course, I'd rather her be with me, but being neighbors wouldn't be too bad either.

It turned out *extremely* well for Drew and Emmett.

I grab my phone from my pocket, typing up a quick email to my complex's leasing office to see if there are any units available.

"Are you ever going to tell me what happened between you two?" Eddie asks, his voice a few notches quieter.

Eddie was there when I came to Lenny's seven years ago—he saw the look on Annie's face when she saw me—and he worked with us at Lenny's for most of those years. I'm pretty sure he knows there is more to the story, but he's never asked.

I made a promise to Annie that I wouldn't tell anyone about us, but it's hard to keep my head on straight when it comes to her.

"There's nothing to tell," I reply, a little too quickly, slipping my phone back in the pocket of my jeans.

"Did something happen at Drew and Emmett's wedding?"

I turn to look at my friend. His green eyes are highlighted under the hospital's fluorescent lights, making the scar across the left side of his face a little more noticeable. His gaze is questioning, one of curiosity, not anything accusatory.

I figured our friends suspected Annie and I hooked up that night because she ended up in my hotel room, but we didn't. She was drunk, and she dropped a bomb on me then fell asleep. I've never been able to ask her what she meant about being tired of pretending to hate me.

I probably never will.

But that night was an eventful night all around—being that Drew and Emmett got married *and* Mia's brother found out that she and Eddie had been secretly dating behind his back. It's not surprising that nobody has ever asked us about it with everything else that went on.

"I wish," I joke, hoping to bring a lightness back to the conversation.

Eddie nods, looking away from me and back at the door to Drew's room.

"We all see the way you look at her, Luke," Eddie says. My whole body tenses. "You look at her like she hung the moon."

I run a hand through my hair, and let out a dry chuckle. *The moon.* It shines through the darkness, always giving glimpses, only showing its full self after weeks of waiting. But that full moon makes all the glimpses, all the waiting, worth it. "No, man. She didn't hang the moon," I answer before I can stop myself. "She *is* the moon."

CHAPTER 10
ANNIE

"I DON'T THINK I've ever felt this tired in my life," I say to Luke as we walk into our—no, *his*—apartment. "I can't even imagine how Drew is feeling right now."

Rosie greets us at the door like she always does, and I give her a few scratches on the head before I make a beeline to the couch.

From the moment we got the text that Drew was in labor, things did not slow down.

By the time we got to the hospital, Emmett told us she was already no more than an hour away from being ready to push —the crazy bitch didn't even have time for an epidural and refused to tell the doctors that her pain was above a five.

After only a handful of pushes, Mia and I taking turns holding the hand Emmett wasn't holding, little Lennon was here.

We went to wait with the boys while the doctors checked on Mom and the newest member of our family, and then we were all able to make our proper introductions to our niece a few hours later.

When my head hits the cushion on Luke's couch, the exhaustion from the work week and the excitement of the past six hours hits me hard. Luke and I both have the day off tomorrow, and I don't even have the energy to stress about not having work as a way to keep the two of us busy—and separate.

"Come take a shot with me," I hear Luke say from the kitchen.

"It's two in the morning, I'm not taking a shot with you," I tell him from the couch. This man's energy never seems to run out.

"Please? It's not every night we become an aunt and uncle," he replies.

Too tired to argue, I grumble, "Fine," and get up from the couch, covering my mouth with the back of my hand as I let out a yawn. The only hard liquor I drink is gin; anything else reminds me of going around the trailer and picking up bottles of vodka, whiskey, tequila, and whatever my dad could get his hands on.

Gin was the only one he didn't like.

It definitely isn't ideal for a shot, but when I get to the counter, it's what Luke pulled out from the cabinet above his fridge, along with two shot glasses.

He pours the gin for the two of us, and we each pick up one of the small glasses. He holds his up in front of me. "To Lennon, the seventh member of the Lenny's crew." Luke smiles at me, and I have to roll my eyes to avoid sinking into those baby blues.

I gave my heart to Luke all those years ago, and I never once asked for it back. The emptiness in my chest became a reminder of why I don't let people all the way in, why I always keep loved ones at arm's length, why I'll never let myself love anyone like I loved Luke.

So maybe it's the exhaustion or the happiness I'm feeling for Drew, Emmett, and Lennon, but I can't ignore the feeling in my chest, the one that feels like my heart is filling beyond its means.

I don't have a heart. Not anymore.

But right now, it feels like I do.

And I can't help but think there is no one else I'd rather celebrate this moment with.

"To Lennon," I echo, holding up my shot glass to clink with Luke's.

We both take the shot, the piney—almost medicinal—taste shoots a warmth through my body as I set the glass down.

Luke coughs into his fist, setting his glass next to mine. "I don't know how you drink that shit."

A laugh escapes me as he shakes his head, his blonde hair whipping across his face, looking like Rosie after she gets out of the bath. "Why do you have it if you don't even like it?" I reach for the bottle, pulling it closer to inspect the label, and notice it's the same one I buy, the same one I convinced Emmett to carry at Lenny's.

"Because you like it," he answers, and the heart I felt a moment ago skips a beat.

"This obsession with me is getting out of hand, Lukey-poo," I tease, needing to gain the upper hand. I back away from the counter, closing the distance between me and the guest bedroom.

The apartment is mostly dark, aside from the light in the kitchen. It's quiet enough to make it feel like we're the only two people in the world.

Nothing good happens at two in the morning.

Because it feels too much like a dream. Like whatever happens in the middle of the night won't matter in the morning.

Luke takes a few steps toward me, and my feet are stuck to the ground. My words must have hit a nerve because there's none of his usual demeanor—no flirty sarcasm, no bright grin, no playful wink. All I see is that same edge I saw before when he told me I was coming to stay with him. The one that shuts me up and makes my brain short-circuit.

"Obsessed doesn't even begin to describe how I feel about you, Annie girl." His words are a kick to the back of the knees, and I am being thrown back in time. Back when I never thought I'd have to learn what it felt like to live a life without loving Luke.

"You don't mean that," I whisper, and he takes another step closer to me. Close enough that if I unglued my feet to the floor, I could close the space between us with a step of my own. "It's been seven years, Luke. It's been over for just as long. This," I say, gesturing between the two of us, "is nothing."

The words feel like sand on my tongue.

They don't feel like the truth.

"You're it for me, Annie, whether you want to see it or not. It's always been you. Always will be."

I feel pressure behind my eyes, so many feelings plummeting into me hearing his words.

The words I wished for in secret over the years.

The words I know he thinks he means but doesn't.

The words I wish meant *something*.

My feet move until I can feel his cool breath against my lips, until our chests are no more than an inch away from meeting, until I can make out every single drop in his ocean eyes.

I hate him for making me feel like this.

I hate him for what he did for me, almost as much as I hate myself for not being able to move on from it.

I hate him for never letting me go.

I hate him for being here, for following me when I tried to run away.

I hate him because I love him. I always have, and I always will.

I fucking hate him.

And I kiss him.

CHAPTER 11
LUKE

KISSING Annie feels like coming home.

My arms find her hips, grabbing her hard enough to leave bruises, her arms looping around my neck and pulling me in closer.

As her lips move against mine, I swallow her soft moans, jasmine and rose overwhelming my senses. This moment makes all the waiting, all the loving her from afar, completely worth it.

Her kisses taste like pine with a hint of cherries, and her body fits so perfectly against mine. I haven't kissed her since I was 18, yet my body reacts to her as if the past seven years were no more than just one night away from her.

My hands roam to her lower back, molding her body into mine as much as I can, so I never forget what it feels like.

Her fingers move up the back of my neck and into my hair, pulling tightly, the slight sting of my scalp like oxygen to the fire inside me.

My tongue slides against her bottom lip, asking politely for access.

I need to taste more of her.

My mind just keeps repeating the mantra: *more, more, more.*

More of Annie.

More of my Annie girl.

More because it'll never be enough.

My bottom lip gets caught between her teeth, and the growl that comes out of me just makes her bite harder.

I should have known that I'm not kissing the Annie I knew in high school. Kissing this version of her isn't just sweet kisses and gentle touches.

It's fighting for control; it's dominating.

It's fucking *heaven.*

And then it stops.

I open my eyes just in time to see her take a step back, her hand going to her swollen lips, her eyes both hazy with lust and widened with worry—maybe even regret.

Against my better judgment, I reach for her, only for her to widen the distance between us, until she's in her room, the door to the guest room closing before I can convince her that this wasn't a mistake.

———

Saying I didn't sleep well last night would be the understatement of the century. It was already past two in the morning when we got home from the hospital, and I remember seeing light coming in from under my curtains when I finally stopped tossing and turning.

By seven in the morning, alternating between dreams of kissing Annie and nightmares of her face when she pulled away, I got up and took a cold shower, knowing sleep was not in the cards today.

Every time I feel like I'm one step closer to Annie, she pushes me fifteen steps back. Last night being a perfect example. She seemingly let me in—making me think all my hard work was paying off—only for her to shut me out again.

I know it felt too real to her. I could tell by the way she looked at me when I told her it's always been her. I heard it in the shakiness of her voice when she said there was nothing between us.

She's lying to herself as much as she's lying to me.

She'll tell me, our friends, herself that she hates me when she doesn't.

She kissed *me*.

That kiss was like nothing I've ever experienced, which isn't hard to believe. No one has ever made me feel the way Annie does—the spark, the heat, the thrill that I feel every time Annie rolls her eyes at something I say or gives me her signature death glare.

I know, with everything I am, that she is worth it.

Last night proved that I'm getting somewhere with her, and the more she tries to convince herself that it's over between us, the harder it makes me want to fight.

I glance at her door, not surprised it's closed, and I tiptoe closer to see if I can hear her moving around. I swallowed my pride when it came to Annie years ago, and I have no shame pressing my ear to the door if it means I might cross paths with her this morning.

Rosie didn't sleep with me last night, and she's not on the couch, so I know she's in there with Annie, and it sounds like they're both fast asleep; there's no movement coming from the other side of the door.

I walk over to the kitchen, my mind turning with all the ways I could keep myself busy today. Knowing I can't sit with my own thoughts too long, I glance at the clock on my oven and see it's just past nine.

Rosie won't stay in bed much past that—lucky for me, I adopted a dog that matches my energy and inability to sit still for too long—and a buzz of anticipation comes over me knowing I'll get to see Annie, but it quickly fizzles out.

Before the kiss, I was hopeful that both of us being off

today would get me a little time with her, maybe convince her to take Rosie for a walk or get lunch. But now?

I know Annie. She is going to avoid me like the plague today.

If Little Miss Lennon hadn't made her grand appearance into the world last night, I could've gone to talk to Emmett about my last shift, but I suppose that's on the back burner for the foreseeable future—there is no way I am on his short list of priorities right now.

The three new bartenders are on their own today and will be more so now that Emmett is on paternity leave. I'll probably still head in later to make sure everything is okay.

My last shift at Lenny's is supposed to be at the end of August, but I want to throw up every time I imagine what my life will turn into if I move back home and work with my dad.

I might be able to put off quitting Lenny's and working at the law firm now that Emmett has his family to worry about—running the bar could be something I take off his hands for a month or two—but that conversation with my dad *also* makes me want to throw up.

A conversation that is weighing so heavily on my shoulders, one I need to get off my chest before it buries me. One that I'll put off a little longer while I figure out what to do with myself today.

I decide to see if my brother is busy, hoping I can take my mind off all this stuff with Annie and my dad, even if it's easier said than done—especially the Annie part.

Bennett is technically my half-brother, just like Caleb, but it has never stopped me from seeing them as family. I sure as hell don't see my parents as such.

"Hey, Lu. You caught us at the perfect time." Bennett answers on the first ring. As a firefighter, I know it's usually a hit or miss on whether or not he'll be able to talk. He alternates between 24-hour shifts and having 48-hours off, and I'm not surprised that he isn't alone—almost always with his best friend, co-worker, and roommate, Jack, who I assume is the "us" he is referring to.

"Hi, Luke," Jack says, confirming my thoughts.

"We're on our way to get breakfast, not too far from you actually. Want us to pick you up?"

I take one more look at Annie's door. Knowing she'll want space after last night, I take out the notepad and pen I've been using for my notes to her all week from my junk drawer.

Holding my phone up to my ear with my shoulder, I write her a quick note that I'm going out with Bennett and Jack.

"Yeah, I'll tag along. See you guys in a few."

The three of us spend the short car ride to the diner a few minutes from my apartment catching up about our jobs, and both Bennett and Jack update me on all the latest Owens and Hastings family drama—both families having their fair share of issues. The biggest one always seems to be how my dad still hates Jack for convincing Bennett to become a firefighter with him.

When we sit down at the diner and each order a coffee, I fill them in on my timeline with the law firm and how my dad won't get off my ass about it.

"So, you're still planning on working with Dad?" Bennett asks before taking a sip from his mug.

"Yeah. I'm sure he can't wait to finally have the 'sons' part of Owens & Sons," I answer dryly, taking a sip of my own coffee.

Jack and Bennett exchange a glance. "Are you still planning on moving home?" Bennett asks. He and Jack have an apartment about halfway between where I live and where we all grew up, our hometown being about 45 minutes north of where I live now.

"That's the plan," I answer. "I'm supposed to move back at the end of August so I can start at the firm, but I haven't looked much for a place. Plus, my boss just had a baby, so things at work have been a little chaotic."

"The bar has been busy?" Jack asks.

"I have been picking up some of the slack since Emmett's been busy with Drew and prepping for the baby. They're my friends too, so I didn't want him worrying about work when there's more important stuff to worry about."

"But your dad wants you to start in September?"

"Unfortunately," I retort without thinking, the dismay evident in my tone.

"You sound excited." I don't miss the sarcasm in his voice. Jack has become almost as much of a brother as Bennett and Caleb over the years, and he is no stranger to what having a dad like Daniel Owens does to one's psyche.

His dark hair is as long as my brother's, Bennett's blonde hair being even lighter than mine. Both guys are tall and in great shape due to their jobs, barely fitting in the booth where they are seated across from me.

I let out a sigh. "It's just hard imagining myself as a lawyer. I like where I am now and what I'm doing now." It's the truth. I like working at the bar, helping Emmett train the new guys, and the social aspect of being a bartender. The same can't be said for being a lawyer. "I'll get over it," I add.

"There was more excitement in your voice over playing 'boss' at the bar than there was about the career you *supposedly* have always wanted," Bennett responds. And he isn't wrong. Ever since I agreed to take his place at the firm, I played the part. I told everyone—friends, family, Annie—that I was declining the hockey scholarship because *I* wanted to, even if it was a lie I wasn't just telling them but myself too.

A lie I've been telling since my senior year of high school.

I shrug my shoulders. "I like that Emmett can rely on me, and I've been running things on my own." I've taken the new bartenders' training schedules, inventory, and the distributors and deliveries off Emmett's plate all week, and things have gone well. "I'm not too bad at it."

"Then buy a bar," Bennett replies. He says it with such

finality that is laughable to me, like it really is that simple. I don't mind playing "boss", as Jack put it, but running Lenny's isn't something I want to do for the rest of my life.

It's something I want to watch *Emmett* do for the rest of my life.

But buying a place that's mine, for me to run how I want to, sounds much more appealing than I thought it would.

No.

I let out a laugh, but there isn't much humor behind it. "I'm sticking to the plan, Ben." I give him a smile that I hope proves to him that I'm fine, even if he just gave me one more thing I have no business thinking about.

"You don't have to be a lawyer," he assures, and I take a page from Annie's book and roll my eyes.

"That's easy for you to say."

Bennett and I don't really talk about my decision to step up and do what our father wanted for him. It's something that has gone unspoken in our family.

Until now, apparently.

"I know the pressure Dad puts on you is partly my fault, and I'm sorry for that," Bennett starts, "but you're an adult. You don't have to do anything you don't want to do."

I hear what my brother is saying, and I want to believe it. It sounds so *possible* when it's out in the open, but there's this nagging feeling deep in my gut that won't go away. This feeling of dread, of not wanting to be an even bigger disappointment than I already am.

"Every time I think of doing something different with my life, I tell myself I can't just back out now, not after all the time and money—Dad's money—I put into it," I protest, arguing a point that I don't even want to make. It feels more like an excuse. "He's not even my biological dad, and he put me through school and now is giving me a spot at his firm. People would *kill* for that."

"You do not owe him anything, Luke. You and I both

know that it took me dropping out for him to even look at you as his son." His voice is harsh, and the words feel like a knife to my chest. But they are the truth.

This is not what I was expecting when I agreed to breakfast this morning, and by the slight rise of Jack's eyebrows and the way Bennett pauses, I don't think either of them were expected it either.

Bennett's words are the same words I've thought to myself my entire life, but I always told myself I was overreacting. Hearing it from someone else's perspective makes it all the more real. All the years of feeling like I wasn't good enough for the family I thought I was born into, just to find out that, for my father, it was true.

It all must show on my face because Bennett adds, "You're my brother. You always have been because all that other shit our parents tried to hide from us doesn't matter to me. You and Caleb matter to me. Caleb is doing what he wants to; I'm doing what I want. You deserve the same. Who gives a fuck what Dad thinks?"

Jack nods, agreeing with my brother. Bennett's right. I don't care what my dad thinks—not anymore—but why can't I feel anything but guilt for not wanting to stick to what I made the choice to do?

"I'll figure it out," I finally say, but there is nothing in my voice that sounds convincing. I can tell Bennett is thinking the same, but he doesn't push it. Our waitress comes over to take our order, and the rest of breakfast is more of catching up and filling each other in on our lives.

I tell them about last night and meeting Lennon, updating them on both Drew and Emmett. They ask about Eddie and Mia, and I fill them in on their courthouse wedding last week and how both the band and Mia's photography business is doing.

Jack and Bennett, along with my oldest brother, have met the Lenny's crew on many occasions over the years. Drew,

Eddie, Mia, and I, being the ones with siblings, always try to bring our brothers and sisters around our friends—Emmett's sister, Lennon, is always around in spirit.

Finally, as we finish our breakfasts, Bennett asks about Annie.

Both Jack and Bennett know my history with her because they had front-row seats to not only our whole relationship but when she up and left me too. The two of them watched the two of us grow up, and they both always gave me a hard time about her, thinking that she was the one who got away.

Little do they know that I love a challenge, and Annie is the biggest one of all.

"You're telling me you have to live with the girl who broke your heart for the next month?" Bennett exasperates. They both got a kick out of me convincing Annie to live with me, not knowing the whole story of who she is now.

I let out a real laugh this time. "It's a living hell," I tell them, deciding that I can disclose more about Annie and me to them than I can our friends. "I just can't get over her, you guys. There's no one like her."

"No one like Vivian Mitchell? She was the quietest little girl I think I've ever known. I don't think she ever said one word to me even though I was at your guys' house as much as she was," Jack recalls with a smile and shake of the head.

The memory of the quiet Annie who used to come over to do homework or study hits me right in the heart.

From the moment our first-grade teacher sat us next to each other, I followed Annie around like a lost puppy. Her shyness intrigued me, even at such a young age, because it was such a stark contrast to me, and all I ever wanted to do was get her out of her shell.

I would talk her ear off, ask her questions, and try to make her laugh, and those moments she gave me more than a nod of her head or a small smile became addicting.

I knew I loved Annie from the moment I saw her, but that

love transformed when we got to high school. Admiring her turned into *needing* her, and it wasn't until we made things official in that she opened up about her parents and her life at the trailer park.

I realized that maybe she needed me as much as I needed her.

When she told me about the shit her parents said to her—especially her mom—she thought I was joking when I told her she should move into my bedroom.

"She's nothing like that anymore," I tell Jack. "Now, she'd tell you anything you want to hear, even the shit you don't," I joke, not being able to fully put into words who Annie is now.

Vivian, as Jack remembers her, hated being called by that name.

We were in fifth grade when Annie told me she wished she didn't have to have the same name as her mom.

I didn't think much of it at the time, not making the connection between Annie hating her name and hating how her mom treated her until much later.

My 10-year-old brain went straight to the conclusion that if she didn't like it, I would call her something else—simple as that.

And from that day on, she was Annie to me.

"Well, be careful. We both saw what it did to you when she broke up with you," Bennett says as the waitress drops off our check. We each throw down a $20 as he continues. "I'm not going to sit here and tell you she isn't worth it because that look in your eyes when you talk about her tells me you're going to do what you want anyway. So, just be careful, okay?"

"Yeah, it sounds like she'd enjoy hurting you this time around," Jack jokes, and, as we're walking back out to the car, I can't help but think about how right he is.

The guys drop me off at my apartment, and I feel a little lighter than I did this morning. Talking about my dad and all the decisions I have to make sucked, but it needed to happen. I have a lot to think about because whatever I decide isn't going to just affect me.

I start heading into the complex at the same time a familiar head of brown waves and cherry lips walks my dog towards me, and I don't even try to hide the grin that forms on my face, the same one I wear whenever I see her.

"Fancy seeing you here, Lukey-poo," she sing-songs as she takes a headphone out of her ear. "Good breakfast with Jack and Ben?"

"Those endorphins from your walk put you in a good mood or something?" I tease. "Why are you being so nice to me?"

Her smile has a sinister twist, and I know she is either planning my demise, or has already put the plan into action. "Is me being nice to you *that* out of the ordinary?" she asks, feigning innocence in the way she bats her eyelashes.

I take Rosie's leash from her. "Yes," I reply without a second thought.

She laughs, and the sound is music to my ears. "You just know me too well," she answers. "I might possibly need something from you."

I open the door and follow her in, knowing all too well that whatever she wants, it's already hers.

CHAPTER 12

ANNIE

"WHAT COULD you possibly need from me?" Luke asks as he follows me into the entrance of the apartment complex. He is in his usual attire of a white Henley and jeans, and his blonde hair seems even more golden with the sun coming through the glass door. I turn around to find his blue eyes on me, their usual sparkle shining bright, and I have to turn forward so I don't trip over my feet at the sight of that smile.

"I'm glad you asked," I counter over my shoulder, brushing my hair behind me as we walk down the hallway to his apartment. "We never got to finish our conversation from last night."

"You're right," Luke says as I pull out my set of keys to his place and go to unlock the door. "I wasn't even halfway done kissing you."

My hands freeze, and my keychain falls out of my hand. My cheeks are already hot from my walk with Rosie, and I do *not* blush—especially because of Luke—but I feel all the blood in my body rush to my face.

Luke bends down to pick up my keys, finishing the job of unlocking the door for us, and it takes me a moment to form any words.

It's not like I haven't thought of the kiss, for much longer than I'd like to admit, but it was definitely not the "conversation" I was talking about.

I could barely sleep last night after closing the door to the guest bedroom.

Half of me wanted to open the door right back up and finish what I started. The other half of me wanted to pack up all my shit and leave without a trace.

Again.

Kissing Luke was like a breath of fresh air—something I could very well become addicted to—which is exactly why it can never happen again.

Even if I wanted to give Luke and me another chance—which I don't—there is way too much to trudge up from a place buried deep inside of me for that to be able to happen.

Luke steps around me to walk into the apartment, and I resist the urge to slap my hand across my forehead.

I am *not* about to let one kiss change anything.

"Well, I was done kissing you." I pour my fake confidence into my delivery and hope Luke didn't notice how long it took for me to come up with a response—and not a very good one.

Before he can say anything else, I get our conversation back on track. "I meant the conversation before we found out the baby was coming."

Luke takes Rosie's leash off and hangs it up by the door. We both follow her into the living room, sitting on either side of her when she jumps up and plops down in the middle of the couch.

Once again playing the part of a perfect buffer.

I'm still in my red workout set from my walk, a sports bra and biker shorts, and I usually have to throw on a sweatshirt when I get back because of how cold Luke keeps the temperature in here. But for some reason I don't care to admit, I find myself needing to throw my hair up in a ponytail because I can't get my skin to cool.

"So you want to talk more about how you were jealous?" he says matter-of-factly, but the smirk on his lips gives him away. I feel the tips of my ears burn, reaching behind me to grab a pillow to chuck at him so he won't notice.

Why did I ever think this conversation was going to be easy?

He lets the pillow hit him, and I wish I threw it harder.

"First of all, bartender, I was not jealous. I told you I just felt bad for the new girl who had to spend every night of the week with you. Second of all, I have no reason to be jealous. She's just some girl you work with."

I regret the words almost instantly, not liking how they sound outside my head. *Just some girl you work with?* I sound *exactly* like a jealous girlfriend.

"Woah, careful there, honey. You're sounding like you might like me a little bit."

The smirk on his face makes me want to bite his lip off. "You wish," I argue, ignoring the term of endearment. I almost resort to sticking my tongue out, but I think it would turn him on.

He doesn't miss a beat. "More than you know."

"I hate you."

"No, you don't."

I close my eyes and let out an exhale because this man is insufferable, and my patience is running thin.

"I wanted to talk about my living situation, but it seems like I might not have to, considering I will probably kill you before our month is up and can just take your apartment from your cold, dead hands."

"You talking about how you want to kill me all the time doesn't have the effect you think it does."

I shake my head. "I'm ignoring that. Not because I don't have anything to say but because I think you'll like it too much."

"Aw, Annie girl. You know me too well," he flirts, throwing my words from earlier back at me.

I resist the urge to outwardly groan. "Like I was saying last night," I continue, needing to remember why I am willingly sitting on the couch with Luke, alone in our—*his*—apartment, suffering through his flirting. "I don't think I want to go back to my old complex. Whether the apartment is found negligent for the break-in or not, it just all put a bad taste in my mouth about it."

Luke nods, finally staying quiet, allowing me to go on.

Good boy.

"And I was thinking," I say, stretching out the words, trying to not avoid looking at his face, even though I'm 99% sure his eyes on me are what is making it feel so hot in here. "Since you—"

"You can stay here," he interrupts, and I momentarily forget what I was about to say.

"No, I mean—" I try, but he keeps talking before I can get the words out.

"You can stay however long you need."

Does he do this on purpose? Make it so hard to pull away.

"No, Luke. That's not what I meant. I thought because you're moving back home, I could take this place."

All the color from his face drains, and I instantly want to take back the words.

A few moments pass before he finally says, "I don't know if I'm moving back home." The words are barely above a whisper. It sounds like he doesn't want anyone to hear him, even though we are the only two people here, and my stomach knots.

"What are you talking about?" I ask, my volume matching his. As if whispering these words will nullify the conversation, make it so it doesn't count. Towards what? I don't know. Count towards me actually caring about what Luke wants to do with his life?

"I was talking to Bennett and Jack this morning, and I don't know if I want to be a lawyer."

Luke must expect me to be more surprised by this sentiment, but my face doesn't change.

I'm not even the smallest bit surprised.

I knew from the moment he told me he wasn't taking that hockey scholarship our senior year of high school, the one he worked his ass off for, that it wasn't the decision he wanted to make.

Both Luke and I come from families that didn't want us, and I think it's part of the reason we held so tightly to each other growing up.

His "father" took him in for the sole purpose of saving face, but I think it was more than that. I think Mr. Owens said Luke was his as a way to hurt his wife and his brother for their affair.

My parents didn't want a child.

Just like Luke, my parents didn't plan on having me, but I didn't find out when I was nine like he did. I was told every day for as long as I can remember that my mom and dad didn't want me.

That I ruined their lives, their relationship, their *everything*.

So I tried to become invisible at home, at school, anywhere. The people who were supposed to love me the most in this world are the ones who wished I was never born.

I grew up wondering why they even decided to have me to begin with. Then, the bullying started in high school, and I wished they never did.

My mom was my first bully, and, somehow, along the way, she taught me how to be the perfect target for my next ones.

There was one person who saw me, no matter how hard I tried to fall into the background, and that person is sitting here telling me his truth as if I didn't know him well enough to know it was a lie to begin with.

Luke was never meant to be invisible. It isn't who he is. So when his father finally saw him, I knew he wouldn't be able to resist, even if it meant giving up what he wanted.

"Okay," I say, stretching out the word. "So don't be one."

Luke throws his hands up in the air before using them to push his hair back. "Why does everyone make it sound so easy?" he asks looking up towards the ceiling, but I stay silent. "Nevermind," he says, exasperated, shaking the hair he just pushed away back in his face. "That doesn't matter. I'm sorry you can't take this place just because I have my own shit to figure out."

Why do I want to tell him that there is nothing to be sorry for?

That I'm here for him, to help him figure it all out.

"I emailed the leasing office last night," he continues, "I'm waiting to hear if there are any units here that are available."

I take in a sharp exhale, a small pressure in my chest forms at the thought that Luke can still be so good to me despite how much of a bitch I am to him.

A thought about Luke and me that I bury down with the rest of them.

"You didn't have to do that."

There's a sadness in his eyes that doesn't look right on his face. A small smile graces his lips, and it makes me miss his wide grin and even that maddening smirk.

I'm too taken aback by the pressure that just keeps growing in my chest to realize he's moved until he's kneeling on the floor in front of where I'm sitting on the couch, his hand gently cupping my cheek as if I'd break with even the slightest touch.

"When will you understand that I will do anything for you?"

He stands up and heads to his bedroom before I can process his words, his touch, *him*.

The door closes behind him, and the pressure in my chest doesn't subside.

I thought the space where my heart was supposed to be was empty, the pieces smashed and broken beyond repair.

Turns out, my heart has been there all along.

It just only beats for Luke.

CHAPTER 13
ANNIE

"WHAT DO you mean you don't want to do anything to celebrate your last summer?" Mia whines, the sun highlighting the golden specks in her brown eyes.

She and I are sharing a patio chair in Drew and Emmett's backyard as we watch Luke and Eddie play fetch with Rosie and Daisy.

"You start rotations in a few weeks," Drew adds from her chair across from us. Her red hair is braided, a few pieces loose to frame her face. Her lack of sleep is barely noticeable behind her new-mom glow as she holds a one-week-old Lennon against her chest.

I wait for her to clarify why my rotations starting constitutes as a reason to celebrate. "Your last hurrah at this stage in your life?" she adds, with an attitude that says *duh, Annie*, but I just keep staring at her, my eyebrows raising. "The kickoff to the last year of vet school?" Even more attitude.

"Those are not reasons to celebrate."

She lets out a groan, her head falling back against the chair. "You're no fun," she exasperates.

I resist the urge to roll my eyes, ignoring both of my friends as they throw temper tantrums. "It's no big deal. I want Saturday to be like any other Movie Night, that way Lenny can be there too."

"But it isn't just any other Movie Night," Mia argues. "We want to celebrate before it's too late. Soon, it'll be August, and you'll be too busy with your last three weeks at the shelter." I try to hide the curve of my lips as she rambles. "Then it'll be September, and you'll be too busy and tired for the next twelve months becoming a bigshot veterinarian, saving the lives of all the cutie little animals of the world."

"True," I start, stretching up the word. I'm still not convinced this weekend should be anything special. "So, Drew can give me her turn to pick the movie," I reply with a smile, only for Drew to give me a mock smile in return and reach into her drink on the table next to her to throw an ice cube at me.

The three of us laugh, putting a pin in the conversation.

Drew goes inside to change Lennon, and Mia and I watch Eddie and Luke run around with their dogs, Emmett shaking his head at the four of them, but I can make out the small smile on his face.

"So, almost another full week at Luke's," Mia says as we watch the boys.

"Almost," I echo with a sigh. My eyes find Luke as he tosses the tennis ball to Eddie for him to throw for Rosie and Daisy.

It's been almost a week since our conversation about Luke not only admitting he didn't want to be a lawyer but how he also admitted to trying to find a place for me before even knowing if I wanted to move back to my old apartment or not.

Luke is taking on most of the responsibility of Lenny's with Emmett staying home with Drew and the baby, so even though he was off, he still went in both Saturday night, and most of Sunday to make sure everything was okay.

I also had this nagging feeling that he was avoiding me

until it was replaced with the urge to punch myself in the face for caring if he was ignoring me or not.

We didn't see much of each other the rest of the weekend, and we fell back into our normal routine when the work week started. Tonight is the first night he hasn't been to Lenny's all week, but I wouldn't be surprised if he heads over there after this.

"Annie?"

I look at Mia. "What?"

"I asked if things were going okay, but you were too busy staring at Luke."

"Don't be dumb," I say as I lightly slap her on the arm. "I was just thinking about how I'm surprised he isn't racing Rosie and Daisy to get to the ball first."

Mia lets out a sigh as if she's disappointed in me.

"What?"

"You don't get to do this forever, you know," she says, raising an eyebrow at me as if daring me to argue with her.

"I don't know what you're talking about," I reply, untucking my hair behind my ears in case they're turning red.

"When are you going to admit you have feelings for Luke?"

"Who has feelings for Luke?" Drew asks, as she closes the screen door behind her, holding a baby monitor.

"Annie," Mia answers at the same time I say, "No one."

"Well, duh," Drew says as she sits down, setting down the baby monitor on the table in front of us. "We all know that."

"You all know nothing," I deadpan.

"We know that both of you have feelings for each other. Luke is obvious about it, and you pretend you don't like it when really you do," Mia informs, proving to me that I'm not as good at hiding my feelings as I thought I was.

"We know that *something* happened between you guys when you were young, the same way *something* happened at my wedding," Drew adds. "We want you to know that we love you and support you, and there is nothing you can tell us that will change that."

I cross my arms, feeling defensive because it's like the walls I've built over the years aren't as strong as I thought they were.

Or, there is nothing strong enough to keep these two out.

I let out an exhale.

I've never felt the urge to open up about Luke to Mia and Drew, only because I don't want them to take on any of my shit. It's mine to deal with for a reason, not theirs.

I can't tell them how it hurts to breathe when I think about what happened between me and Luke.

I can't tell them that I finally feel like I have a heartbeat again after all these years of thinking my heart didn't work.

I can't tell them that being near Luke is so fucking confusing because all it does is bring up all these feelings and memories I have no business remembering.

If I tell them, it can be used against me—a way to hurt me.

That's what happens when you let people all the way in.

"I know what you're thinking." Drew sighs. "I know that look."

"What look?"

"You're thinking of all the ways to keep us out," Mia answers for her, and I can't hide the surprise on my face at the fact that I think these two bitches are mind-readers.

"It's what you do, Ann," Drew continues. "You keep us at arms-length, and you think we don't notice."

"That's not true," I argue. "You two are my best friends."

"Exactly," Mia counters, grabbing my arm from where it's crossed over my chest, and wrapping her hand around mine. "That's how we know when you're pushing us away."

"We know you," Drew urges, getting up to sit on the other side of the patio couch Mia and I are on. "We know you pull away when you think you're asking for too much, but I'm telling you right now that there is nothing you can do that will ever make us love you any less."

I feel a sting in the back of my eyes. "You guys don't get it. I'm not the kind of person who people want to keep around. I do more harm than good, and you'll see it, one way or another." The words feel therapeutic to get out, but the weight on my shoulders doesn't lighten. "I'm going to do something that'll make you see that I'm not worth all of this."

Drew grabs my other hand with both of hers, and I look at her, tears welling up in my eyes. "You are not a burden, Annie. Not to us or Emmett, or Eddie, or Luke. You are our family."

I let a tear fall from the corner of my eye, the first tear I have let fall in I don't know how long. Drew's eyes glisten, and she looks at Mia.

"We know what it's like to feel like you have to be strong, even at your weakest," Mia assures me, "and we have both felt the universe actively working against us, especially when we're barely holding ourselves together."

Drew's hands squeeze around mine at the same time a few more tears race down my cheeks. With the hand not holding mine, Mia tucks the hair framing my face behind my ear. "But it will also give you people who will hold you together if you need to fall apart."

"I wish it were that simple," I whisper, closing my eyes.

"It *is* that simple," Mia stresses, and for a second, I let myself believe her.

Both Mia and Drew have shown me that the friends and family I had before I found them were not the kind that I deserved. I know that.

But I can't shake this feeling that Mia and Drew are too good to be true.

And I hate myself for thinking that.

"Whatever happened to you, Ann, you can tell us," Drew says.

"I've never talked about it."

"Whenever you're ready," Mia adds, "we're here."

The two close in on me, hugging me from both sides, making true on their promise to hold me together when I'm seconds away from falling apart.

"They never let us join their group hugs," I hear Eddie joke from a few yards away. The three of us laugh before releasing one another, all of us wiping our eyes as the boys approach.

"Or their heart-to-hearts," Luke adds with a fake sadness in the form of puppy-dog eyes and a jut-out lip.

I'm thankful for the laugh that bubbles in my throat, one that must surprise Luke by the way his eyebrows raise at me.

"All good?" Emmett asks, and it takes me a second to realize he's not asking Drew.

"All good," I reply.

The six of us shoot the shit and chat on the patio for another hour before we all head our separate ways.

Drew and Emmett fall back into their new routine as parents.

Mia, Eddie, and Daisy head home to their apartment.

Luke heads to Lenny's.

I head back to Luke's with Rosie, my heart feeling a little fuller than it did this morning.

CHAPTER 14
LUKE

I'M happy Annie decided to let the girls do something special for her. The girl deserves a night all about her, especially when she doesn't think starting her fourth year of veterinarian school is something to celebrate.

God knows I'd love to be the one giving it to her.

It's officially been two weeks since Annie moved in, yet I can't remember what my apartment felt like before she was living here. Her jasmine and rose scent has fully infiltrated the place, and I find her endless amounts of cherry chapsticks and lip glosses everywhere I turn.

I usually leave them where they are, but I couldn't help myself from pocketing the one I found on the kitchen counter yesterday.

Rosie has spent one night with me since Annie moved in. I can't say I blame her for wanting to cuddle up next to Annie every night. I fall asleep thinking the same goddamn thing.

"Where did the girls say they were taking Annie tonight after dinner?" I ask Eddie from the passenger seat of his truck.

"Bowling," he answers as he stops at a red light.

It was supposed to be the girls' Movie Night tonight, but Drew and Mia convinced Annie to do something different.

Annie compromised, wanting to keep things on the chill side, opting for dinner and bowling. I figured they would use our Thursday Happy Hour at Drew and Emmett's to plan it, but the conversation they had on the patio when the guys and I were playing fetch with the dogs looked much more serious.

I haven't seen Annie cry since high school.

Resisting the urge to ask her about it was not easy, knowing she would use Mia's how-to-punch lessons and knock my teeth out.

And I like using my teeth to smile and make Annie blush.

Within an hour of the girls being out tonight, Eddie was already texting me that he was bored and wanted to crash girls' night. We didn't want to intrude on their dinner, but we agreed that anything after was fair game.

The sun is starting to set, and Eddie is tracking Mia's location on Find My Friends so we can make sure we beat them to the bowling alley.

"Interesting choice, considering Annie turns into Emmett when she bowls," I laugh.

"Grumpy and mean?" Eddie jokes.

"Grumpy and *meaner.*"

Emmett is home with Lennon, refusing to leave her side, and he called us idiots for crashing girls night, even though we know he would be here with us if Lennon was old enough to be left with a sitter.

Since he can't be here, we decided to do something partly in his honor.

"Where did Emmett say the shop was?" Eddie asks as he looks left and right, waiting for the red light to turn green.

"It's just up here," I say, pointing to the sign with a big rose and tattoo gun on it.

When we stopped by his house to see Lennon earlier

tonight, it came up that Emmett's buddy who does his tattoos just opened his own shop.

I knew exactly what Eddie and I would be doing while the girls were at dinner.

I also took it as a sign from the universe when I heard the name of it.

"Roses and Thorns Tattoo Shop. Right there," I direct Eddie as the traffic light turns green.

Annie likes to pretend she doesn't remember all the memories we have together, and that's okay. I remember them for the both of us. Like how she refused to let me use her crayons in second grade because she said I flattened the tip of them. Or how we sang a duet at our choir concert in sixth grade. Or how I asked her to be my girlfriend with a single rose and gave her one on that day every year until she left.

The name of the shop was a sign that Annie isn't someone you give up on. The same way when she told me that the golden retriever at the animal shelter's name was Rosie.

I like to think the universe is on my side when it comes to making Annie fall in love with me again.

Emmett let his buddy, Casey, know that we were coming, and we both had small ideas that wouldn't take too long. Eddie goes first, getting a sun with a rain cloud on the outside of his forearm, filling in an open space on his arm. Casey tattoos in an American Traditionalist style, so the tattoo fits perfectly with the others Eddie has gotten over the years.

Once Casey finishes with Eddie, he cleans up and re-sets his station. I show him the kind of pieces I want and where I want to place them on my thigh, and within the hour, we are on our way to officially crash girls night.

We get to the bowling alley a good ten minutes before the girls, so we grab a lane and start putting on our rental shoes.

I try to ignore the flip in my stomach as we wait. It feels like I'm back in high school, going on my first date.

No.

It is much more nerve-racking than that.

I can't stop pacing or glancing at the door, but all my nerves melt away when I see Annie walk in.

She's walking between Mia and Drew, and even with the bowling alley's black light and neon patterns all over the floor and walls, Annie looks drop dead gorgeous. Her brown waves are pulled halfway back in two little ponytails, her red tube top accentuating her tan skin. Her brown eyes are framed with her long lashes, and her lips match her top.

She looks good enough to eat.

It takes a second for her and the girls to notice, but when she does, her face is priceless. She goes from surprised—wide eyes and an open mouth—to happy and smiling, to glaring at me like I just "pissed on her campfire" as she would say.

"Surprise!" Eddie yells as the girls walk up to our lane, but my mouth is dry, and I have to clear my throat to avoid an embarrassing crack in my voice.

"What did we say about these stalker tendencies?" she teases. "I mean, come on, bartender. Following me around? What are you, a dog?"

I know what she wants me to say.

She wants me to argue.

She wants me to push while she pulls.

But there's only so much pushing someone can do.

She thinks I'm a dog? God knows she has me on the tightest leash.

I look her right in the eyes. "Woof."

I watch her eyes slightly widen before they roll, and then her teeth sink into her bottom lip as if she's trying to hold back a smile.

Maybe it's the adrenaline from the tattoo or the high I feel from seeing her, but I feel brave enough to grab her by the arm and pull her in for a hug. "Last year of vet school, Annie girl." She smells more like roses today, and I smile to myself at the thought. "I'm proud of you." It takes a second, but her arms wrap around my waist, and she relaxes in my hold as I press my lips to the top of her head.

When we pull away, she's wearing a soft smile, and I instantly feel undeserving of it.

It's too beautiful.

I expect her to cover it up with a roll of the eyes again, or maybe a shake of the head, but it doesn't go anywhere. Instead, her grin widens as she jokes. "Exactly what I wanted tonight, two *more* people to beat me at bowling." She turns to look at Eddie, his arm around Mia whose eyes are fully on Annie and me.

"You're not *that* bad," Drew chimes in, her eyes also zoned in us. "I'm just watching tonight, so I'll give you all the pointers."

I let out a chuckle, my own lips forming a grin. I look back at Annie. "Come on, honey. Just pretend it's my face you're aiming for, you'll hit a strike every time."

"Sounds like a plan," she answers, reaching up to pat my cheek, before turning around to grab herself a bowling ball.

———

Annie really does suck at bowling, but at least she's having fun. By the last game, I think she had a total of 75 points between the three games we played.

By her fourth turn in our first game, she already discovered all of the *incorrect* ways she could throw a ball down the lane. I offered to ask one of the workers to put up bumpers for her, but she responded with the middle finger.

"Do you *try* to be that bad?" Eddie asks Annie as the four of us head outside. Drew left sometime during the second game, no doubt tired and itching to get home to Emmett and the baby.

"Yes, Ed. That's exactly what I do. I'm secretly hiding my

insane bowling skills from all of you. I'm actually a professional bowler," Annie answers, her voice oozing with sarcasm that makes all of us laugh.

We walk to the corner of the parking lot where both Eddie's truck and Annie's car are parked, lucky that the girls didn't notice Eddie's truck when they got here, and say our goodbyes to Eddie and Mia.

"Give me your keys," I say to Annie as we walk towards her car.

"I only had one drink at dinner," she counters.

"Just let me drive you home."

"Yeah, Ann," Mia yells to us, "let him drive you home!" Her voice takes on a teasing tone, and I can see the tips of Annie's exposed ears are pink.

"Whatever," she sighs, handing me her car keys.

"Love you!" Mia shouts as Eddie closes her door for her, shaking his head with a smile as he waves to us.

We get into Annie's car and we drive home in a comfortable silence, the only sound coming from the song playing, "Underscore" by Definitely Maybe, and the rush of the wind coming in through the open windows. It isn't until we are a few minutes from home that Annie says, "Have you talked to your dad?"

It isn't what I thought she would say, but I answer anyway. "Not yet."

She nods her head, but she doesn't say anything else.

And neither do I.

A few moments pass before she speaks again. "Do you regret not taking the scholarship?"

I sigh as we turn into the parking lot of our—*my*—apartment complex.. "I regret a lot of things." It's the truth, but I know that's not the answer she was looking for.

"Luke," she urges, but I don't answer until we're parked.

"Yes."

I kill the engine, but neither of us makes a move to get out of the car.

"I hate the thought of you giving up your life for a man who didn't see yours as more than an inconvenience."

I let my head fall back on the headrest of the driver's seat, and close my eyes. "Me too."

"So stop," she says, surprising me. My eyes open as I turn my head to face her. Her expression is tight, her eyebrows are furrowed, and she looks mad. But for once, it feels like the anger isn't at me.

"You don't have to protect me, Annie girl."

"Someone has to."

I reach out to her, stretching my arm over the center console.

She looks down at my hand before carefully putting her hand in mine, and I let go of a breath I didn't even know I was holding.

"Is this just a ploy to steal my apartment?" I joke, breaking some of the tension in the air because it's like second nature to me.

It makes her chuckle, and I squeeze her hand. "No," she replies, staring at our interlocked fingers. "It turns out I actually don't completely hate spending time with you."

"Good," I answer quickly, maybe too quickly, because her head snaps up, her eyes finding mine. "Because you're stuck with me for two more months."

She shakes her head, letting out an exhale, but she doesn't let go of my hand. "I only have two more *weeks* in your apartment, Luke. Mine should be ready by then."

"You said you didn't want to move back there," I tell her, "and your new apartment will be available starting October 15th. So, technically we're both right. About two months and two weeks from today."

A small gasp escapes her lips. "There's a unit available? Here?"

I nod. One of the benefits of being Daniel Owens' bastard son is the hush money and trust fund he set me up with, money—thankfully—never being a problem for me. But I know Annie would hate me if I told her I already put the deposit and first month of rent down for her to reserve the place, so I keep that to myself. "And it's yours, if you want it." *Or you can just stay with me forever,* I want to add. But I don't want to scare her away when I've already gotten this close.

"I—" she starts, "I don't know what to say."

"'Thank you, Luke. You're my knight in shining armor' is a good place to start," I tease, but the joke doesn't land. Her hand pulls from mine, taking all the warmth with it.

"That is the *last* thing you are to me," she snaps, her brows furrowed and her eyes narrowed. I have whiplash from how fast she flipped on me.

What the hell did I do?"

"Annie, I was just kid—"

I can't even finish my sentence because she's reaching across the car, pulling her keys out of where I left them in the ignition, and slamming the car door behind her.

CHAPTER 15
ANNIE

I CAN'T STAY HERE for two more weeks.

Being here is severely fucking with my head.

My head, my body, my heart, it's all reverting back to what I worked so hard to put behind me.

When did I turn back into the scared, shy little girl that needs Luke—of all people—to come fix everything and make it all better?

Pathetic.

I shut the door to the apartment behind me, knowing Luke isn't too far behind, but he can open the damn door himself.

I head into the guest bedroom and start packing up all my stuff. It's a mess in here, and there is no way I can get everything out in one trip, but I pack what I need for a night before grabbing my phone to call Mia.

No.

I can't involve her in this.

I have to handle this on my own.

I'll sleep in my car if I have to.

I cannot stay here.

"Annie?" a voice booms from the kitchen, the door slamming behind him. "What the hell just happened?"

I ignore Luke as I continue shoving shit into my bag.

"What are you doing?" he asks, coming to a stop in front of my opened door.

"Leaving."

"What? It's almost midnight. You're not leaving." He steps toward me. I feel his hand come to my shoulder, but I shrug him off.

"Yes, I am." I zip up the bag I have opened on my bed and finally turn to face him. "This was never a good idea. There's too much history, too many feelings. It's not fair to either of us."

"What are you talking about?"

"This!" I yell, gesturing between the two of us. "Living together, spending time together, it's bringing up old feelings for the both of us. It's not healthy."

"These aren't old feelings, Annie. They never went away. Not for me."

"Well, they did for me," I snap.

He shakes his head. "You don't mean that."

"Don't you dare," I spit, poking him in the chest, "tell me how I feel."

"You can lie to yourself, but you can't lie to me." He grabs my hand, holding it tightly. "We can be so much more than this. Please give me a chance to show you."

I try to pull my hand from his grip, but he's either holding on tight, or I'm not trying that hard to pull away. "I don't give a fuck about what you think we could be."

"I'll give one for the both of us."

I shake my head, finally ripping my hand out of his and step back. "No. Being here. With you. It hurts too much."

For every step I take back, Luke takes another forward.

He places his hands on my upper arms, holding me in

place. "It doesn't have to hurt, Annie. Tell me what I did wrong, please. I'll do anything."

"It's not worth it," I whisper.

He bends down to try and meet my eyes that are staring at the space in front of me. "Whatever it is, it cost me everything."

Finally, I look at him, pain etched across his features as he waits for me to respond. A small part of me knows I'm not angry, not anymore. But I know I'm not okay.

"You'll never be my stupid knight in shining armor, Luke. Because you weren't there when it mattered most."

———

Luke left my room Saturday night without another word.

I could've—*should've*—told him.

But I didn't.

Aside from when we get together with our friends, Luke and I have exchanged less than twenty words in the last three weeks.

He's giving me space—or maybe taking the space he needs away from me.

I found out from Mia that Luke was putting off his dad's firm until Lennon was a few months old and Emmett was back at the bar regularly—I was sad to hear he's still planning on going to work for the son of a bitch.

I wanted to talk to him about it.

But it isn't my place.

I've thought myself to death about all of this Luke stuff, and I need to talk to him about what happened at Grant's party and why I left. Then I—the both of us—can have some well-deserved closure. I can't cut him out of my life, it's not possible, and I'm finding that I don't really want to. But I don't want this shit hanging over our heads anymore.

We'll get our closure, and then we'll be friends.

But I didn't realize how much I would miss him after these three weeks.

He still leaves me notes on the counter or texts me when he'll be home. I still make enough of my dinners for him, and he leaves out my stuff to make my matcha in the morning. We're under the same roof, so I still see him, but I still miss him.

And that scares me.

I've been able to distract myself long enough with finishing up my veterinarian assistant shifts at the animal shelter and prepping for my rotations that start next week, but living in this limbo isn't fair to either of us.

Today was my last day at the animal shelter, so Mia, Eddie, Drew, Emmett, and one-and-a-half-month old Lennon are meeting me at Lenny's to celebrate.

Luke closes the bar on Fridays with Ava, one of the new bartenders, so I've decided that tonight is the night we talk without me biting his head off.

"What's your first rotation?" Drew asks. She has Lennon strapped around her chest like a mini backpack, and Emmett is standing behind her chair at the bar.

"My first two weeks will be at my school's teaching hospital, and then I'm doing four weeks with the Milwaukee Zoo."

"Do you know what you're thinking of doing after this year?" Emmett asks, his arm wrapped around Drew's chair.

"Not really. That's what this year is for. Figuring out what I want to do."

"Enough about school and work for now," Mia announces from the chair to the left of me, Eddie on the other side of her. "Tonight is about celebrating what you've already accomplished, not what you're about to."

She smiles and holds up her drink. "Luke!" she yells to the far side of the bar as Drew holds up her White Claw, and Emmett and Eddie hold up their beers. "Come here!"

Luke turns to see us all holding up our drinks and rushes over with his water bottle he keeps behind the bar.

"Cheers to Annie," Mia says as Luke holds up his water bottle next to our glasses. "We know you're going to kick ass with your rotations!"

"To Annie!" my friends echo, and my eyes find Luke. I should've known his eyes would've already been on me making my stupid heart skip a beat. "To our Annie girl," he adds before clinking his water bottle with our glasses.

The bar is crowded for a Friday, groups of regulars and people our age filling up the booths and high top tables and a whole lot of college kids who walked over from the baseball field down the road with all their equipment.

"How are the new bartenders?" Eddie asks Luke, nodding toward Ava who is working the bar tonight. She looks to be a year or two younger than me, with strawberry blonde hair and dark blue eyes. Freckles are sprinkled over face, and she carries herself well.

She's cute and quiet, and I think the regulars will get a kick out of making her blush.

She reminds me a little of the old me.

"Good, I'd say. Things have been pretty smooth with Ava and the other two guys," Luke says as he scoops ice into a few cups below the bar. "I've been trying my best to hold down the fort," he adds, grinning at Emmett who gives him a nod.

"Hey, Luke?" Ava calls to him, and she gives us a little wave as she walks over. "Um, my boyfriend just got here. He's down at the other end of the bar. Do you mind if I take my break?

"Sure," he answers with a shrug of the shoulders. "Back at it in fifteen?"

"Of course," she answers, a slight blush forming under her freckles. She gives us all a smile before heading to sit at the bar with her boyfriend.

"He's a dick," Luke says under his breath.

"What? Who?" Mia asks, all of us leaning in.

"Ava's boyfriend," Luke answers. "Ava is a super sweet girl, and he is just always so mean to her. Last time he came when we were working, I overheard him accusing her of cheating on him and then asked her to cover his drinks."

"Ew," Drew says, a sour look on her face. "Why do such nice girls always end up with assholes?"

Emmett snorts. "You would know," he teases, alluding to when he and Drew first started dating and her asshole ex-boyfriend showed up here only for Emmett to throw him out on his ass.

"She'll realize it sooner rather than later," Mia adds as we watch Ava's boyfriend point at Ava's chest with a scowl and say something I can't quite make out.

"Hopefully," Luke adds. "I've heard the guy say more nice things about his fancy white truck than he has about Ava." He lets out a humorless chuckle. "Anyway, do you guys want anything before I go make my rounds?"

We all say we're good, and Luke spends the next fifteen minutes waiting on tables and getting drinks for everyone, but I can't keep my eyes off the couple in the corner—my thoughts about the conversation Luke and I need to have floating to the back of my mind.

I have a bad feeling.

CHAPTER 16
LUKE

ANOTHER NIGHT, another crack in my chest from having to pretend that everything is fine for the sake of Annie and our friends.

On the outside, I'm giving her space, and everything is fine.

On the inside, I'm fighting every urge to lock us both in the apartment and make her tell me what she meant about me not being there when she needed me most.

I've racked my brain for the whole month of August trying to figure out what I did that would make her say that I wasn't there when she needed me, and there are years of memories to think through.

And there's been no time for me to think of what the fuck I'm going to do once Emmett comes back. The time I gained from the excuse I gave to my dad about not being able to leave Lenny's yet won't last forever.

I've been avoiding his phone calls like the plague—he barely said a word to me when I told him I wouldn't be able to start at the firm in September. Caleb has been calling me too, wanting to find out what my plan is after Bennett told him about our conversation at breakfast.

In all honesty, I know what I want to do.

And I know it's not going to be what my dad wants to hear.

So I'm putting it off.

Even though I'm not training at the bar anymore, and the three new bartenders know what they're doing, I've been here enough over the past three weeks that I can give Annie her space.

The nights I'm not here, I go to the hockey rink with my buddies from law school to blow off steam.

I set down some drinks for the baseball team taking up the whole back corner of the bar, trying not to trip over their bat bags they brought in with them.

I pull my phone from my pocket, glancing at the time and seeing it's been about fifteen minutes since Ava went on her break.

Usually, I wouldn't be too much of a stickler about it, but the bar is pretty packed, and I could use the help.

As I approach where Ava and her boyfriend are sitting at the bar, a few feet away from Annie and the rest of our friends, I hear what's-his-face say something about what Ava is wearing.

"Seriously?" the guy says to her as I approach. "You really have to show your mediocre tits to get some attention?"

"I'm not showing them off, Jett," Ava answers, and her eyes dart to me. Her voice is small as if she is embarrassed that I heard the exchange.

"Ava?" I politely interject, "I need you back behind the bar." *And away from this guy,* I think to myself.

"Fuck off, man. We're in the middle of a conversation." I don't know how many beers Ava served him, or if he was drinking before he got here, but I can hear the slight slur in his words. He turns back to Ava. "Seriously, why are you dressed like such a slut?"

"Hey," I say, my voice taking on a harder tone. "Don't talk

to her like that." Whether she was covered from head to toe or dressed how she is now in her Lenny's tank top and jeans, I think this dick would find any excuse to insult the girl.

"I said, 'fuck off'. This is between me and my girlfriend." He pushes his arm out towards me, and I let him push me back a foot or two. I've handled worse drunken spats at the bar during my time at Lenny's, and I don't care to play "who's more macho" in these types of scenarios.

I hold my hands up, and try one more time. "I think it's time for you to go. Ava, I need you back behind the bar."

It's like my words went in one ear and out the other. Ava looks like she's about to cry, yet her boyfriend just doesn't let up.

"Is this fuck the reason you're dressed like that?"

I'm two seconds away from throwing my hands up and letting the cops deal with this when a voice from behind me chimes in, and it doesn't look like we're getting out of this the easy way.

"So you're mad your girlfriend has *tits*?" I hear the familiar voice behind me, and she doesn't sound happy. "Your hot-ass girlfriend can't wear a shirt that, god-forbid, shows an inch of cleavage? You're *that* insecure?"

"Annie," I say, and she shoots me a look. I hold my hands up in surrender and would wish mercy on Jett if he wasn't such an asshole.

Jett looks Annie up and down, and I know he just signed his own death warrant.

He shrugs his shoulders, a nasty smirk on his face. "Takes a slut to know a slut."

Annie's head falls back as she puts a hand on her stomach to dramatize a cackle that our boy, Jett, was not expecting. Ava is soft-spoken, quiet. She kind of reminds me how Annie used to be. Jett is used to being able to say whatever he wants to a girl who will just take it.

He's in for a wild ride.

"Good one. I've never heard a 'slut' comeback before. What's next? I'm fat? Ugly?"

"You look like you hear those a lot already," he retorts, a slimy, satisfied grin on his face. Jett has to be in thirties, and Ava is, at the most, my age. The look on his face shows his age at the same time it shows his true colors, and I hope Ava sees them.

"Ooo, burn," Annie teases. "You proud of that one? It must have taken a lot of brainpower."

I have to mask my chuckle with a cough in my fist, as Jett stands up, only having a few inches on Annie but absolutely none on me. I know Annie doesn't want me stepping in, but I'm here if she changes her mind.

He leans a few inches from her face, his fully-poured beer in his hand. "Watch your mouth. Wouldn't wanna see you get hurt."

Annie doesn't back away, her voice hard. "Is that a threat?"

"Why don't you keep talking, and we'll find out." Jett's grin only widens as if he's enjoying all of this. He doesn't say anything else, but I see his arm move before I can pull Annie out of the way.

The prick fucking throws his drink all over Annie, beer coating her white tank top and trousers she wore to work today.

Her mouth is open, forming an "O". I don't think I've ever seen her this mad—and that is saying something. Jett's face twists to mine, and he utters his famous last words. "Control your girl."

This time it's my turn to laugh. "Dude, you have no idea what you just did." And before he can look back at where Annie is standing, she's gone.

Annie is passing by the booth of college kids, grabbing one of their bats from their bags and storming out the front door.

Realization must hit Jett at the same time it hits the rest of us because it turns into a race to get out the door. Mia and Eddie are the first ones out the door behind Annie, me, Jett, and Ava right behind them. Emmett, with a protective arm around Drew and Lennon, catches up with us by the time we get outside—along with the rest of the bar.

And what a sight we find.

Annie is already at the *only* white truck in the parking lot, swinging the bat in her hands. The first crack of the windshield sends a shiver up my spine, and we all watch as she continues, a devious smile on her face as she destroys Jett's prized possession.

I make a mental note to delete the camera footage for the parking lot when I get back inside, but I have a feeling that Jett won't involve the police after a whole bar witnessed him threaten Annie.

"What the fuck?!" Jett booms, and I can't even pretend to feel sorry for him. His hands go to his head, pulling the thin strands between his fingers before turning to me.

"Aren't you going to do something?" he yells, but it comes out more as a whine. There's a look of pleading in his eyes as he looks from me to his truck.

Annie finally decided it had enough and starts walking towards us.

"What do you expect me to do?" I counter with a shrug of my shoulders. "You pissed her off."

Making her way through the crowd, Annie rests the bat on her shoulder and walks over to the group of college kids, who are looking at her in awe.

She holds the bat out to no one in particular. "Thank you for the rental, boys," she chides, adding a wink for good measure before three different kids reach out to grab the bat from her, all mumbling different "you're welcome" sentiments.

While the baseball team has heart-eyes, I look over at Jett

who has steam coming out of his ears. The guy is smarter than he looks because he just storms over to his beaten-up truck, hops in the driver's seat and speeds off as the rest of the patrons cheer.

I see Mia and Eddie run up to Annie, Emmett and Drew—with Lennon in tow—right behind them. Mia's hands go to Annie's cheeks, cupping her face and pulling a smile from her while Drew shakes her head trying to hide her own smile.

Eddie and Emmett each hold up a hand, making Annie grin ear-to-ear as she reaches up to slap her hands against theirs, and I tear my attention away from Annie to look at Ava.

"You okay?" I ask her, resting my hand on her shoulder.

She exhales. "I'm okay." Giving me a small smile, she turns to make her way back inside, and I hope tonight showed her that she deserves much better than a guy like that.

"Hey, bartender."

I turn around to find a beer-soaked Annie.

There's a flush to her face from that handy work on Jett's truck, her cheeks almost as red as her lips.

"Hey, honey."

There's a few feet between us, and she closes the distance with a step forward. This is the closest I've been to her in three weeks.

Now that the excitement is over, the crowd has gone back inside, along with our friends, so it's just the two of us.

The sun set at least half an hour ago, and with nothing but a few street lights, the Lenny's neon sign, and the moonlight, it feels like we're the only two people left on Earth.

"That was quite the show," I say, balling my fists to resist the urge to trace my fingertips over the smooth skin of her arms.

She shrugs. "He deserved it."

"I'm sure Ava appreciated someone standing up for her

like that." I put my hands in my pocket as I rock back on my heels.

"That wasn't for Ava."

I lift a brow and cock my head, confused as to who else it would be for.

"I mean, yeah, I would have stepped in for any girl in that sort of situation, but—" she uncrosses her arms to tuck her hair behind her ears, her white tank top is soaked through, showing the outline of the white, lacy bralette she has under.

I pull my hoodie off over my head, leaving me in a black Henley and shorts, and I put it over her head before she can tell me to fuck off.

"But what?" I ask, a small crack in my voice I hope she doesn't notice, as she pushes her arm through my sweatshirt.

She looks so small in my hoodie, the bottom hem hitting her mid-thigh, her hands barely sticking out of the sleeves, and the hood on her head dropping down on her forehead. I have to hold in a chuckle.

"He touched you," she whispers, and all signs of humor fade.

I nod, but I still don't get what she's trying to say. My face must be easy to read because she rolls her eyes and sighs.

"I saw him push you, and it pissed me off."

"So, let me get this straight," I start, needing to clarify that I am *indeed* hearing what Annie is saying or if the guy actually knocked me out in the bar and the past ten minutes have been a dream. "You saw the guy push me, so you came over, ripped him a new one, and then when he took it too far, you bashed his truck with a baseball bat. Because he 'touched' me? Not because he called you names or poured a beer all over you?"

She crosses her arms again, and the tips of her ears pinken. "Well, when you say it like that," she says through her teeth, "it makes it sound much worse than it was."

I can't explain the feeling in my chest at the thought of

Annie wanting to protect me. It's similar to the rush I feel when she tells me to shut up or pouts her pretty lips, but I don't think it's a feeling I can ever go so long without again.

"You like me," I say, a grin on my face.

"I can't stand you."

"Admit it. You like me."

"I'll admit I don't like seeing anyone *else* put you in your place. That's my job."

"Don't be a brat."

"Don't be a dick."

Somehow, in the last five seconds, we ended up chest to chest, and now we're at a standstill. It's been weeks since we've talked—*really* talked—and there's so much between us that needs to be said. But, at this moment, I can't remember anything except for what it feels like to kiss Annie.

"What are you going to do about it?" I push, knowing Annie fights the hardest when she's scared.

Just like she did when her apartment got broken into, and she didn't want to ask for help.

Just like when she feels me getting close to her, so she pushes me away.

Just like when those feelings for me come up to the surface, and she tries to bury them even deeper.

"Absolutely nothing." Her voice is like venom, but I'd let her sink her teeth into me if it meant I could feel her lips.

"You sure about that?" I tease, and I'm no more than an inch away from her lips, my hands pulling out from my pocket to find her hips.

She sucks in a breath, placing her hands on my chest, but she doesn't push me away. Instead, she closes her eyes, and I take my chance, even if it's the last thing I ever do.

My lips crash into hers, and I pull her into me, holding her hips to make sure she stays right here. But when has she ever done what I wanted her to do?

Annie pulls back, a hand going to her mouth. Her eyes

meet mine, and it looks like she's about to say something. I hold my breath, hoping I didn't just make another mistake that'll just push her further away.

Then, with a slight shake of her head, "Fuck it," she says, and her fingers fist my shirt, her nails lightly scratching my skin underneath, pulling me back in and pressing her lips against mine.

I've said it once, and I'll say it again.

Kissing Annie is like coming home.

CHAPTER 17
ANNIE

TIME STANDS STILL as his lips move against mine, and it's nothing like the kiss in the kitchen. That one went from zero to one hundred in a matter of seconds.

This one? It's already at a thousand.

One of Luke's hands loosens from my hip and moves up my body until he finds the side of my neck. I'm still covered in beer under Luke's sweatshirt, the hood still up on my head, and we're outside a crowded bar where our friends are probably wondering where we are, but neither of us care.

He grips the side of my neck, urging me to tilt my head to give him better access as our kiss deepens; our tongues are tangled, competing for dominance and control.

My skin feels as hot as the sun, and pressure builds in my belly. A mix of emotions should be filtering through my brain right now—dread, nerves, confusion.

I should really stop this because we need to finish our conversation from the night he and Eddie surprised us at the bowling alley, but my mind is blank. The only thought in my brain is *how long can I make this last?*

Maybe this was always bound to happen.

Have I been running away from what was meant to be?

I could say I feel myself falling back in love with Luke, but that would be a lie.

I've never stopped loving him.

"Are you guys still out here?" I hear, and I don't even register the voice until Luke's lips freeze against mine, and I realize we are no longer alone.

"I told you to leave them alone!" Drew complains to Mia, slapping her in the arm.

"How was I supposed to know they were going to be making out—I mean *up*," she corrects herself after another slap on the arm from Drew.

I let go of my death grip on Luke's shirt, wiping a hand down the front to get out the wrinkles, and I look up to find him smiling at me with swollen lips.

"Looks like we were caught," I whisper.

"Good. I'm done keeping my feelings for you a secret."

My eyes roll. "As if you ever did," is all I say, even though what I *should* be saying is we *really* need to talk.

Mia and Drew come over, Eddie and Emmett with Lennon now strapped over his chest, right behind them.

"So, is this a thing?" Eddie asks, gesturing between the two of us.

"No," I say, at the same time Luke says, "Almost." I turn to him, confused, but he just winks at me.

"We have some *things* to discuss," I explain to our friends, who I'm sure are only hearing the answer they want to hear, which is *yes, this is a thing*. I turn to Emmett, finding Lennon asleep in her carrier, kissing my finger and pressing it to the top of her little head. "I'm going home."

"Me too," Luke says, and we all laugh at the eagerness in his voice.

"You got three more hours until close," Drew says, and we all laugh harder.

"Maybe I'm not cut out for this whole 'boss' thing," he jokes.

"You're just filling in. If you were *actually* the boss, you could close whenever you wanted," Emmett explains as his tattooed hands interlace lightly across the carrier on his chest.

"So *you're* going to close early for me?" Luke asks hopefully.

"No."

Luke shrugs his shoulders. "Worth a try." He turns to me, throwing an arm over my shoulder like it's the most natural thing to do. "See you at home, Annie girl." He presses a kiss to the top of my head before giving a salute to our friends and heading back inside Lenny's.

The rest of us say our goodbyes, and I'm thankful, after such an eventful night, my best friends give me a reprieve from answering all their questions. I know it won't last long, but I'll have until at least a couple days to prepare.

"I'll see you guys for Sunday dinner," Drew says as I pull her and Mia in for our group hug, and I can't believe it's already September.

"Yes. Our house at six," Mia adds.

"Perf," Drew and I answer at the same time, and then we all say goodbye for the night.

Only, for some reason, my night feels far from over.

———

I hear the front door of the apartment shut, and I glance at the clock on my bedside table to see it's just past midnight.

I've been tossing and turning since I got into bed, no longer smelling like a whole work day with animals and stale beer—there's been butterflies in my stomach since leaving the bar.

Not the cute kind that you get before your first date.

No, these fuckers are the kind that are just there to remind you of all the things you should be worried about when thinking about what's to come.

And what's to come is a conversation that I'm really not ready to have.

Would it be easy to fall back into the role of pretending to hate Luke? Yes.

Would it be even easier to go out there and kiss him until I forget my name? Also yes.

But I can't keep doing this. Not to me, and most definitely not to him.

We need to talk about what happened the night of Grant's party. The video I saw of him and Devin. The reason I left in the first place.

I'll be the first to admit that this high school bullshit is just that. *High school bullshit.* It shouldn't matter all these years later. I shouldn't let it dictate me in the ways that it does.

But after seven years of reflecting on what happened, that night was a culmination of being bullied by the girls who were supposed to be my friends, my parents telling me what a waste of space I was, and a whole relationship built on the promise that Luke and I—no matter what—were enough for each other.

And that night, all of it coming to a head, felt like all my fears were proven true.

All of this to say, it ends. *Tonight.*

We get the closure we need, and we can get over these feelings that should've faded a long time ago.

"Annie?" I hear, followed by a small knock on my door. Rosie's head pops up from where she is laying at the edge of my bed, and she jumps off as the door cracks open.

After tonight, some might consider me brave.

I did smash the truck of a grown man for touching someone who doesn't even belong to me.

But when the door to the guest room slowly opens, and I pretend to be asleep. Using the term "brave" to describe me is an insult to the word.

"Annie?" I hear again, this time a little louder, but I keep my eyes closed and my breathing steady, even though I feel like I'm about to hyperventilate.

Years of theater and faking confidence has prepared me for this endless minute of waiting for Luke to lead Rosie out of my room to let her out. It isn't until I hear the front door open and close again that I open my eyes, bringing my hand to my forehead in a slap, cursing myself for being such a wuss.

No.

This is not who I am.

Not anymore.

I ask for what I want. I tell people what's on my mind, whether they like it or not.

When Luke gets back inside, I am going to march out there and tell him that we need to talk. No flirting, no back-and-forth, and no kissing.

Definitely no kissing.

I push the covers off me and swing my legs over the edge of the bed, getting up before I lose my nerve. I start pacing the kitchen, my mind reeling over what I'm going to say and how this is all for the best.

I'll tell him what happened, and he can finally know why I left.

Then we'll agree to move on.

I hear the jingle of keys and the turn of a lock, and I freeze, telling myself that if I move now, I can be back in bed before the door opens.

But it's too late. The click of Rosie's nails on the floor echoes in the quiet apartment as Luke kicks off his shoes and closes the door behind him.

"Hi," I say, not wanting to give him a heart attack when he turns and sees me in his kitchen.

Luke looks up at me, his lips in a smirk on the side of his face. I'm in a pair of sweatpants and an oversized t-shirt, but I still feel goosebumps cover my skin.

"Hey, honey," he replies, and there's an unfamiliar feeling in the air. It isn't awkwardness or tension; it's almost like a sense of anticipation, like both of us know something is about to happen, but we don't know what.

That's a lie.

I know what.

"Luke," I start, ready to rip my newly-restarted heart from my chest and lay it all out for him, but I don't get the chance.

In two seconds, Luke is in front of me, his arms scooping me up under the legs placing me on the kitchen counter. The cool granite is a stark contrast to the warmth of his arms, and my mind instantly blanks when our lips meet.

As he kisses me with that same urgency I felt outside Lenny's tonight, the thought of a heart-to-heart about our messy history and even messier breakup all so we can get *closure* sounds like a stupid idea.

His hands find the tops of my legs, gripping tightly as he pulls them open, stepping between them, so I can feel his body against mine. My hands snake up his arms, feeling his warm, golden skin under my fingertips, as I move them up to wrap around his neck.

The first swipe of his tongue against mine sets my insides on fire, and I can't fight the urge to fist my fingers in his blonde hair, angling his head for me.

Our tongues dance, and my body longs for friction as the pressure in my belly deepens. We both notice at the same time that the counter is the perfect height for me to feel his hard length against my core, and it's like he can read my mind as he grinds his hips against me, a small moan escaping from my lips but sounding so loud in the quiet apartment.

"Tell me you want this," he whispers against my lips, and I don't know exactly what *this* is. But, the more he kisses me, the more he rubs his body against mine, the more I drop my defenses and convince myself that giving into Luke is exactly what I need to do.

"I want this," I whisper back, my grip tightening in his hair, and I pull him back to me, hoping my kisses leave him bruised.

He pulls back an inch, and I stifle the whine I almost let out in protest.

"Are you sure?" he asks, his eyes glued to mine, darkened by lust. "Because this isn't just a one-night thing for me, Annie."

I resist the urge to pull my eyes away from his, the reality of how close I am to tearing down the walls I've put up between us threatening to come crashing down on this moment.

"I can't promise more than tonight."

Something flashes in his eyes, a look of longing, of hurt, but then it's gone. His hand cups the side of my head, "Then, I guess that's good enough for me." He pulls me in, and I see stars. We're a mess of kisses, touches, and desire, our clothes suddenly feeling like too much of a barrier between us.

"Take off your shirt," I tell Luke, and he does it without a second thought. I make quick work of my t-shirt and sweatpants, throwing them to the ground as Luke stands in front of me, his chiseled chest and corded arms like a fantasy come to life. His cheeks have a slight flush and his blue eyes are fixed on me, making me feel like I could burst into flames any second.

"You're perfect," he says, stepping between my legs and peppering kisses along my jaw and down my neck to my exposed breasts.

My brain completely turns off as he sinks his teeth into the sensitive skin on my chest, licking away the sting with his tongue, and I feel him smile against my skin.

"Cat got your tongue, Annie girl?"

I hum in agreement as one arm holds me in place on the countertop and the other finds my breast, my peaked nipple between his fingers as he whispers, "So you're telling me all I had to do is get you naked to shut you up?" There's an edge to his voice I haven't heard in so long, I thought I imagined it in the first place.

The same edge that makes me completely susceptible to anything this man says to me.

Like move in with him.

That edge brings mine back to life. "I'm not naked." Not my best comeback, considering the only clothing I have on is my underwear, but it's all I can manage as he moves his lips down my chest, his tongue tasting my skin until he meets his fingers on my nipple, circling his tongue around the sensitive peak, making me lean my head back and let out a moan I'll be embarrassed about later.

He moves across my chest, repeating the maddening movement of his tongue on my other breast, and I lean back on my hands behind me, exposing myself to him. He moves back and forth across my chest, alternating between using his fingers and mouth until I am a complete and utter mess.

"Luke," I plead, and I don't even know what I'm asking for.

"I got you," he whispers against my skin, bringing his lips to mine and kissing me deeply before pulling away.

I open my eyes just in time to see him jog into my bedroom, the sound of the drawer in the bedside table opening and closing, and Luke coming back with that little blue toy he's been obsessed with since he packed me a bag the night of the break-in.

I haven't used it since I moved here, and I honestly forgot that I threw it in that drawer almost two months ago.

"What are you doing?" I ask through my haze of lust when I hear the familiar buzz of the toy come to life.

"I haven't stopped thinking about you using this since I found it in your room."

"I still can't believe you went in my underwear drawer to pack that," I quip, but the breathiness of my voice cancels out any nonchalance I try—and fail—to use. "How did you even know it was in that bedside table?"

"Now is not the time to talk about what you call my 'stalker tendencies'."

"You're lucky I'm too turned on to think straight right now," I say as he presses kisses on my jaw."

"Do I turn you on, Annie girl?" he teases.

"I'm going to kill you."

"Not before you show me how you use this little toy of yours," Luke coos, his lips against my ear as he drags the toy across my chest and down my stomach, itching closer and closer where I need it.

It's a clitoral stimulation toy, and the first and only sex toy I've bought myself. It's kept me satisfied over the years during dry spells, but I've never used it with a partner before.

"Oh, you'd like that wouldn't you," I say, but I'm already taking the vibrator from his hands.

He loops his thumbs under the band of my underwear, helping me shimmy them off as he drops to his knees in front of me, putting him eye level with the most intimate part of me.

"I know how you like me on my knees for you." The feeling of his breath against me is nothing compared to the kisses he begins to place on my inner thighs, getting closer and closer to where I want him most.

"Luke," I breathe, and I should've known he'd read my mind.

He lets out a groan as he slides his tongue up my slit, tasting me for the first time. With one swipe of his tongue, I feel like I'm about to fall apart. "Now," he says, looking up at me, "show me.

CHAPTER 18

LUKE

THIS IS WHERE I BELONG—ON my knees for Annie.

She looks like a dream sprawled out on my kitchen counter, her brown eyes almost black with lust, and her lips swollen from my kisses. My dick throbs when I see my bite mark on the top of her breast, and I am already impossibly hard after getting just one taste of her.

While I'd be fine spending the night with my head between her thighs, making her scream my name over and over, I've been thinking of her with this little blue toy of hers for weeks now.

I can't take my eyes off her as she sucks her bottom lip into her mouth, biting hard as she places the toy on her clit, her head falling back when she feels the sucking sensation right where she needs it. I lean in and kiss the fingers that are holding that toy to her pussy as she lets herself fall back on the counter and begins rocking her hips.

Annie's moans are like music to my ears, and I grip her thighs, pulling them apart as I watch her move the toy against her dripping pussy. Then my eyes catch on something on her hip.

I don't remember Annie having a birthmark there.

In the darkness, I can't quite make out what it is, and then she pushes one of the buttons on the toy and it speeds up, making me completely lose my train of thought.

I can't take it anymore.

I unzip my shorts, pulling them down with my briefs enough to pull my cock out, and I'm already seconds away from embarrassing myself when I slide my hand down my length.

"Fuck," I breathe as I watch her, and a groan escapes my throat as my name falls from her lips, my hand fisting my cock as I jerk myself off to the sight of her getting herself off.

And then she's there, falling apart, and I'm right behind her, her name falling from my lips.

"That was the hottest thing I've ever seen," I announce when we finally come down from our high. Annie turns off her toy, setting it down beside her as she pushes herself up on her elbows. She rolls her eyes, but there's a smile on her face and a flush to her cheeks.

She looks down at me, and her eyes slightly widen when she takes in the sight. When she sinks her teeth in her bottom lip, I concur that she likes what she sees.

"Look at what a mess you made," she purrs as she reaches her arm to the right, turning on the sink next to her. Then, she hops off the counter and walks into the guest bedroom, her ass swaying with each step.

"Clean yourself up, bartender," she says over her shoulder, "and sleep tight."

And then she shuts the door behind her.

———

There's a new feeling in the air when I wake up this morning, last night still fresh in my mind. The sun feels like it's shining brighter, my mind feels clearer, and my heart feels like it's beating louder than usual.

And I know it has everything to do with Annie.

Last night was incredible for more than one reason—one being how I'll never get the image of her on my counter out of my head.

Annie *finally* let her walls down around me. She'll deny it, but I know she did.

I know my work is far from over, and I know that there is only one possibility for how the aftermath of last night will unfold.

First, she'll lie to both herself and me and say it meant nothing.

Then, I'll do everything in my power to show her that it meant *everything*.

I can hear Annie showering when I make my way out of my bedroom. I slip on a sweatshirt and a pair of shorts and find Rosie waiting for Annie outside the closed bathroom door, her head popping up when she sees me walk up to the door.

Annie can pretend all she wants that last night didn't shift things between us, but I refuse to let her convince herself that it was just a one-time or *spur of the moment* kind of thing.

I knock twice on the bathroom door, not giving her time to say anything before I walk in, the steam from the hot water clouding the bathroom and my view of her through the glass shower doors.

"What the hell do you think you're doing?" she squeals, sliding the door enough for her to peek her head out. Her brown hair is thrown up in a messy bun to keep out of the water, and her tan skin is covered in bubbles from her body wash—the scent of jasmine immediately invading my senses.

I open the cabinet above the sink, pulling out my toothbrush that sits beside the one she put in there. "Brushing my teeth," I answer as I grab the toothpaste we share, squeezing some on my toothbrush before walking over to the shower.

"You couldn't wait?" she huffs, and I want to kiss the pout

off her lips. She watches me as I reach into the shower, and she fights to keep her expression neutral as I put my toothbrush under the water, getting it wet.

"Nope," I answer, popping it into my mouth.

"The sink is right there," she quips, sliding the glass door shut, but I'm not about to leave her alone.

I let a few seconds pass, knowing I'm already past pushing my luck. "What do you want to do today?" My voice is a little mumbled around the toothbrush, but she answers right away.

"What have I told you about minding your business?" I can't see her through the glazed glass, but I can make out the silhouette of her mind-numbing body.

The body I had my hands all over last night.

I have to stifle a groan at the thought, right along with imagining how easy it would be to step into that shower with her—even if I'm unsure that I'd make it out alive if I gave into that temptation.

I spit into the sink, rinsing my toothbrush in the sink. "I thought we could spend the day together."

The shower turns off, and she pulls down the towel hanging over the glass door—*my* towel. I'm sure she's already armed with some sassy rejection, but I don't give her the time.

"I have some errands to run." And while these *errands* aren't necessarily fun or romantic, they won't scare Annie away. Bombarding her with roses and surprise beach picnics would have her running for the hills. "I have to stop by the ice rink to reserve my rec team's practice nights for the month of September and pick up dog food. You can come with me."

She slides the shower door open with one hand, the other holding the towel wrapped around her, and steps out onto the bath mat. "I don't want to spend the day with you." The white cotton makes her pink cheeks even more noticeable, and her big brown eyes are narrowed on me. She looks just like a gift waiting to be unwrapped, her long tan legs glistening with droplets of water.

I'm staring, but I don't care.

Annie does.

She steps up in front of me. "Hey," she says, snapping her fingers in my face. "It's nothing you haven't seen before. Get over it."

"Never." I shake my head, hoping to bring thoughts back into my brain. "While I'd much rather look at you wrapped in *my* towel, get dressed. The rink opens at nine."

"I'm not running errands with you." She looks down at the towel she's holding around her, and I follow her gaze. "And it's *my* towel now."

I don't even register what she says because my eyes are now fixed on the bite mark just above where she's holding the towel around herself, the sight of the red indent going straight to my groin.

She sees my eyes still on her chest, looking down and shaking her head. "Didn't know you liked to bite," she teases. She's trying to sound like she couldn't care less, like she's just giving me a hard time, but I know better.

"There's a lot you don't know about me, Annie girl."

She rolls her eyes. "What I do know is I have my own errands to run. So, move." She squeezes past me to get through the door and over Rosie who is still laying just outside the bathroom, heading straight to the guest room, but I don't give her time to close the door, being only a step behind her. "Perfect. We can make any stop you need when we're out. I'll even buy you a matcha."

She ignores me as she pulls a pair of underwear, shorts, and tank top out of the laundry basket at the foot of her bed, her room even more of a mess than the last time I peeked inside it. Turning around and wanting me to leave for her to change, she huffs, "Do you mind?"

"Not at all. Go ahead and drop the towel, honey." I give

her a smirk and cross my arms, leaning against the door frame. "Like you said, it's nothing I haven't seen before."

Her brows furrow, and I can almost see the thought of throwing something at me cross her mind.

She just has to ask me again, and I'll leave her alone, but instead, she shrugs her shoulders and smiles, calling my bluff. "Fine." She drops her towel and my knees go weak. "I need to pick up some baking supplies. We can stop at the store after we pick up Rosie's food."

My head falls back just as the towel hits the floor, and I don't even care about the groan I make. Partly because I'm annoyed at how she never fails to do the opposite of what I think she's going to do. The other part because she has no idea what her bratty little tendencies do to me.

I reach out, gripping the door hard enough for my knuckles to turn white. "We're leaving in ten minutes," I growl, and I shut the door before she has time to tell me no.

CHAPTER 19
ANNIE

SOMEWHERE BETWEEN LUKE reaching into the shower this morning to get his toothbrush wet rather than use the sink that was *right* there, and him shutting the guest room door with a literal *growl*, I told myself that I couldn't avoid this conversation we need to have any longer.

But it's not the conversation I thought we needed to have.

I let my feelings for Luke get the best of me last night. I don't regret it. I don't think there's anything *wrong* about what we did. It was one of the best orgasms I've had.

Knowing Luke was there watching me while I got myself off was a literal wet dream come true, but it definitely complicates things.

It was so much more than something physical.

It felt so good to let the walls I've built so high come down, and now that I know what it feels like, I don't want to put them back up.

Letting people in is hard for me. I learned early on in my life that people tend to use your weaknesses against you, especially the people closest to you. It happened with my parents; it happened with my four closest friends.

It even happened with Luke.

When you let people in, you give them total power over you.

It's taken me years to build walls tall enough that people can't climb over them and strong enough that no one can break them down, but I am exhausted.

I thought keeping people at arms-length was the only way I would feel safe, but I was wrong.

People like Mia and Drew, Eddie and Emmett, they make me feel safe. I can let my walls down around them—I *willingly* give them the power to hurt me because I know they never will.

And last night, Luke made me feel that way too.

But my mind can't help but spiral when I think about our history, the memories, his betrayal. I can't go through that again. I don't think I'll make it through it alive this time around because there's so much more to lose.

I thought it would be easy to put space between us.

And when that didn't work, I thought the answer was closure.

But there's no such thing as closure when it comes to Luke.

It's time to tell him—tell him *everything*.

I look over at Luke at the front desk of the local ice rink. He's making the middle-age receptionist blush as he gives her his golden smile and devastating ocean eyes all so she lets him reserve extra rink time for his rec hockey team's September practices that start Monday.

The whole way here, I wanted to just rip off the Band-Aid. I wanted to tell him that we needed to talk—that I hate him for making me love him; that I love him enough to dig up the memories I bury the deepest because I'm slowly realizing that he's my biggest weakness of all.

But I couldn't.

My mind was too busy spinning from all the times he looked over at me from the driver's seat and his face lit up at the mere fact that I agreed to run these stupid errands with him.

And that I would do it over and over again if it made him smile like that.

My mouth felt dry when I let him reach over his center console to put his hand on my thigh, his thumb rubbing lazy circles against my skin as he drove, my hand itching to take his in mine, neither of us saying anything about it.

I turn back to the rink, slipping my hands into my pockets as I lean back and watch the kids and parents skate across the ice, opting for a *cooler* summer activity.

I see a little blonde boy with his dad, struggling to keep his balance for a moment as he holds his dad's hand. After a few skates together, the boy lets go of his dad, picking up speed as he glides along the ice, a huge smile on both their faces.

The little boy reminds me of the first time I saw Luke on the ice. We were just kids, and it was during the simple times where you just invited your whole class to your birthday party. Mr. and Mrs. Owens rented the whole rink in our hometown for twenty first-graders to skate around for Luke's seventh birthday, and Luke had a permanent smile on his face, caring more about going around the rink as fast as he could than any of the guests, presents, or cupcakes.

"All set," I hear, and I didn't even realize he walked over to where I was waiting for him.

"Oh, great." I shake my head, bringing myself back to the moment. "Pet store time?"

He looks out to the rink and then back to me with a sparkle of mischief in his eyes. "What size shoe are you again?"

———

"I haven't seen you on the ice in years," I tell Luke as we return our rental skates.

He looks out to the rink and then back to me with a sparkle of mischief in his eyes.

We spent an hour or so on the ice, and it was more fun than I'd ever admit to him.

Luke is a natural on the ice, gliding in his skates with the same ease of walking. Me, on the other hand, has the same amount of gracefulness as a baby giraffe trying to walk on its new legs.

He was skating circles around me. *Literally.*

It took me going around the rink twice before I let go of the siding, just to hold on to him so I wouldn't fall, and I'm positive his arm will be bruised tomorrow.

I don't feel bad about it though.

He left his own marks on me last night.

"You never accept my invites to come watch my rec games."

I scoff. "Liar. Mia, Drew, Ed, Emmett and I have been at the last three. You just haven't gone to one all summer."

We wave to the receptionist as we walk outside, the sun is high with no clouds to block it, the blue sky being just a shade lighter than Luke's eyes.

"Well, excuse me for having a bar to run," he answers, pulling his car keys from his pocket.

I laugh, but the sound comes out hollow. My voice takes on a more serious tone. "You never told me what you decided to do about your dad's firm."

Luke's smile fades. He runs a hand through his hair, as we walk to his car. "Well, the spot is ready and waiting for me. It has been since I graduated."

"Duh," I reply.

He stops mid-step in the parking lot and turns to me. I stop walking and find a shocked expression on his face. "Wait a second. No 'who would ever want you as a lawyer' or 'wow, so you are smarter than you look, Lukey-poo'?"

I roll my eyes and keep walking. "I'm not a *total* bitch. I know you're smart. You made it through law school without even an ounce of interest in being a lawyer."

"How do you know I don't want to be a lawyer?" he asks, coming into step beside me.

"Are you kidding? You practically died of happiness when you got that hockey scholarship and then six months later you suddenly wanted to be a lawyer? Working with your *dad* of all people?"

He reaches his arm behind his head, his hand rubbing his neck as he rounds his car to the driver's seat. I open the passenger side door, climbing in at the same time Luke turns the car on. "Sometimes I forget how well you know me," he admits, and my heart skips a beat.

I try to mask the smile threatening my lips. "You're not that hard to read." And it's true. Luke isn't hard to read. He's happy 99% of the time, and that 1% of the time he's mad, sad, frustrated, or feeling any other emotion, it's written all over his face.

"I like to think I can say the same about you," he says, and I resist the urge to look anywhere but out the front windshield, feeling his eyes burn a hole in the side of my head.

The words are on the tip of my tongue.

I feel like my lips are about to burst with everything I need to say to him, all the questions I want to ask, all the answers I want to give him.

I want to tell him that we spent seven years apart because I was too scared to face him after I saw the video of him and Devin.

I want to ask him why he did it—why he threw away what we had and why he never told me that he cheated.

I want to give him a chance to explain.

And most of all, I want to promise him that I'll ruin him

for anyone else if he ever even thinks about hurting me, but I want him to see that, in reality, I need him to promise me he'll never do anything to hurt me again.

But instead, I ask, "Did you tell your dad you're not taking the job he has for you?"

Luke sighs, leaning his head back on the car seat. "I've been putting it off."

"Shocking," I deadpan.

He turns to face me. "Telling Daniel Owens what he *doesn't* want to hear is easier said than done."

I can't help the protectiveness that overwhelms me at the thought of Luke with his father. The man used Luke as a power play against people who hurt him, keeping the truth from him until it was too late for him to have a relationship with his biological father.

To me, it's simple. The man doesn't deserve to call Luke a son.

But to Luke, it's so much more complicated.

"Then why don't you tell him to fuck off?"

Luke snorts. "Why don't *you*?" he jokes.

"There's a lot more I'd rather tell him." I huff. "Starting with how he barely acknowledged you as a son until he needed something from you. Not to mention how he took advantage of you and your need to gain his approval—which, by the way, was completely valid to want as a literal *child*—and ending with how much time and energy you put into something *he* wanted. Not what you wanted."

Luke doesn't say anything for a few seconds, so I finally turn to face him. His mouth is slightly parted and his eyes glisten.

"What?" I ask, feeling like I might have crossed a line.

He clears his throat. "Careful, Annie girl." The tips of my ears heat at how low he keeps his voice. "Your feelings are showing."

"I don't know what you're talking about," I say instinctively. I cross my arms over my chest, looking back at the front windshield. "So if you're not going to be a lawyer, what are you going to do?"

Luke shifts in his seat, his head falling forward until he hits his forehead against the steering wheel. He sighs. "I don't know. I mean, I went through all the schooling, didn't even have to take the bar because the state of Wisconsin doesn't require it as long as you meet all the course requirements and character and fitness standards. I have a position at a firm that guys I went to school with would do anything for. It makes me feel like shit for giving that up."

"Why?" I can't help but ask. "Sure, it's annoying watching someone have something handed to them that they don't deserve, but that's not the case with you, Luke. You worked your ass off to be deserving of that job for years, and you did it for someone who doesn't deserve even a second of your time."

Luke shakes his head, his forehead still resting against the steering wheel. I watch him from the corner of my eye. "I want something that's *mine*. Something I can be proud of; something I can put the hard work into because I want to, not because I have to. I just don't know what that *something* is."

Neither of us acknowledge that he had that with his hockey scholarship—that he could've played on a Division 1 team, pursuing something *he* wanted—and gave it up.

"It's not too late to find it," I answer quietly, wishing I had something more to say to him.

"Yeah, maybe," he responds before letting out an exhale. "Either way, I know I have to tell my dad. I just know that when I do, I'll most likely never talk to my parents again."

"Parents are overrated anyway," I say it as a joke, but it's the truth to me.

People deserve parents who want them, who love them, who cherish them. I've never had that, and neither has Luke. He just held on to the idea of them longer.

"So," he starts after a few quiet moments, "what do you say we end this heart-to-heart here and get our dog some food and maybe a new toy or two?"

As always, Luke knows how to brighten a space, always being the one to lighten the mood when it begins to dim.

He's like the North Star, shining brighter than everyone else around him, and you can't help but follow him through the dark.

"She's not my dog." I laugh, but the argument feels moot at this point.

I turn to look at Luke, my heart feeling like it's seconds away from bursting from my chest from how much I hope he never loses his shine.

"Whatever helps you sleep at night, honey."

CHAPTER 20
LUKE

WHAT IS it that people say about the definition of insanity? That it's the equivalent of doing the same thing over and over again and expecting a different result?

Whatever it is, I think I am certifiably *insane* because the way Annie is looking at me right now makes me think that my years of trying to make her love me again have finally paid off.

I was joking before when I teased her about her feelings showing, but I know my Annie girl, and I know that she'll always keep her feelings under wraps. I can appreciate it, though, especially if she gives me glimpses like she is now.

Gone before I can think too much about it, she turns to look forward, pressing her feet against my dash and leaning back in her seat. "I believe I was promised a matcha for running these errands with you."

"Coming right up," I say, putting the car into drive and pulling out of the ice rink parking lot.

———

"Remind me why we have to drive 20 minutes to *this* pet store for Rosie's food?" Annie asks as we exit the store, taking the last sip of the iced matcha I got her on the way here before tossing it in the trash can we pass.

"Because," I say, feigned offense in my voice, "our Ro-Ro deserves the very best."

"I won't argue with that," she says, opening the backseat door of my car for me to put in Rosie's big bag of food and the plastic bag of toys we picked out for her. "I meant it more as why did we pass three *closer* pet stores to come out this way."

I don't have any other reason for coming out this way other than the fact I wanted to spend more time with Annie. Listening to the songs she played in the car, hearing her sing for the first time since she made us all go sing karaoke one weekend three years ago; I forgot how much I love her voice.

I kept driving, wanting to prolong the car ride, until she got suspicious as to where I was headed. I was lucky there was a place for us to stop at when I was only half-paying attention to where I was going.

"This one is Rosie's favorite," I lie, shutting the door and opening the passenger side door for Annie.

"She's not here," Annie replies, not missing a beat.

"Is there anything I can say that you won't argue with?"

"Nope," she answers with a smile.

"Brat."

"You like it."

I shake my head and laugh because what I want to do—throw her into the backseat of my car and *show* her how much I like it—-wouldn't be appropriate.

"What errands did you need to run?" I ask her when we both get into the car.

"I wanted to get some baking things—flour, sugar, cocoa powder, other ingredients and supplies. That kind of stuff."

"For the cake you're making me?" I tease, and I make a

mental note of one more errand I need to run, one I need to do without Annie before she gets home from her first day of rotations on Monday.

"Ha, funny," she deadpans before adding, "We have Sunday dinner tomorrow at Mia and Eddie's, so I need to make a dessert." A moment passes before she continues. "But I guess some baked goods could count as my rent since you won't let me pay you anything for it."

"Exactly," I answer. I would never make her pay me for staying at my place for a few months. "I'm already thinking of all the desserts you can make me between now and October when your new apartment is ready."

Her words make a movie of memories play out in my head—all the times she baked me a birthday cake and how much better they got over the years. The first cake she ever baked me was for my 12th birthday, and it was borderline liquid when we cut into it.

The last one was for when the Lenny's crew got together to celebrate me graduating law school at my apartment. They were all the to watch me walk across the stage and get my diploma. That cake was the best thing I ever tasted; I've had literal dreams about the dark chocolate cake and the peanut butter frosting.

Well, maybe second best—Annie tastes pretty damn good.

She laughs. "I can't believe I'll be living down the hall from you in just over a month." She lets out a sigh, "But in all seriousness, with rotations starting, my stress level is about to skyrocket, meaning I'll need something to do to keep me sane and help me relax. Get ready to eat cookies and cupcakes for every meal starting Monday."

"I can think of some things I can do to help you relax," I flirt, never missing a chance to push her buttons. It's like second nature to me after this long.

Annie reaches behind her to grab her seatbelt, willing her

face to stay the same. "But if it has to do with you, it *definitely* won't keep me sane."

She clicks her seatbelt in and tucks her hair behind her ears. "I would hope not," I quip. "I would hope it would drive you crazy, just like it did last night."

This time, she can't control the small inhale she takes and the widening of her eyes.

Got her.

She turns to face me, ears red and her signature death glare in full effect. "Drive."

———

I drop Annie off at home, helping her bring in her bags of baking supplies and the stuff we got for Rosie, and let her know I need to stop over at Lenny's.

She looks like she's about to offer to come with me, but I saw the sparkle in her eyes when she was throwing all kinds of stuff in the cart at the grocery store.

She's itching to get started on dessert for tomorrow night.

I head back the way we came, stopping to get the perfect present for Annie. Her birthday is coming up at the end of September, and I haven't given her a birthday gift in years. The last time I did was a bouquet of roses for her 19th birthday, and she told me that she'd rather me just drop off the face of the Earth as a gift.

Then she took a lighter and set the flowers on fire.

And because she, of course, wants the one thing I won't give her—leaving her alone—I haven't gotten her anything since.

Until this year.

I'll frame this year's gift as an early birthday gift and a *congrats-on-starting rotations* gift. I know she won't be able to resist being happy about it, especially after I saw the state of her old stand mixer after the break-in.

After picking her up a new one—a bright red one, that reminded me of her lips after she puts her cherry lip gloss on —I actually did stop at Lenny's because I could never lie to Annie. I told her I was coming here, so I did.

Ava's working with one of the other new bartenders, Mickey. The two look like they have everything under control, so I give them a quick wave before rounding the bar and heading back to Emmett's office to make next week's schedule.

But before I can, I hear a voice I haven't heard since high school.

"Luke Owens?" the voice booms, and I turn to find Grant, my buddy from my high school's hockey team, sitting at the end of the bar.

He was our goalie; big and built enough at 17 to buy us alcohol at the local gas station and not get carded. His dirty blonde hair is a little darker now, and he has more facial hair than he did the last time I saw him.

"I haven't seen you since the night before we all left for college. How've you been?" He stands up from his chair at the bar as I walk over to him, taking his held-out hand and letting him pull me in to slap his hand on my back.

"I'm good, man. It's nice to see you." The last I heard of Grant, he was going to college with three of our friends on the team a few hours north of here. All four moving on from their hockey careers and all four reluctantly being followed by their high school girlfriends—the girls Annie used to be friends with.

I didn't keep up with many people from high school, quickly finding a new group of friends in college and then law school. Plus, I had the Lenny's crew. I didn't really need anyone else.

And seeing Grant makes me feel like my mind is reverting back to high school and like the past seven years didn't happen, and I'm not a fan of the feeling.

"You still with Devin?" I ask him, not having thought about her since that night she whisked Annie away and then I didn't see her for four months.

Grant shrugs his shoulders. "We've been on and off over the years, but we just moved in together not too far from where we went to college."

I nod my head, not really caring for this small talk, but I don't want to be rude. "What brought you back?" Lenny's is across town from where I grew up, so it's not too crazy to see people I knew in high school out this way every so often. It's just not at all often they come here, seeing as though it's a small dive bar in the midst of more trendy, popular places.

And for people like Grant and Devin, I would expect them to flock back to our hometown if they're ever out visiting this way—I wouldn't put it past them to be the kind of people stuck in that high school mindset.

"We're in town for the week. You remember Penelope? Devin's friend? She's getting married at some place in downtown Milwaukee, and you'll never guess who she's with now," he answers, and I really hope my face doesn't show how much I don't care about this.

It must not because, when I don't say anything, Grant continues like he never really wanted my response anyway.

"Alek's *brother*. Remember him? He was two years older than us. She dumped Alek a week after we all moved into our dorms, and then ended up with his brother." He shakes his head.

I have a vague memory of Penelope and Alek dating, her following him to college, but it's really none of my business what happened between all of them, especially after we drifted.

"Crazy stuff, man," Grant says, taking a sip of his beer. "Anyway, what brings you here?"

"Oh, I work here," I answer.

Grant's eyebrows raise. "You're a bartender? *Here*?" He

lines the word "here" with disbelief and borderline disgust, as if he can't believe I would work here, and I cross my arms.

"I do. I'm running the place while the owner is out on paternity leave." I want to ask him why he seems to have a problem with that, seeing as though his face makes it seem like I just told him I kick puppies and push over toddlers for a living, but he voices his confusion before I can.

"Damn, I'm surprised. When I heard you were giving up playing hockey to be a lawyer, I just figured you'd be one by now."

I resist the urge to pull an Annie and roll my eyes. My skin is prickled with annoyance, and I want nothing more than to tell him I'm done with this conversation. "That was the plan."

"My dad saw yours not too long ago, told me you were still planning on going to work with him."

"Things changed," I answer, and that's all I'm giving him. I'm ready to give him a goodbye, but he stops me in my tracks.

"Whatever happened with Viv—I mean, Annie?"

Grant is literally the last person I want to talk about Annie with, seeing as though no one from our high school would believe me if I told them Annie isn't the shy theater kid she was back then.

"She's good," is all I say, quickly adding that I got to go and pretending to agree that we should get together sometime.

I never make it back to Emmett's office because I head out the front door and drive straight home. I'm not going to sit and listen to someone, who I know doesn't deserve to know the amazing person she grew into, ask about Annie.

ANNIE

BY THE TIME Luke got home after the mysterious errand he had to run, I already had two different brownies almost ready for dinner tomorrow. I would've had three, but I don't work as fast without my stand mixer, and I only have old-fashioned mixing bowls and wooden spoons at Luke's place.

I made us both dinner, and I didn't let myself dwell on how natural it felt to have such a domesticated evening with Luke.

Of course, because it's us, we bickered. He flirted; I tried to shut it down. I told him that he was being stupid, and he teased me about being a brat.

As *normal* as a night can be for us.

We argued over dinner about the *Twilight* franchise—me forever arguing with Mia and Drew, and now Luke, that the first one is the best one—and we fought over whether or not the movies would be better with different casting—me saying no, him saying yes.

We finally decided we would watch the first one, Luke being overly familiar with the series as a whole because of how much I talked about the books with him when I read them in middle school.

"I blame you for how well I know these movies," he tells me halfway through.

"You're the one who didn't tell me to shut up when I would give you chapter synopses as I read the series."

"Why would I have told you to shut up? It was the only time you would actually *talk*," he teases. I try to block out the memories of the old Annie, trying to forget how much of a wallflower I was growing up.

"This is why you should be careful what you wish for, just look at me now," I tease back.

"Speaking of that," Luke starts, his eyes on the TV screen from where he's sitting next to me on the couch. It felt natural to stretch out next to him, putting my feet in his lap. And somewhere between the opening credits and the first-time Bella sees Edward, he started to idly rub the tops of my legs. "You'll never guess who I saw today at Lenny's."

"Who?" I ask, watching as Jasper flips the baseball bat in his hand in arguably the best scene of the movie.

"Grant."

Neither of us hit the mute button, but everything goes silent— Luke, the TV, Rosie playing with one of her new toys at Luke's feet. The world around me drowns out, and I feel like I'm being pulled deeper and deeper underwater.

My throat burns with the need to breathe, but I can't suck in any air. My breathing is shallow and my lungs start to burn.

I bring a hand to my chest to steady myself, trying over and over to take in a full breath. It takes a couple tries, but I finally get some air in.

What the hell was that?

Luke somehow ended up knelt in front of me, but it's different from the last time he was on his knees for me.

Last night, it made me feel desired, in control, *powerful.*

Right now, it makes me feel exposed, small, *weak.*

"Annie?" Luke whispers, or maybe shouts. I can't tell

through the pounding in my ears. "Annie?" he says again, and this time it sounds more clear.

"What?" I answer, and my voice cracks.

"Are you okay?" he asks, his features taught with concern.

I clear my throat, shaking my head and tucking my hair behind my ears. "Of course I'm okay. I just—" I pause. I take one look into his baby blues, and I try to ignore the pressure building behind my eyes. "I just haven't thought of Grant in years," I lie, but the concern etched on Luke's face doesn't fade. "Brings up a lot of memories."

Luke tilts his head; his hands are on my knees as he's knelt in front of me. I clasp my hands together, and they feel clammy and cold. "Did something happen at Grant's that night?" he whispers.

He's asked me about that night before, when he first started working at Lenny's, but I shut it down. Told him to never bring it up again.

It makes sense that he'd come to this conclusion, that *something* happened that night, not only because it's the night I left but for my reaction to hearing that he saw Grant tonight—does Grant even know what happened between Devin and Luke? Are Grant and Devin still together? Was she there? Did Luke see her too? Did she say anything about that night? Why would they come *here*? To Lenny's? To *my* place?

I nod, not trusting my voice right now, but Luke doesn't push. Instead, his hand cups my cheek, not letting me look anywhere but his eyes. "I know those girls—Devin and all of them—were your friends. And I know something happened between you all."

My stomach drops, and I want to shake my head and plug my ears, anything to avoid thinking about bullying that still affects me more than I'd like to admit, but Luke holds me in place, and I feel the warmth of his touch over my entire body.

"I also know that you didn't deserve to lose your friends just because you guys weren't interested in the same stuff."

I close my eyes.

"I don't know everything that happened," he continues, "but I am so sorry it did. I can see it still affects you."

I never blamed Luke for anything leading up to Devin showing me the video of him. He had so much going on between his family bullshit and hockey. I could've confided in him, or anyone for that matter, when the bullying just got worse, but I didn't.

That's my fault. Not his.

I shake my head, and his hand on my cheek drops to the pile of our hands on my lap. "There's nothing you could have done," I say, finding my voice, wiping a tear that came loose.

He asks again. "What happened at Grant's party, Annie?"

My eyes find his again and the walls come up before I can stop them—like a defense mechanism that initiates without me even thinking about it.

"What happened the night before, Luke?"

I read the confusion all over his face; it's as easy as reading a book I've read a thousand times. There's something like guilt there too, maybe for what happened that night with Devin or maybe for never telling me, but it's there.

"I—" he starts, "honey, I was so drunk that night. I barely remember the night before. Why? Why are you asking about it?" His voice shakes, and there's an urgency to it.

I stand up from the couch, not even registering what he says. Luke loses his balance a little before standing up with me. "Forget it," I say, and I feel the familiar crack in my chest because it sounds like an excuse. Just when I found my heart again, just when I realized it wasn't broken beyond repair, it shatters again hearing him question *me* rather than tell me the truth.

"Annie," he pleads as I walk to the guest room. "Please,

tell me what I did, and I will spend my entire life making it up to you."

I stop just outside my door, and so many emotions hit me right in the stomach. Did he really think I'd never find out he cheated on me? Does he really think that I'd forget it after all these years? Devin showed me that video and told me they hooked up.

How could I not believe her when I was seeing the two of them right in front of me, playing over and over again on her phone?

"I can't do this right now," I finally say, but I'm unable to turn around. If I see him, I'll fall apart. I'm not like Drew or Mia, I'm not strong enough to look him in the eyes and tell him that what he did may not have meant something to him, but it was everything to me.

It was every single comment from my parents about being a waste of space. It was every single rumor that those girls spread about me. It was taking away my sense of worth bit by bit until there was nothing left. It was every convoluted message I internalized about how I wasn't worth the trouble.

The lesson I know all too well: the person closest to you has all the power to hurt you.

And for me, that person is Luke.

So why am I wishing I could fall into his arms, so he can make it all better?

I resist the urge, hoping I can go to sleep tonight and convince myself that this has all been a bad dream.

That Luke never ran into Grant.

That Luke never asked me what happened the night I left.

I wish I could go back to the blissful ignorance of this morning, thinking to myself that maybe Luke and I finally would have our second chance.

But second chances aren't meant for people like me.

"Goodnight, Luke," I whisper, before walking into the guest room and closing the door on us.

CHAPTER 22
LUKE

SHE PUT her walls back up.

Just when I thought I'd never see them again, she built each and every one even taller and stronger than ever.

She asked me what happened the night before.

What the hell *did* happen the night before Grant's party, and why is it a complete blur?

I know I drank a lot with the guys that night, more than I ever had before, and it was years ago, but did I really blackout the night I destroyed my relationship with Annie?

I've been pacing outside her door all day, hoping to see her, but she's been avoiding me. She only comes out when I'm not around—either when I'm letting Rosie out or when I'm in my room.

My hands are in the pockets of my jeans, and I feel the tube of cherry lip gloss I stole from Annie's a little while ago. I carry it with me as a reminder of her, along with the tattoo on my thigh that has finally fully healed. Both are secrets I keep for myself, aside from Eddie who was with me for the tattoo.

We're supposed to leave for Mia and Eddie's for Sunday

Dinner, and I know Annie wouldn't miss it, so I'm biding my time, just outside her door.

We need to leave now to make it there by six.

And I'm getting impatient.

I need to see her.

Just when I'm about to knock on the door, it opens. Annie is wearing an oversized t-shirt and jean shorts, her brown hair slicked back in a bun at the back of her head. Her lashes are long, framing her big brown eyes, and I spot a few freckles on her nose from being out in the sun this summer.

I can also see the slight redness to them, and my chest cracks.

I clear my throat. "Um, ready to go?" I ask, hoping we can both just ignore that I was waiting outside her door like some kind of stalker.

She nods, and it's out of character.

Why isn't she telling me to fuck off, or rolling her eyes at my "stalker tendencies"?

She stalks past me, grabbing the containers of brownies she packed up. One minute, the brownies were laid out on a cooling rack on the counter. I go outside to take Rosie around the block, and when I come back, they're in her containers.

"Are we bringing Rosie?" she asks quietly, and her voice sounds familiar yet foreign.

"You heard your mom, Ro-Ro. Let's go see your sister," I say, grabbing her leash from where it's hanging by the door, and hoping to get *anything* out of Annie—asking for a smile would be delusional, but an eye roll, a death glare, a quip about her not being Rosie's mom.

I need something from her.

Hearing the noise of the leash, Rosie hops off the couch and comes to sit, her tail wagging as I bend down to clip it to her collar, but still, Annie doesn't say anything.

As I stand, I see Annie has already opened the front door of the apartment and started walking down the hall.

The car ride to Mia and Eddie's is the same.

Annie doesn't say a word.

I watch her out of the corner of my eye as I drive, and her usual edge, that confidence that I've watched blossom over the last seven years, is gone.

————

I knock on the door to Mia and Eddie's, holding the containers of brownies Annie made. One has frosting, the other powdered sugar. Emmett, Annie, and Mia like brownies with frosting, and Drew, Eddie, and I like powdered sugar on ours. It took one Christmas four years ago, arguing over which way is better, for Annie to say she'll just make both.

"Shit," Annie mutters under her breath, but I don't have time to ask her what's wrong before Drew opens the door. Eddie and Emmett are on the couch, Eddie holding Lennon in his lap as she stares at the faces Mia is making at her from the floor.

"I'd say something about me having to play host while they occupy my baby, but I feel like we all share houses at this point," Drew says with a smile, grabbing the containers of brownies from me.

The three of us follow her into the kitchen, Rosie proving Drew's point that each of our homes is as much of ours as they are each other's, waltzing right into Mia and Eddie's place like she owns it, plopping down with Daisy on her dog bed.

Mia looks over at us from where she is on the floor in the living room, and her smile instantly drops when she looks past me and sees Annie a few steps behind me.

"Ann, what's wrong?" Mia asks, and the entire room shifts. Drew sets down the brownie containers and turns to Annie, the guys looking up from Lennon and directly at us.

"I—" Annie starts before slapping a hand against her forehead and letting out a shaky exhale. "I forgot the powdered sugar for the brownies."

She says it like she's a second away from crying, and I think we all know she's not upset about forgetting something at the grocery store. Drew and Mia immediately fall into action.

Drew walks over to Annie, gently placing a hand on her arm like she is tending to a wounded animal. "It's okay. We can run and grab some," Drew says before turning to the living room. "Right, Mia?"

Mia is already up from the floor and walking into the kitchen. "Absolutely. We can go right now. The boys can handle baby duty and dinner until we get back."

Mia is already grabbing her purse and keys, and Drew is pushing Annie out the front door. I try to catch Annie's eye, but she won't look at me. Drew looks over, meeting my eyes, giving me a little nod that says, "We got her."

I feel so many emotions rush through me as the door shuts behind the three of them, but I don't have time to process them before I turn back to the living room, where Emmett and Eddie look at me, Eddie still holding Lennon. "You wanna tell us what that was about?"

A laugh escapes my throat, one free of humor, at how I'm supposed to answer that question. "I have no fucking clue," I say, running a hand through my hair before basically throwing myself to the ground in front of the two of them.

Mia and Eddie's apartment is about the size of mine; a big living room that connects to the kitchen, with a dining table that separates the two rooms. Their living room has a white fluffy rug in front of the couch, and I feel the material tickle the back of my neck as I lay back, pressing my palms into my eyes until I see stars.

"Well, you can either tell us your side of the story," Eddie continues, gently putting Lennon into her portable rocker as

Emmett watches his every move. "Or, we can hear Annie's side of the story from the girls later tonight. Your choice."

I let out a groan, only for Emmett to kick me in the head. "Ow," I mumble, letting my arms fall to my sides. My vision is blurry as my eyes re-regulate to the light.

"What did you do?" Emmett growls, and it actually sparks a little fear in me.

Emmett took a while to warm up to me. Whether it was because he suspected some sort of history between Annie and me or because I made every effort to counter his grumpiness when I started working for him, I'll never know. The two of us built a relationship solely because I refused to let him not like me.

I spent our shifts together trying to get him to talk to me, smiling at him, and asking about his day even when he looked like he wanted to kill me, but it worked. We're more than coworkers or friends—we've become family along the way.

But right now, Emmett doesn't feel like that.

Right now, he feels like someone who will hurt anyone who hurts Annie.

Emmett and Annie rarely acknowledge their history. Emmett is over a decade older than us, but he's known Annie since she was a kid with her dad always bringing her to the bar he frequented before he left her and her mom.

Emmett hadn't seen her since she was in middle school when she randomly turned up for a job the summer after we graduated high school, a lot happening to the both of them during their time apart.

I sit up from where I'm lying on the floor and shake my head, pushing myself up to standing and walked over to the dining table where there are stacks of plates and bowls and piles of silverware. "I honestly don't know what I did, but I know I did something."

Eddie and Emmett follow me, Emmett keeping Lennon in his line of sight but following Eddie to the table.

I start setting the table, just to have something to do with my hands.

"How do you not know what you did? Annie is always the first to tell you when you do something to piss her off," Eddie mentions, holding out a hand to help me set a plate for all six of us.

I look over at the oven, seeing a timer for twenty more minutes. "Aren't we on dinner duty until they come back?" I ask, not being able to look either of them in the face while I avoid Eddie's question.

"The lasagna is basically done. Just need to throw the bread in the oven and toss the salad, but we'll wait for the girls," Eddie answers.

I nod because what he's really saying is "talk".

So I do. I start at the beginning when I met Annie in first grade, all the way until the last time I saw her the night of Grant's party, and I can't stop. I tell them about running into Annie at Lenny's and seeing her for the first time in months, and I try to put into words how it felt to see her—that new person she was.

I talk about my feelings for her and how all they've done is evolve over the years, and I tell them about how I can't picture my life without her.

My shoulders feel lighter and lighter the more of our story I share with Emmett and Eddie, who genuinely listen and ask the occasional question as they help me set the table. They never once make me feel guilty for not telling them the truth about Annie and me, and I'm grateful for that.

While I'm at it, I tell them about how she's always been there for me, during all the shit with my dad and my decision to give up what I wanted to do to please him. They know the complexities of my parental dynamics, all of us at one point over the years confiding in each other about our issues with our own families. They echo Annie's sentiments about doing what I want, not what I think my dad would want.

I tell them about my decision to not become a lawyer and how I want something that's mine, and that I just don't know what it is yet.

I see a thought cross Emmett's face when I say it, but I don't pause to ask him about it, wanting to get everything out before the girls get back.

I know Annie doesn't want our friends to know our whole history, but I can't do this anymore. I can't keep my feelings for her to myself if I'm going to get her back.

I need help figuring out what the hell I did wrong in the first place.

"Wait, was she with you that night before the Grant guy's party?" Eddie asks. We finished setting the table, so we're now just standing around the set dining table. I'm leaning on the chair in front of me, rocking back and forth on my heels.

"No," I answer, "but I had a lot to drink, and I didn't drink at Grant's party the following night because of it." I exhale. "I honestly barely remember that night."

Eddie crosses his arms as Emmett leans back on the kitchen island behind him. "But Annie said *something* happened that night?" Eddie's brows are tight, his green eyes concentrating on me.

I shake my head. "The hockey team got together with our coaches for dinner that night, and then we all decided to go to one of our teammates' house because his parents were gone for the weekend. Grant was always able to get alcohol at a gas station by the high school because he never got ID'd."

I rack my brain for any other memory of that night. "I remember taking shots—a lot of them. We did one for every guy on the team who wasn't pursuing hockey in college." I shiver at the thought of how much alcohol was consumed, seeing as though only two guys on the team were sticking with hockey in college.

"So what? A handful of shots in a few hours?" Emmett questions.

"More like eighteen shots in less than two."

Eddie's eyes widen as Emmett shakes his head. "No wonder you don't remember shit," Emmett scolds. "You're lucky you didn't need your stomach pumped."

While I completely agree, I don't want to dwell on how I was 18 and stupid with no knowledge of alcohol limits. "It's safe to say I blacked out."

"I'm assuming you don't remember anything after taking the last couple of shots?" Eddie prompts.

"Barely," I answer, wracking my brain for any memory from that night, a night I never thought twice about until now.

"Are you sure you didn't say anything or do anything that could've hurt Annie's feelings? We know you wouldn't hurt her, but that's a lot of alcohol and you were young."

I shake my head, my hair whipping my cheeks. "It was just the guys from the team. They barely knew Annie, just knew her as my girlfriend and a friend of their girlfriends."

"Was she friends with any of their girlfriends?" Emmett asks, all of us invested in getting to the bottom of this.

"Yeah, but—" My body freezes, and I feel like I want to vomit. It's as if my body is having memories that my brain can't quite conjure up. My skin feels tight and hot, like I'm coming down with a fever, and everything feels like it's going in slow motion. I feel like I'm trying to move through water, but I can't get my arms or legs to move fast enough.

"What is it?" I hear Eddie ask, but I close my eyes. The memory is there, but I can't make it out.

What happened to me that night?

CHAPTER 23
ANNIE

GOOD THING DREW and Mia didn't pursue theater—neither of them can act for shit.

We walk through the front doors of the grocery store, and both are trying to act like my reaction to forgetting the powdered sugar for the brownies was completely normal. Like I didn't just nearly burst into tears in front of all of them because of it.

They didn't say anything to me on the ten-minute car ride here, Mia driving with me up front and Drew in the back seat. They didn't try to console me or ask what was wrong; we all just listened to whatever playlist Mia had on.

Now, they're pretending not to watch me out of the corner of their eyes as I lead us to the baking aisle.

"So," I start as we walk to the shelves with the different types of sugar, "you're not going to ask me?"

"Ask you what?" Drew asks, trying—and failing—to act like she isn't wondering what's wrong.

I roll my eyes and feel Mia's hip lightly bump mine.

"There she is," Mia says. "I don't know where she went, but the Annie I knew was *not* the one that walked into my apartment tonight."

I shake my head and hold back a smile. "Luke told me he ran into someone from our high school yesterday," I explain, reaching out to grab a bag of powdered sugar, hugging it against my chest. "It put me in a funk."

"Any particular reason why?" Drew asks, and I don't ignore that the three of us are about to have this conversation—one I've never had with anyone—in a goddamn grocery store.

The aisle we're in is currently empty, so I exhale before continuing. "I had a hard time in high school." I don't know why I don't call it what it was, say the word aloud—*bullied*. I was bullied in high school, but I can't get myself to say it. "One of the guys he ran into was dating a girl who used to be my fri—" I can't even get the word out because I hear a voice behind me that makes my blood run cold.

"Vivian Mitchell?"

I don't turn around.

It's like deciding to open up about this conjured her into existence—a sick joke if you ask me. This is what I get for trudging all this up and bringing it into the open.

Maybe, if I stay where I am, looking at Drew and Mia's confused faces that are looking past me at the person who is now walking towards me, she'll go away. Or, maybe, if I'm lucky, the ground will swallow me whole.

Why did I think taking a second to explain to Drew and Mia why I wasn't myself tonight would be the end of it? Why did I think the universe would be on my side? That I can run in here, forget that Luke ran into Grant and dug up all the feelings I've desperately tried to keep buried, grab this powdered sugar, and just enjoy the rest of my night with my friends before I start the toughest year of my education tomorrow.

Of course not, luck has never been on my side.

"Vivian?" I hear it again, and this time, the voice is closer.

"Do you know her, Ann?" Mia asks, her hand gently grabbing my elbow. My arms are still crossed over the bag of powdered sugar I'm holding to my chest, and if I squeeze my arms any tighter, the plastic might pop.

"Can we help you?" Drew says, her voice polite, but I can tell that she is wary because of my reaction.

I finally turn around, and any traces of the new and improved Annie melt away. I'm no longer the girl who takes no shit or bashes the truck of a grown man with a baseball bat.

I'm the girl who is afraid of her own shadow because it might be taking up too much space.

Devin looks the same, just older. Her brown, almost black, hair is still pin straight, but it's cut to fall just above her shoulders, and she has harsh bangs across her forehead. Her blue eyes are similar to Luke's—only I wish I could float in his. Devin's eyes have always had something lurking below the surface, something that will swallow me whole.

"It's been so long," she says, and the smile she has on her face, as if she's happy to see me, is insulting. "Grant told me he ran into Luke, but I didn't think that meant I'd see you."

My first instinct is to ask her what the hell she means by that, that she has no business even *thinking* of Luke, but my mouth feels dry. The words don't come.

When I don't say anything, she continues. "I've meant to reach out over the years. I really do feel bad about how we left things."

"You feel *bad*?" I grit out, finally finding my voice, and I feel my nails dig into my palms as I clench my fists.

"Of course I do," she exclaims, almost as bad an actress as Drew and Mia. She's holding a basket with a few groceries over one arm, the other she brings to her chest. "I only showed you the video, so you'd know the truth. I know you might not see it that way, but I did it for *your own good*."

"Video?" I hear Mia ask; I feel Drew's wariness behind me, while all I feel is anger coming from Mia.

"Oh, sorry," Devin says, looking past me at Mia and Drew. "I'm Devin. I was friends with Viv—"

"Annie," I interrupt, but it's no more than a whisper.

Devin looks at me. "Did you say something?"

"I go by Annie."

"Oh, right. I could never get used to Luke calling you that." She laughs, but it's more of a cackle. "Anyway, you seem to be doing," she pauses, looking me up and down, and I feel smaller than I have in years, "well."

There's so much I want to say, but I feel trapped inside my body.

"And for what it's worth, if it weren't me, it would've been some girl he met in college." She shrugs her shoulders, and she tries her best to look genuine, like she actually believes what she is saying or that it's helpful in any way.

If I didn't know any better, I might have missed the patronizing look with the familiar trace of triumph on her face.

"We're leaving," I hear Mia say over my shoulder, and I feel both her and Drew place a hand on my back, leading me forward past Devin. As we pass her, I avoid her eyes, watching the floor as we walk down the aisle. *"And for what it's worth,"* Mia says over her shoulder, "being a mean girl in your twenties is embarrassing. Get a fucking life."

———

Walking out of the grocery store is a blur. One of the girls bought the powdered sugar, the other helped me to the car. The whole time, I couldn't stare anywhere but my shoes, trying to at least hold it in until I got to the car.

Drew put me in the backseat with her, and before Mia could even drive out of the parking lot, I was crying into Drew's lap.

It's the first time I think I have truly cried—not just a few tears—since the night Devin and the other girls sat and watched me in the corner of Grant's parents' basement.

But I'm not crying because of what just happened.

I'm crying because of how I let someone like Devin have so much power over me for so long. Someone who was supposed to be on my side but turned on me the first chance she had. Someone who I trusted to be there for me, to support me, but used my deepest fears against me.

Devin knew how much Luke meant to me; she knew how being loved by him felt more like a dream than a reality—those are the types of things you tell your best friend when you're young and in love.

My feelings for Luke are so tied up in this whole situation, and I go back and forth on being embarrassed about it to wanting to slap myself in the face for not doing something about it sooner.

I feel Drew's fingers in my hair as she lets me cry, and I feel Mia's hand wrap around mine. Through the tears, I see her arm reached behind her, and one hand on the steering wheel, and it makes me cry even more.

I don't feel like I have to be strong—they're giving me the space to fall apart. And just like they promised, they're here for when I'm ready to put myself back together.

After a while, the car stops moving. I don't know if Mia took the long way home, or if these ten minutes just felt like hours, but we are parked outside Mia and Eddie's apartment complex.

I let go of Mia's hand and push myself up from Drew's lap, wiping my hands across my cheeks. My first instinct is to apologize, but they stop me before I can. "Don't," Drew and Mia say at the same time, and I see both their eyes glisten as I look back and forth between them.

"Don't you dare apologize for falling apart," Drew says.

"And I won't apologize for going back there and punching that bitch in the face," Mia says, turning around in the driver seat. "Seriously, Ann. I've never seen you like that."

"Me either," Drew adds.

I sigh. "I haven't felt like that. Not since moving here, meeting you guys."

"Do you want to talk about it?" Drew asks.

I feel myself nod, and now there's no going back.

"Wait," Mia says, before getting out of the driver's side and rounding the car. She opens the car door to the backseat that is vacant next to me and squeezes in until I'm squished between the two of them.

I can't help but laugh. "We can go inside. The boys are probably ruining dinner as we speak."

Drew waves a hand. "All they have to do is pull out the lasagna when the timer goes off. They can handle that."

I shake my head, but I feel my lips curl in a smile. Even with my cheeks still wet from my tears and my eyes swollen, smiling feels good, even if it's just for a second.

I take in a deep inhale, and I feel Drew grab my left hand and Mia grab my right as I exhale. "I was bullied in high school." Drew lets out a small gasp and Mia squeezes my hand. "I didn't realize it still affected me so much until tonight."

"Of course, it affects you," Drew says, her teacher side coming out. "There are so many studies that show bullying has a lasting effect into adulthood. That is nothing to be ashamed of."

I nod. "We were friends before that, Devin and me. We had other friends too, Penelope, Bea, Eliza, we were all close going into freshman year. Then something changed. I wanted to audition for the school's musical, and Devin and the other girls wanted to try out for cheerleading. I didn't think much of it at the time, and I thought we would still be friends who were just into different things.

"I got the lead in the musical my freshman year, and it

was a pretty big deal. Freshmen were usually in the ensemble, but I was able to land the main female role. I was so excited to tell them."

I remember running down the hallway and finding Luke, barely being able to get out the words. He hugged me and said he was proud of me, but I told him I had to go and find Devin. I couldn't wait to tell her—my best friend.

"When I told them—Devin and our other friends—they seemed happy for me. I didn't think anything was wrong until I came to school the next day and found out Devin and the girls didn't make the cheerleading team. I felt like a complete asshole for making the day before all about me, and I wanted to apologize. But I didn't have a chance because I heard the rumor about how I got the role."

Even though it was years ago, I still remember the shame and embarrassment I felt, and I wish I could go back and tell my younger stuff that it wasn't my fault I felt that way.

"Rumor?" Mia prompts, and I turn to her.

"They told everybody that I got the role because I offered a blowjob to the music director."

"Are you fucking serious?" Mia exclaims, her voice sounding much louder in the quiet car. "There's *so* much wrong with what you just said."

"Um, let's start with the fact that you thought you had to *apologize* for being excited about an achievement to your *friends*. Fuck that. Fuck them," Drew adds, her voice just as loud and just as pissed.

"And to start such a horrible and *harmful* rumor! Does she understand not only how wrong it is to say that but how damaging and dangerous it is?" Mia stresses, her hand closing so tightly around mine, but I don't think she notices.

"Do you think she's still at the store?" Drew asks, and I can't help but laugh at the sentiment, knowing my best friends would fight for me.

I shake my head before either can jump back in the front seat. "She's not worth it."

"Well, I'm sure it all didn't stop there," Drew says, alluding to the bullying. As a teacher, she knows all about the dangers and patterns of it. It usually doesn't just go away.

"Nope," I say, accentuating the "p", leaning my head back on the car seat. I let go of their hands holding mine. "The rumor circled and faded when something more interesting came along. The rumor would resurface every time I got a good part in the school's musicals or plays, but the damage was already done." While I was a target, I wasn't a good one. I didn't react the way they wanted me to, but little did they know I was just too scared to react. I didn't scream or cry or beg them to stop. I just took it. I took every shoulder check in the hallway, every trip over someone's foot, all the whispers when I walked by, all the times I walked into a room and everyone pretended I was invisible.

I wished I was.

Every day.

But being too scared to react just made them try harder.

So hard that teachers started to notice, but I wouldn't let them do anything. Too scared that it would just make it all worse.

I sigh. "I was terrified to go to school because I didn't know what to expect when I got there, but I was more terrified to stay home and explain to my parents what was happening."

"And let me guess, you didn't want to be a problem or a burden for your parents," Drew rhetorically asks, leaning her head back next to mine. A small, sad, knowing smile on her face.

"You might not believe this, but I was really good at not taking up space when I was a kid." I go for self-deprecating humor, but it doesn't warrant the reaction I thought it would.

"You deserve to take up space, Ann," Drew reassures, and I didn't realize how much I needed to hear it.

I don't like how I've felt about myself these last 24 hours, ever since Luke told me about running into Grant. I don't like thinking that the confidence I've grown is fake or forced because I'm not the girl who needs to play a different role to feel like I deserve to be here.

I'm done feeling that way.

"I like you better when you take up space hitting grown men's trucks with baseball bats," Mia adds, making us all smile.

"I just didn't need to be reminded that I was meant to be seen and not heard, or that they didn't even want me in the first place," I explain, resisting the urge to flinch at my own words. I'm so used to hearing them in my own head, but I didn't remember how harsh they were when said aloud.

"Their loss, because *we* want you," Mia replies, her head falling onto my shoulder as she leans back.

"Good, because you're stuck with me now," I joke, but I mean every word. I make a mental note to talk to both of them—after I walk them through this mess—about therapy and the process that comes with it. Both of them, their husbands too, are huge advocates for it after how much they found it helped them.

Tonight showed me that if I want to be done with these feelings, I have a lot of work to put in and a lot of shit to trudge up. Not only with the bullying and the stuff with Luke, but the shit with my parents too.

I don't want to let it affect me so much anymore, and it's way too heavy to keep carrying around.

Drew asks, "So, what does all of this have to do with you and Luke?"

The smile on my face quickly fades, but my walls are already down, might as well stomp all over them, so I couldn't build them back up even if I wanted to.

"There was a party the night before everyone left for college. I only went because Luke wanted to."

"So, to clarify, you and Luke did date?" Mia asks, and I realize I haven't explained the history Luke and I have.

"Long story short, we met in first grade, grew up together, became close friends, and started dating in high school. He asked to be my boyfriend one night when we snuck out to walk on the beach by the lake. He gave me a rose, and we had our first kiss, and blah, blah, blah. The rest is history."

"Aw, is that why you got the rose tattoo on your hip when we went out for Drew's birthday two years ago?" Mia's voice is high and hopeful.

"I don't know what you're talking about," I reply too quickly, which I am realizing I say a lot when I don't want to answer questions. "Anyway," I continue, "we went to this party and Devin and the other girls came up to Luke and me and said they wanted to talk. Something about wanting to spend time with me before we all left for school, so I told Luke I'd be back and went off with them."

"Why don't I like where this is going?" I hear Mia ask, but it's more to herself than anyone else.

I should've known better than to go with them, to believe they wanted to spend time with me. I was naive to think they wanted to apologize, and I know that now.

Maybe it's why I've been so stubborn, so embarrassed, to tell anyone about all of this. I spent four years being the target of these four girls—and they knew exactly how to hurt me because they were my friends first—yet going with them was like giving them permission to let them hurt me that night.

They were the ones who taught me that allowing yourself to get close to someone gives them all the power to hurt you.

"Once they got me away from Luke, Devin told me they wanted to show me something. Apparently, the night before, she and Penelope went to the house where all the hockey guys were. Penelope was dating the guy who was hosting, and, well, Luke was on the hockey team, and—" I pause because I've never had to put this next part into words outside my head before. "He hooked up with Devin. She showed me a video of her on his lap, and they were kissing."

Apparently, her and Grant had been on a break, and I wouldn't put it past Devin to think this was killing two birds with one stone—getting back at Grant and hurting me in the process.

I look directly in front of me, feeling both Mia and Drew freeze beside me.

"The video was only a minute long of them making out before cutting off as Devin stands up and holds her hand out to Luke, but she was all too eager to fill in the blanks for me."

"He cheated?" Mia questions, her voice now a whisper.

I nod my head.

"Does Luke know about the video? Or that you saw it?" Drew asks. "And are we sure we believe what she said?"

"No, and I don't know, but it was hard to believe anything else after watching the video of the two of them. I almost told Luke last night, but I got so mad at him when he said he didn't remember anything happening that night. I'm pissed we're in this situation at all. I mean, it's been seven years. I should be over it by now. And if it's all been some big lie, then you guys are going to be bailing me out of jail when I beat the shit out of her."

Drew shakes her head, trying to hide an inappropriate smile and my inappropriate response to dealing with conflict. "There might be more to the story."

"And you guys deserve your second chance. Annie, Luke is so in love with you, it hurts *me* that he can't have you," Mia adds.

I blow out a breath that comes out a little like a laugh but then turns into a groan. "I know, you're right. But seriously, seven years? Last night, Luke said the night was a blur because—"

I don't even finish the sentence

It's the first time I've ever told the story to anyone, actually said the words out loud.

It's also the first time I realize that Luke had been drinking the night before Grant's party.

I sit up straight and immediately feel like I have to get out of the car.

"What?" Mia and Drew speak at the same time.

"He could barely remember the night because he was *drinking*." I finally say, looking back and forth at both of them, and I can't believe I could ever be so stupid.

"Okay," Mia says slowly, "but what does—" her eyes widen, coming to the same conclusion as me.

"He said the night was a blur," Drew reiterates, and I feel like I'm going to throw up.

CHAPTER 24
ANNIE

I RUN to Mia and Eddie's apartment as fast as my feet will go, Mia and Drew right on my heels. The powdered sugar is long forgotten in Mia's car, along with everything aside from the realization that Luke was drunk the night Devin recorded him.

How could I be so stupid? Letting this go on for so long.

I'm going to kill her.

But first, I'm going to tell Luke that I love him, and that *I'm* going to be the one spending my whole life making it up to him.

When we finally get to the apartment, Mia quickly unlocks the door, only for us to be greeted by the boys. Luke and Emmett both have bags of to-go containers in their hands, Emmett also strapped with Lennon across his chest, and Luke has Rosie's leash in his hand as she sits beside him. Eddie is cleaning up the kitchen and dining table, and all six of us look at each other for ten solid seconds without saying anything.

Finally, Luke breaks the silence. "We're leaving." He grabs my arm, and the edge in his voice is the one he uses when he doesn't want me to argue.

"Wait," I manage to say before he can drag me out into the hallway. "We need to talk."

"We do," he says before adding, "and like I said, we're leaving."

"Go," Drew says as Mia pushes me closer to Luke.

I escape Luke's light hold on my forearm to wrap my arms around Drew and Mia, hoping that all the words of gratitude and love and thanks get across with how tightly I hold onto them.

"Go," Drew repeats as Emmett comes up behind her, kissing her on the top of her head, making her cheeks go bright red.

"We're here when you need us," Mia adds, leaning back on Eddie's chest as he wraps his arms around her.

I blow a kiss to a sleeping Lennon and give Emmett and Eddie both a quick nod before walking out of the apartment with Luke.

"She's had a lot of dealing with feelings tonight, Luke!" Mia shouts.

"And she has a big day tomorrow," Drew adds, reminding me that my rotations start tomorrow, so there's even more of a reason to get all this shit figured out *tonight*.

"Luke used a lot of brain power tonight!" Eddie yells.

"Go easy on each other!" They yell at us in unison, and I think I even hear Emmett's voice too, but I don't have time to laugh because I'm too busy following Luke down the hallway and through the front entrance of the complex.

He isn't slowing down, and he hasn't said a word since he said we're leaving, not even a goodbye.

His features are tightened, and there's an urgency to his step. He's walking with a purpose, and I don't even have time to be confused as to what happened with him and the guys in the 45 minutes we were gone.

"Luke, stop," I say, finding my voice with him again, and he does.

He turns to me in the middle of the parking lot, Rosie wagging her tail as she looks up at him and then at me.

"We need to talk," I repeat to him.

His features loosen, and he gives me a small smile, but it isn't his normal one. His normal smile is golden and shiny, full of happiness. This smile is sad, and it makes my heart hurt. "I know, honey. But, we're not doing it here," he answers. "Let's go home."

The car ride back to the apartment is loaded. There's tension in the air, and neither of us talk. It gives me a second to register everything I'm feeling, and these feelings aren't going to be going away anytime soon.

Not until Luke and I talk about what happened between him and Devin that night.

Not until I apologize with everything I am that I left without an explanation.

Not until I tell him that I love him and will do anything to make up for the last seven years of pushing him away.

Once we're inside, Luke empties the bag he had with to-go containers of salad and lasagna, a bag of bread, and my brownie containers.

"I never got to put the powdered sugar on these," I say, opening one of the containers to find only a few brownies left with powdered sugar already dusted on them.

"Mia and Eddie had powdered sugar," Luke answers before I can ask, walking over to the living room. "And we divided up all the food and dessert evenly," he says, answering the other question I didn't get a chance to ask.

I close the container and sit down next to him on the couch, not able to ignore the fact that we were just here, in this exact position, almost 24 hours ago, yet I feel like my whole world was flipped on its axis.

"Luke," I start, but he holds up a hand, cutting me off. I can't fight the furrow of my brow as I resist the urge to slap his hand away.

"I know you're not too keen on giving me what I want, but please, I need to say this."

My features relax, and I bring my knees to my chest as Luke runs a hand through his hair.

"That night, before Grant's party," he starts, and I almost resort to clapping a hand over my mouth to stop myself from talking. He looks bothered—no, haunted. Like whatever he's about to say isn't going to be easy. That's what keeps me quiet. "I told you last night that I don't remember much of it, but I was talking about it with Emmett and Eddie tonight—and you can be mad at me for talking to them about us later," he quickly adds that last part, before continuing, "I remembered something."

I nod, not trusting my voice at the moment, not when this conversation has been years in the making.

"I remember sitting down on a couch in Alek's basement and feeling hands rubbing up and down my chest. Then there's this weight on me, like someone sitting on my lap, straddling me almost." He shakes his head, and my fists clench at the torment in his voice, at how hard he's straining for memories of something that would be easier to not remember.

Something *I'm* making him remember.

"Luke, you don't have to," I start to say, but he stops me before I can say anything else.

"No, this is important. You deserve to know what I did."

The words put a literal hole in my chest, and my eyes start to water, but not for the reasons he thinks. He thinks he's explaining a night where he got drunk and cheated on me, but it is so much worse.

"I don't remember any girls being there that night. It was just the hockey guys. But the more I thought about it, the more Eddie and Emmett asked me questions to help me remember. I think someone tried to kiss me that night. I don't know who it was or what I did because then the memories are literally just black and all I remember is waking up on that same couch the next morning." His eyes find mine, and I watch a tear fall from one and then the other, and then my own tears follow. "I'm so sorry, Annie. I don't know why I would even do something so awful, and it's even worse that I can't remember."

"Luke, stop."

"Please, Annie. I'll do anything to make it up to you. Please," he begs, and I don't deserve it.

"Stop," I say again, a little harder this time, just so he'll listen. "You have nothing to be sorry for."

His face twists in confusion, and I reach out and grab his hand, bringing it into my lap. "Listen to me. The night of Grant's party, Devin and the other girls showed me a video of you and Devin." I used to think of that night and feel sadness completely wrack my body, weighing me down like an anchor being thrown in the sea.

Now, I see red and only red.

And it takes everything in me to keep my voice even as I continue, wishing I could wring Devin's neck right here instead. "She was in your lap, holding your face as she kissed you. I think that's what you're remembering."

"No. No. She wouldn't do that. She was your friend. I know you guys weren't getting along, but she wouldn't have stooped to *that* level. Plus, I would've stopped it." His voice trails off before he adds in a whisper, more to himself than to me, "If I had known, I would have stopped her."

Luke's head is shaking as he processes so many things at once. He doesn't know how bad things got with Devin and me, and how could he when I brushed off the rumors she started as childish and immature or told him it was the girls sneaking backstage to hide my costume was a harmless joke?

I never told him about why I would eat lunch in my English teacher's classroom or why I would avoid the hallways as long as possible to avoid getting tripped or shoulder-checked.

He didn't know Devin would stoop that low because I never told him she already had.

"Luke, sweetheart, this isn't about me right now. This is about you." I squeeze the hand I'm holding and reach out my other hand to cup his cheek, just like he does with me. "You couldn't have stopped it because she had the power. You didn't." I pause, taking a small inhale because it is taking everything in me to not walk out of this apartment and drag her here by the hair to show her the hurt she's caused. "What Devin did, you were drunk and couldn't consent."

He shakes his head, letting out a humorless laugh. "We were kids."

"We can't just brush over it."

"We're not brushing over it, and I understand the severity of it. I do," he grabs the hand I have on his cheek, turning it to leave a soft kiss on my palm, "but, I'm not letting us only focus on that when I wasn't the only one hurt. And that the night was only the start of it."

"What she did, it doesn't matter that you were kids. It was *assault*. And it's not okay."

"I know, it's not. But *I* will be okay."

I want to tell him to stop doing what he always does—trying to stay so positive, even at a time like this. There's nothing positive about this; there's no bright side or silver lining.

He doesn't let me tell him though because he adds, "I'm sorry it took so long for me to remember."

I shake my head. "Don't you dare apologize. You have nothing to be sorry for. I'm the one who is sorry. Until last night, I didn't know you were drunk in the video—drunk enough to not even remember the night."

"You're not the one who should be sorry." He reaches his

fingers to my cheek, carefully putting a piece of hair behind my ear.

"I assumed the worst and never gave you a chance to explain."

How can he be so *good*? Even at a time like this?

"Honey, you thought for *years* that I cheated on you. And that I was lying about it. That's why you've been pretending nothing ever happened between us. That's why you left."

I huff and drop my hand from his cheek. "Are you kidding me? I've been preparing myself for weeks to tell you all of that, and here you are just saying it for me."

"How many times do I have to tell you? I know you pretty damn well." He smiles at me, grabbing my hand and joining it with our others in my lap. "I know you, better than I know myself. And I know that you weren't keeping your walls up around me and everyone else for no reason. I knew something happened, and I knew no one, especially not me, was going to make you talk about it. So, I took what you would give me. I played the long game, and I figured in the meantime, I would try to make you fall in love with me again."

"You didn't have to do that."

"Of course I did. And I can be very persuasive."

"No, idiot. You didn't have to make me fall in love with you again because I never stopped loving you in the first place." My lips crash into his before I can think otherwise. My arms loop around his neck as his snake around my hips as he pulls me on top of him, my legs instinctively going to either side of him as he leans back on the couch. "I love you," I say against his lips, making his arms instantly tighten around me.

"I love you," he echoes, and the three words hold more meaning than the world's longest love confession.

There is still so much more to say, but I let our rushed touches and the swipes of our tongues be enough answers for now.

Luke pulls back, and I have to bite back the embarrassing

whimper I almost let out. "Does this mean I'm yours?" he asks, and the smile that makes my heart skip a beat is back and better than ever. His blue eyes are shining in the low light of the living room, the sun of the early summer evening peeking through the blinds.

I roll my eyes. "Are you asking me to be your girlfriend?" I tease, thinking the term sounds so trivial after everything we've been through.

"No, silly. I'm asking if *I* can be your boyfriend."

"I'd say yes, but I don't see a rose this time around." The memory of the first time he asked is now at the forefront of my mind for the second time tonight.

"It's funny you say that." He taps the tops of my thighs, helping me ease off him as he stands up, unzipping his jeans.

"What have I told you about keeping it in your pants?" I scoff, but I can't fight the smile as he tugs down his jeans, thinking he probably has roses on his boxers or something.

"You said you wanted a rose," he replies, and he turns to the side with rose-free black boxer briefs and his jeans at his knees, his thigh exposed but not uncovered. "How's this one?" he adds, but I can't look at his face. I'm too busy staring at the rose tattooed on his thigh, the one in black and gray ink, about the size of my palm, with thorned vines. It's similar to the style of Eddie's tattoos—what he told me is American Traditional—so the rose is bold and stark against Luke's skin.

"When the hell did you get that?" I can't help but exclaim; my feelings for what this rose is and what it stands for going straight to my chest. The placement and look of it going straight to my core.

Luke smirks, raising a brow. "You like it?"

"Tell me when you got it," I demand, crossing my arms and trying to look him in the eyes and not where I *want* to be looking at him right now.

"I got it for you."

"I said, 'when', not 'why', dummy."

"Same difference."

I give him a smirk of my own, standing up, ready to take back the upper hand. "Copycat."

Confusion dawns on his face before he's hit with a realization. I had an inkling he might have spotted my little secret the night he had me sprawled on his kitchen counter, but he never said anything.

"Show me," he commands.

My rose tattoo is on my hip, so I hook my thumb in my shorts and bring them down a few inches for him to see.

"Looks like it's official, huh?"

"What, that I'm yours?" I look down at my small stemmed rose, the fine line tattoo contrasting with Luke's, and the boldness of his and the softness of mine doesn't escape me. "This isn't some brand of ownership."

"Oh, mine is. I'm yours, Annie girl. You own me—every part of me. Always have, always will."

CHAPTER 25
LUKE

ANNIE LEFT before I woke up this morning for her very first day of her vet school rotations. She has a few weeks at her school's teaching hospital and then a few weeks at the zoo to start off her long year of rotating between different places to work under all kinds of veterinarians.

I made sure her stuff for her matcha was out and ready for her before I went to sleep last night, along with her lunch packed and a note wishing her luck.

The events of last night are still a fresh wound on my skin, and I can't stop thinking of everything that was thrown out in the open after so many years.

There's a stinging pain at the thought of how one night had such an impact on Annie and me, but that pain reminds me that it's not all in the past.

Something I have only been able to imagine, but it is finally a reality: Annie said she never stopped loving me.

She loves me.

I get to be hers.

And I'm not letting anything get between us this time around.

After the surprise of not only my rose tattoo but *her* rose tattoo, we spent the night on the couch with the Sunday Dinner leftovers and talked about anything and everything.

It was the first time since we were teenagers that we just let the conversation ebb and flow however it felt right, talking about anything and everything—the conversation moving through our past, our present, even our future—almost like we were making up for lost time. And because it's us, we still bickered and argued, flirted and teased, but it would've felt wrong without it.

Annie and I have been able to see what the other has been up to over the years, sharing celebrations, holidays, birthdays, and achievements with the Lenny's crew, but it has always been from afar.

Last night, she didn't feel so far away anymore.

We talked until the sun set; Annie couldn't keep her eyes open, tired from the emotional weekend and in need of rest for her first day. Her head was on my lap as I told her that I was going to call my dad and tell him my decision to not take the position at his firm.

Her eyes looked heavy as she listened, reaching for my hand that was idly drawing circles on her arm, and she told me she was proud of me.

I could've talked to her all night, but it was the eve of a very big day for her. I walked her to the guest room, hoping she would let me follow her in. She didn't, but she kissed me goodnight, and that was enough for me.

For now.

It felt like the beginning of something new and exciting, and I have to keep reminding myself that we can't just pick up where we left off, no matter how much I want to. We finally have our second chance—something I never thought we'd get—and we need to do things right this time.

We were kids the first time around, latching on to each other as we grew up because it felt safe in the midst of the madness unfolding around us. Falling in love with Annie was as natural and seamless as breathing while losing her felt like the ground was crumbling from beneath me.

I lean back in Emmett's desk chair, my mind not where it needs to be to finalize this schedule. I've been staring at my laptop screen all morning, my mind going back and forth between wishing I could go back and change what happened in the past to being somewhat thankful for it.

I've never been someone to waste time being angry about something out of my control. I try to stay positive, see the bright side of things, or find the silver linings—I always have. Even through all the shit with my parents and the time I spent chasing a goal that was never mine to begin with. I like to think that the choices I made brought me to where I am supposed to be.

Without my mom's affair and my dad taking me away from my biological father, I wouldn't have been able to grow up with Bennett and Caleb.

Without the time I spent in college and law school, I never would have ended up at Lenny's or found Emmett, Drew, Eddie, and Mia.

I know I would've found Annie. I'll find her in each and every lifetime.

There's a silver lining in all of it.

And yet, I can't help but feel this intense anger thinking about that night at Grant's. I was taken advantage of that night by a girl who had the sole purpose of hurting the person who mattered most to me.

I don't like to hold grudges, but being used as a pawn in Devin's sick game isn't something I can easily get over, especially since it cost me so much for so long.

It would be easy to blame Annie for not telling me sooner. She could have come to me that night, or even the next morning—hell, she could've told me when I asked her at Lenny's months later—but I can't.

I can't blame her for protecting herself.

I can't blame her for doing what she thought was best.

Especially not when I didn't give her a choice on whether or not she could keep me out of her life.

Knowing Annie, how strong she is, how much she's overcome, how many odds were working against her, I can't imagine the pain she must have felt that night when she thought I cheated on her.

It's easy to think that cheating happens, that people get over it. But it wasn't just that, not for Annie. I was the only person she let herself believe wasn't going to bail when things got hard. She let me see her, every part of her, in ways that no one else had. We grew up together, supported each other, fell in love with one another, and she thought I was throwing that all away.

How could I fault her for protecting herself? For doing what she had to. For *finally* putting her and her feelings first, above anything and everyone else.

I don't blame her for these past seven years, for the years we could have spent together, because I got to fall more in love with the person she became, the person she grew into—the bold, strong, confident woman who speaks her mind and takes what she deserves.

Devin, on the other hand, is easy to blame.

Not only for what she did to me, as hurtful and problematic as it was, but for what she did to Annie. For hurting her out of spite and selfishness, and for not caring about the lasting effects her actions would have.

I exhale, feeling like Annie and I deserve to rid ourselves from this night that has haunted us for all these years; that starts with confronting Devin and getting this weight off our shoulders.

My phone buzzes on the desk next to my laptop, bringing me back to the moment.

I glance at the screen, seeing a text from Caleb and a text from Bennett. Caleb's text being a reminder that I promised to talk to my father today about my decision. Bennett's text wishing me luck about the former.

I pick up my phone, ready to get this conversation over it, when my phone rings.

"Hey, Ben, I just saw your text, and no I haven't talked to him yet."

"Figured maybe you could use a pep talk before you dialed up our dear old dad," he jokes, and it genuinely makes me laugh. I like to think that I got my positivity and laid-back demeanor from Bennett, Caleb being the more responsible and on-top-of-things as the oldest brother. "Caleb said you still haven't called him."

"It's barely nine in the morning, my day started an hour ago."

"You know Caleb, always the go-getter. Plus, I wouldn't blame you for putting it off. Speaking from experience, it's not an easy conversation to have."

When Bennett told my dad that he was quitting law school, I was still in high school, and I remember thinking a gun went off for how loud my dad's voice boomed at my brother. It was an all-out screaming match for hours, both going taking turns throwing insults until Caleb got the two of them to calm down.

I haven't seen Bennett and my father in the same room together since that night, and I doubt that will be changing anytime soon.

I'm not worried, though. I'm not Daniel Owen's biological son like Bennett and like Caleb. They were the ones who were bound to follow his footsteps, not me. I'm prepared for an uncomfortable conversation that further proves I'm a disappointment in the eyes of my father, but it's nothing I'm not used to.

I've made my peace with it. I have the family that matters to me, and what Daniel Owens thinks of me is no longer a concern of mine—which is exactly why I need to stop putting off this call.

"I'm not worried," I reply, "I have much more important things to deal with than how dad will take the news."

"Is one of these important things making progress with figuring out what happened with Annie?" Bennett asks, and I don't miss the slight teasing in his voice.

Since I met him and Jack for breakfast about a month ago, I've kept Bennett updated on my courtship of Annie. The last update I gave him was from Friday when she beat the shit out of Ava's boyfriend's truck, and I swear Bennett laughed for a whole five minutes. Partly at the situation but also at how much of a lovesick puppy I sounded like when I told him how she did it because the prick pushed me.

What happened after we went home that night, I kept to myself.

"About that," I start, aimlessly spinning a pen I found on Emmett's desk around my fingers. "I think I finally did it."

"You got her back?" Bennett asks with a hopeful tone in his voice as if this affects him as much as it does me.

"I got her back, man," I answer, a huge smile on my face. "Everything about the night she left and why she did was thrown out into the open. She apologized, even though she really didn't have to, and I told her I was hers if she was willing to have me."

"Congrats, little brother. I'm happy for you."

"Thanks, Ben. We still have shit to work through considering so much has changed since the last time we were together, but I have a good feeling."

"Me too. I'm glad to see you taking charge of your life, with Annie and this stuff with Dad. You got your whole life ahead of you, and I'm glad to see you living life for *you*."

"It feels good. And it'll feel better once this stuff with Dad is off my shoulders, which I should really get to."

"Right, don't let me keep you. Just wanted to check-in. Seriously, Luke, I'm proud of you."

My throat feels tight at the words I don't hear often. Words I heard from Annie last night, words I'm hearing now from my brother, words I went my whole life *wishing* to hear.

I clear my throat. "Thanks, I appreciate you saying that," I say, hoping Bennett hears the sincerity in my words. "I'll let you know how it goes with Dad," I add before we say our goodbyes, and I hang up.

Before I lose the nerve, knowing that I won't feel like this after hanging up on the upcoming phone call, I dial my dad at his office, figuring I'll have a better chance of reaching him if I call him at work than on his cell.

"Owens & Son's. This is Maria speaking. How may I help you?" I tell my dad's assistant who's calling, and she puts me on hold before transferring me to him. I inhale while I wait, mentally preparing myself for the disappointment I'm about to face.

The phone call clicks off hold. "Luke?" I hear my dad's assistant say.

"Still here," I answer.

"Your dad asked what this call was referring to?" she asks, and my grip on my phone tightens.

He can't even take my goddamn phone call?

I pinch the bridge of my nose, leaning back in Emmett's desk chair. "It's about my position at the firm," I say, trying to keep my voice polite and even.

"He assumed so," Maria replies. "He asked me to confirm whether you will be accepting the position or not."

My annoyance gets the best of me. "Can he not ask me this himself?"

"Your dad is very busy. If you'd like, I can take a message and he can call you back when he has a chance."

I stand up from where I'm sitting, my feet pacing back and forth across Emmett's office. The annoyance I feel prickling all over my skin begins to burn, frustration making it hard to see straight.

I was stupid and naive enough to think I was *at least* worth more to him than *this*—that I deserved the decency of something as simple as a conversation.

My feet pause, stopping me from pacing a hole in the floor, and I shake my head, knowing that I really should be diagnosed clinically insane, because why did I think that doing this—expecting my father to see me as more than a bother, a problem, a *burden*—over and over again would lead me to different results.

"No," I say into the phone, wishing things could be different but knowing they never will be. "I will not be taking the position at the firm."

I hang up the phone before I can even hear if Maria says anything, and I close my eyes, taking a deep breath. It's such an ugly feeling, holding onto hope that you mean something to someone you care—*cared*—about.

At least there's a silver lining in all of this.

Today marks the last time I will ever have to deal with Daniel Owens.

CHAPTER 26
LUKE

ANNIE SHOULD BE HOME from her first day any minute now.

I didn't let the conversation with my dad—or lack thereof—affect the rest of my day, and I had to finish the schedule before my midday shift started.

I purposely gave myself a shift that let me be home in time to see Annie when she got home from her first day of rotations, her days being the equivalent of a work day, along with work she has to bring home and do before repeating it all the next day.

She warned me about how busy she'll be because this year involves long hours of hands-on clinical training across all the different specialties. She has to manage cases while also adapting to different teams before rotating to a new placement and doing it all over again. I hope that I can make things less stressful for her—I plan on doing so whether she wants me to or not.

I hear her keys outside the door, Rosie hopping off the couch to meet Annie, just as I press a big, white bow to the top of the stand mixer I got her yesterday.

Maybe now that she's my girlfriend, she'll be okay with me buying her presents.

My Annie girl deserves the very best.

"Happy First Day!" I shout as she walks through the front door. Her brown waves are twisted back in a clip, pieces falling out to frame her face.

She's dressed in black scrubs and her white tennis shoes, a white lab coat and her stethoscope hung over one arm, her backpack hung over the other.

She smiles when she sees me with my arms out as I stand in the kitchen, intentionally blocking my gift for her, but also wide open in case she needs to fall into them.

Her lips curve into a smile, and she looks like she wants to roll her eyes at my antics, but I can see her ears pinken as her smile grows and she walks towards me.

She drops everything she's holding on to the floor and wraps her arms around my waist. My arms immediately pull her in close and lean down to press a kiss to the top of her head that's resting against my chest. She smells of her usual scent of jasmine and roses, and a hint of antiseptic hits my nose.

"Did you have a good day?" I ask into her hair, and I feel her nod against my chest.

"I'm tired," she mumbles against my chest, making me chuckle. She lifts her head to look at me. "What?"

"I like tired Annie—she's cuddly."

Her eyes narrow, but she doesn't let go of me. "You're lucky you're cute. And that I'm too tired to think of anything brattier."

"Lucky for *you*, I'm going to ignore that—except for the part where you called me cute—and still give you your surprise."

She bites her bottom lip to hold back her smile. "Surprise?" she asks, taking a step back from me and instantly seeming more awake than she was ten seconds ago.

"To clarify, I got this for you *before* we got back together, so just imagine how much I'll spoil you *now*."

She puts her hands on her hips. "Just because you're my boyfriend doesn't mean you can spoil me."

Boyfriend.

She called me her boyfriend.

The word makes me feel all warm and fuzzy inside, even though the term doesn't feel like enough. Not after everything we've been through.

I clear my throat, trying to hide the emotion clogging it. "We can save that conversation for another time because . . . Surprise!" I move out of the way and her eyes widen as her hands go to her mouth. The red stand mixer is bright against the dark countertops, and it fits just right in the space under the cabinets. "Now, you can do all the stress-baking you want."

"Luke, this is—" she pauses, walking over to the counter, "this is too much."

"You deserve it, Annie girl. Plus, don't forget all the desserts you promised me."

This makes her laugh. "How could I? Only cookies and cupcakes between now and October 15th, remember?" Her smile is wide, exactly how it should be, and it makes her brown eyes sparkle.

It doesn't take much to make me happy, but seeing Annie smile reminds me that she isn't as outward with her own happiness. Seeing Annie smile makes me feel like I've won a prize, like my hard work paid off, like I'm deserving of something special that she doesn't just give out to anyone.

And I finally got her back.

Fuck starting slow or not picking up where we left off.

We have so much lost time to make up for.

"Or forever." The words slip out of my mouth before I can stop them, but I would've said them even if I took the time to think about them. "Move in with me." I don't even have to hear her answer to know that I will be letting the complex know first thing tomorrow that I no longer need the hold on the unit down the hall.

"I already live here, dummy."

"Don't act like you don't know what I'm asking."

She turns from the stand mixer to me, leaning against the counter. I can read what she's feeling on her face, even as she tries to will any emotion away.

She's surprised, so she'll pretend she wasn't.

She's scared, so she'll fight me.

She's hopeful, so she'll tell herself this is too good to be true.

"I'm going to shower," she says before walking as fast as she can to the bathroom, always doing the exact opposite of what I want or expect her to do.

I can't help but smile at the way she rushes out the words, trying to hide all those feelings to no avail. I resist the urge to tease her about it and instead pick up all her stuff she dropped on the floor a few minutes ago and just walked past. "And I'll heat up the rest of the leftovers from last night for dinner." I set her backpack down at the chair on the other side of the kitchen counter and lay her lab coat and stethoscope on top.

I don't even care if I spend the rest of my life cleaning up after her. As long as it's in *our* apartment, *our* house, *our* home.

I hear the shower start running through the cracked bathroom door as I pull out the to-go containers from last night and heat us up the leftover lasagna.

I know this will be the first of late dinners over the next twelve months of Annie's rotations, but I want to be at her side every step of the way—supporting her, praising her, cheering her on.

After warming up the food and cleaning up the kitchen a little, I hear the shower turn off. A few minutes later, Annie comes out wearing her stupid little cherry pajama set that I haven't seen since she wore it to the hospital the night Lennon was born.

"Don't you think that's moving a little fast?" she asks, warily. "We just got back together." Her voice is a notch quieter and more serious than it was before she showered, but she didn't say, 'No, Luke. I'm not moving in with you'.

I round the kitchen counter with our dinner and sit down. "All the more reason to go full steam ahead." I pat the seat to my left for her to join me.

"Luke, I don't know. We still have a lot to figure out."

"So, we'll figure it out together," I answer. "Come sit down. You need to eat."

I can see the conflict in her eyes. She doesn't want to accept that she doesn't have to do it all on her own anymore. I'm here for her to ask for help, and I'm going to help her even when she doesn't ask.

We eat in a comfortable silence; the only noise is the TV playing in the background from when I was watching before Annie got home.

I keep an eye on her as we eat, and she looks like she's miles away. I can almost see the wheels turning in her head, so I don't even bother saying anything.

Still, she doesn't say anything as I grab her empty plate, rinsing both our plates and silverware in the sink before putting everything into the dishwasher.

I grab each of us a brownie, one with chocolate frosting for her and one with powdered sugar for me. Putting each of them on a paper towel, I push hers towards her, knowing she'll want to get to bed soon but always needing a sweet treat after a meal.

There's a soft smile on her face when the brownie is in front of her, her features not as tight and drawn as they were before. Whatever spiral she was in before is starting to unwind in her mind, and I hope she talks about it instead of rushing off to bed like she did with the shower.

She breaks a piece off and pops it into her mouth and chews slowly, her eyes on the counter in front of her.

We're both finishing our last bites when she finally says, "A lot has happened in the last few days, we're not the same people we were when we did this the first time." She looks down at our hands in her lap before looking back up at me.

"Trust me, I know that better than anyone. I knew from the moment I found you at Lenny's all those years ago that you were not the same girl I knew four months before."

I've never told Annie how I watched her for longer than I'd like to admit before she saw me that day. She doesn't know how surprised I was to see her or how I felt frozen in place when I heard her tell that old guy at the bar to fuck off. She has no idea that I recognized her from the outside but felt like she was a stranger on the inside—one that I wanted so badly to get to know.

"And I knew I was going to fall more in love with you the more I got to know this new version."

"I treated you like shit for *years*, Luke." Her voice is raw with emotion, it's laced with anger as she raises her voice.

She balls up the paper towel her brownie was on and throws it onto the table, bringing her knees into her chest, her eyes on the counter in front of her.

"I pretended that everything that happened between us meant *nothing* to me. I threw it all away without going to you first. *You.* The person who I trusted more than anyone. I just ran away from it all, only to waste all this time over something that wasn't even your fault."

I lean forward on the counter, reaching to tuck a piece of damp hair behind her ear. My fingers trail down her neck, around her jaw, until my fingers find her chin, and lift her face so I can make sure she looks at me when I say, "You and I both know that you did what you did to protect yourself. I will never blame you for that." I press a kiss to her forehead. "You are so strong, Annie girl. You built walls around that heart and pretended like it didn't exist, and I will never fault you for that."

She shakes her head, and I drop my hand. I need her to look in my eyes when I tell her all of this. I round the counter and sit back down in the chair next to her, pulling her hand into my lap. "Look at me, honey. I want you to seriously listen to what I'm about to tell you."

I can tell she wants to scoff at me, but she doesn't. Instead, she looks up and finds my eyes. "You did not waste any time. Things happen the way they do for a reason, and now we have our second chance. A second chance that I have no intention of wasting." I squeeze her hands in mine, giving her a soft smile. I watch as her lips curve upwards, and she squeezes back. "So, I'm going to say this one more time—move in with me."

Her smile fades, but she doesn't let go of my hands. I take that as a good sign. "I want to say yes, but—"

"But what? There's no buts. Say yes."

"What about rotations? How are we going to make it work? I'm barely home, working over 40 hours a week, plus research and reports, and all my additional requirements for evalu—"

"We'll figure it out."

"What about what you're going to do? You have your own life and your own decisions to make with what to do with—"

"Annie." I stop her because she'll keep going until she tires herself out, trying to think of all the reasons this won't work, even though I know that it will. "Say it with me, 'we'll figure it out.'"

"No, because you're just saying that we'll figure it out so I move in with you."

"So, it's a yes? You're moving in with me?"

"No, I did not say that."

"But you want to."

"I'm still not opposed to burying you in the backyard."

That catches me off guard, causing a laugh to escape my throat. "I'll help you dig the grave. Just say yes," I plead, seconds away from getting down on my knees.

"Yes to you helping me dig *your* grave?" And, by the way she's trying to hide the smile on her face, I know she already agreed to moving in with me. Now, she's just giving me a hard time.

I huff out a breath because that threat doesn't go away just because she's my girlfriend, and I think she really is going to kill me. "Do you actively try to be a brat, or does it come naturally?"

She rolls her eyes as her lips curve into a smirk. "It's as natural as breathing, bartender." She stands, and I know she's about to head to the guest room. Little does she know, I have no intention of letting her sleep anywhere but in bed—with me—ever again.

I stand from my chair, blocking her way. "So, it's a yes?"

"Are you done with that?" She takes a little step closer to me, tilting her head a few inches to keep her eyes on mine. She crosses her arms, sitting into her hip.

"Still haven't heard the word." I look down at her.

We stay in our stand-off, waiting to see who will be the first one to back down. We both know that her answer is yes, and we both know she won't give me the satisfaction of just saying the damn word.

We also both know that I will be the one to back down.

"Come here," I say, swallowing her gasp when my lips press against hers.

I grab her by the hips, picking her up, and her legs immediately wrap around my waist. The material of her pajama shorts is soft and thin against my palms as I hold her against me.

Annie's arms wrap around my neck, pulling me in. Her lips taste like chocolate and cherries, and I've never tasted anything more perfect.

I don't break the kiss as I walk us to my bedroom—*our* bedroom.

CHAPTER 27

ANNIE

I CAN FEEL the heat and passion in Luke's kiss as his lips reacquaint themselves with mine. I went seven years without kissing Luke, and I survived. Now, I can barely go an hour without thinking of how his bottom lip feels between my teeth, how his tongue dancing with mine sends me into oblivion, how our lips fit so perfectly together.

He walks me from the kitchen to his bedroom, and it's the first time I've been in here since I moved in—actually, it's the first time *ever*—and I'm too overwhelmed, in the best way, with all of these emotions flooding through me. Luke kicks the bedroom door closed with his foot, before walking over to his bed, and laying me down.

When he breaks our kiss, my eyes slowly open as I adjust to the darkness of the room. His blonde hair frames his blue eyes as he stands above me.

He reaches for me, his hands trailing up the tops of my legs, up my stomach, and to my chest, finding the straps of my pajama top.

His eyes meet mine, silently asking for permission, and I resist the urge to roll my eyes and take the tank top off myself.

Instead, I reach for the thin strap over my shoulder, bringing it down slowly before doing the same to the other, and I feel his patience being tested as his fingers come to the bottom to help me pull it off over my head.

There's something about Luke's movements, the look in his eyes, the tension in the air, that makes me feel like we have all the time in the world. It's easy to want to rush into this, to lose ourselves in each other and not think of what comes before or after.

But I want to savor every moment and feel every feeling I convinced myself I didn't have.

I want to make up for lost time.

Not just because this is Luke, the boy I lost my virginity to. He's the one who I've loved my entire life, the one who makes me feel more seen than anyone else in the world.

Not to mention the man who demanded I show him how I use my vibrator right in front of him.

But because he's been patient with me for years; he knows me better than I know myself; he reminds me that everything's going to be okay, as long as we're together.

We'll figure it out.

Together.

A low groan escapes Luke's throat, and that's when I realize I said the words out loud. His hands slowly glide up my waist, his body leaning down over me, so he can press feather-light kisses to my skin. "Together," he repeats, his breath tickling my skin.

His lips are warm against my chest, igniting a fire in my belly. Pressure builds between my thighs as he swipes his tongue against the top of my breast where he left a mark the last time—one that I watched fade over the days.

As if reading my thoughts, he grazes his teeth against my skin, biting hard before tending to the pain with his tongue, making me moan at the slight pain mixed with pleasure.

"Mine," he whispers against my skin, his palms finding

my breasts, massaging one with each hand before taking my nipples between his fingers.

My hands find the back of his head, threading through his hair as his lips move across my chest, kissing, nipping, sucking, biting, anything to taste me. "Mine," I echo, the word falling so seamlessly from my lips.

Luke takes one of my breasts in his mouth while massaging the other, and I close my eyes as the pressure builds, my back arching more into his mouth as I pull at his hair, and he groans in response. He moves his mouth to my other breast, swirling his tongue around my nipple, grazing his teeth against the sensitive skin.

Every drag of his tongue, every touch from his fingers, every noise he makes goes directly to my core, and he doesn't stop until I'm a complete and utter mess beneath him.

He kisses back up to my lips, and I feel his hands trail to my pajama bottoms, his fingers hooking under the elastic.

"Trying to get me out of my pants, bartender?" I tease, feeling his lips curve into a smile.

"Always," he retorts, sliding my shorts down and off my legs, leaving me in just my underwear.

He pushes himself up from where he's leaning over me, standing to his full height before pulling at the collar of his shirt until it's off and on the floor with my shorts.

I don't even hide how my eyes take him in as I lay on the bed in front of him—from his corded forearms, to his toned shoulders, to his defined pecs. I follow every hard line of his chest, until I see his hands undoing the button of his jeans, but not taking them off.

I push myself up until I'm on my knees in front of him, my head coming to right below his chin even when I'm on the bed. "Come here," I purr, reaching out to grab him by his unbuttoned jeans, pulling him closer until our lips meet again.

His hands find the side of my face as I slide his jeans

down, reaching into his boxer briefs and stroking against his hard length, eliciting a groan from him that I swallow up.

I slowly guide my hand up and down, Luke kissing me deeper with every stroke.

"Honey, if you keep doing that," he whispers against my lips, "I'm going to embarrass myself."

"No need to be ashamed. I know how long you've waited for this." My voice is much breathier than I'd like to admit, my teasing coming out more as suggestive than I had planned.

Luke grabs my wrist with one hand, pulling it from his boxers and holding it between us. "Don't be a brat," he says through gritted teeth, but the flare in his eyes tells me to do the opposite.

"Don't be a tease," I echo, and his other hand finds the hem of my underwear, just below my stomach, and I suck in an inhale, dripping with anticipation.

"Tell me, Annie girl, if I ripped these off of you," he tugs on the elastic band, letting it snap back against my skin, "and stick my fingers in that tight pussy of yours, how wet would you be for me?"

My lips are parted, my eyes half-shut, and my brain can't even form words to say, too drunk with lust and his low voice to even be embarrassed by it. This is that edge I know Luke keeps below the surface of his otherwise composed, carefree demeanor. I've seen it when he made me move in here, when he told me to use my toy, and I think my new favorite pastime will be seeing how far I can push him until he shows this side of him.

With one hand still holding my wrist, the other slowly plays with the hem of my underwear, the smirk on Luke's face telling me he knows exactly what he's doing to me.

But who am I to give him what he wants?

I pull my hand from his grip before standing up from the

bed, so I'm right in front of him. I watch him as he watches me, and I know he's waiting for me to challenge him. The same way I'll be waiting for him to call my bluff.

I hook my fingers into the hem of my underwear, pulling them down until they fall to the ground. "Why don't you find out?"

And just as I hoped, I watch his eyes darken, his lips crashing into mine until the back of my knees hit the back of the bed, and I have no choice but to lay back down.

Luke kisses me until I'm on my back, his body lying next to mine as he leans down to kiss me, his hands trailing all over my body until they descend down my stomach and between my legs.

I moan with anticipation, needing the pressure building to subside, and Luke knows it. He kisses me deep as he pushes a finger into my pussy, swallowing the noises I make as he fills me. "So wet for me," he says against my skin as he slowly pumps his finger into me before adding a second, his thumb finding my clit with such ease, like my body was made for him.

"Could be wetter," I breathe, grabbing onto his wrist and bringing his hand to my lips. I take his fingers in my mouth, circling them with my tongue, tasting my own arousal. Luke watches my every move, eyes following as I move his hand back down my body, and push his fingers back into my pussy, basking in the feeling of him inside me and the heat of his gaze.

"Right as always, sweet girl," he praises as his fingers move inside me. His thumb circles my clit with each thrust of his hand, his lips moving against mine, and it's all too much. I feel the pressure building inside of me, and my skin feels as hot as the sun. I let myself feel all the sensations, letting go of every ounce of control and giving it all to Luke, and I fall apart.

Luke works me through my orgasm, whispering more words of praise against my skin, bringing me back down from wherever I was just thrown into. I blink my eyes open, and Luke's eyes are on me, a look of triumph on his face.

It's cute that he thinks he's the one in charge.

CHAPTER 28
LUKE

I MUST HAVE DIED and gone to heaven because having Annie naked and flushed in my bed is like nothing I've ever experienced. I bring my fingers to my lips, finally being able to taste Annie like I want to and now knowing I'll never have enough. I didn't get even close to enough of her that one night in the kitchen, and I plan on getting my fill tonight.

She turns to look at me, my body pressed up against her side while she's on her back, and her eyes are heavy-lidded. She gives me a smirk, matching the one on my face. "You going to clean up the mess you made, bartender?"

And I didn't think I could get any harder than when I watched her taste herself on my fingers before sinking them back into her pussy.

"You're going to be the death of me." But we both know full well that I would die a happy man if it's by her hands.

"That's what I've been telling you for years. You just never listen," she says, as I work my way down her body.

I whisper against her sensitive skin, "Just can't get enough of me." Her hips roll, trying to get me where she needs me.

"I can just grab my toy if you're going to keep talking," she taunts, pushing herself up onto her elbows.

"You think your little toy can do a better job than me?" My lips press kisses to her inner thighs, getting her all worked up all over again.

"Since you want to sit and talk, I don't think I'll ever find out," she answers, but the last word comes out as a moan because my lips are on her pussy before she can finish the sentence.

I like Annie's fight, her fire, her sass, but I think I might like her more when she's writhing underneath me, unable to form a single thought. She arches into my mouth as I grip the inside of her thighs tight enough to leave bruises, and I'm seconds away from blowing my load with every little noise she makes.

I circle her clit with my tongue, needing her to come on my face just like she did on my fingers before she comes all over my cock.

"Fuck," she breathes, and I love feeling her eyes on me. I bask in her attention, making her take everything I have to give her. Licking, sucking, nipping at the sensitive flesh, and watching how she reacts to it.

I pride myself on how well I know Annie, but I haven't been able to get to know her like this—and that changes tonight.

I push two fingers inside of her and her lips rock with every thrust. I feel her getting close, tightening around my fingers, so I don't stop until she's coming apart all over again with my name on her lips.

Her brown waves cascade against my light blue comforter, her soft skin littered with my marks, and I might have to chain her to this bed after tonight.

As I kick off my jeans, I kiss my way up her body until I find her lips, letting her taste herself on me as I move my mouth against hers.

"I could watch you come all night, Annie girl," I tell her, feeling her fingernails drag softly on my back, looking into her big brown eyes, "but if I don't get inside you in the next ten seconds, I'm not going to make it." I grab her by the hips, flipping us, so she's on top, my boxer briefs being the only thing between us. "There's condoms in the nightstand. Whatever you want, consider it done. Please, just fuck me," I plead, and I'm not even embarrassed about it. This girl has complete control over me, and I wouldn't have it any other way.

"So pretty when you beg," she coos. "I'm cleared and on the pill," she says, reaching between us to help me out of my boxer briefs, my cock finally out and begging for attention.

"I'm cleared too, tested at the beginning of the summer." Her hands are wrapped around my cock, lightly stroking up and down, so the words come out as a cry for mercy.

"Well, you have been very patient tonight," she purrs, and she looks so much better with me underneath her.

"Please. I'll be so good for you."

She pushes up on her knees, angling my cock just below her pussy. All it would take is for me to use my grip on her hip to slam her down, but I don't.

I wait for her.

"Promise?" she asks, a smirk on her swollen, cherry lips.

"Promise," I grit through my teeth, both of us knowing full well that anything she wants from me is already hers, no need for promises.

Her teeth sink into her bottom lip as she bottoms out on my cock, and I now know for a fact that I've died and gone to heaven. I groan at the sensation of being inside her, and it takes everything in me not to pound up into her.

"Ride me like you own me, sweet girl. God knows you do."

And she does.

She moves her hips against me, taking everything she needs from me while giving me more than I could ever ask for. She rests her hands on my chest, her fingernails leaving marks on my skin that I hope turn to scars.

I help her ease herself up and down, letting her control the speed as I lose myself in her.

With how sensitive she must be by now, it doesn't take long for her to get close, her pace picking up, losing her rhythm. I take control, moving her against me, pushing up into her, hitting just where she needs to come undone with me right behind her, and I don't know if I'll ever recover.

It takes a moment for me to come back to earth, feeling Annie fall on top of my chest, her hair tickling my skin. I roll us onto our sides, gently pulling out of her and pressing a kiss to her forehead before running to the bathroom and coming back with a warm cloth.

I ease her onto her back, her eyes heavy and body relaxed, and she watches as I gently wipe her sensitive skin and her inner thighs before throwing the cloth towards our pile of clothes to deal with later.

I pull her into me, her legs intertwining with mine, her head resting on my arm as I hold her close to my chest.

A few moments pass, and I wouldn't be surprised if she fell asleep.

"You're telling me I missed seven years of *that*." Her voice comes out muffled with her lips against my chest, and we both burst into laughter.

I lean back to look down at her, my cheeks hurting from how hard I'm smiling. "I'd say it was well-worth the wait."

CHAPTER 29
ANNIE

SAYING that the rest of the night, the week, the month, was a dream would be an understatement, and—for once—I am okay with eating my words.

Luke was right.

We will figure it out, and we'll do it together.

The whole month of September flies by for more reasons than one.

Rotations are kicking my ass. Having a full-time job without the monetary benefits, in addition to hours of work to bring home with me, all to do it all again the next day, but I finally feel like I am using what I've learned the past three years.

I'm in my first week of my second rotation, this time at the Milwaukee Zoo, working at the zoological teaching hospital. I know it's early to be deciding what I might want my main focus to be when I'm finally done with my rotation year, but I knew I would like working with the staff at the Animal Health Center.

This rotation is the one I talked to my advisor about over the summer, and I'm really interested in the AHC program they offer for fourth-year veterinary students.

With the stress of rotations, I thought a new relationship, especially one with someone as clingy—in a good way—as Luke was going to be just one more thing to worry about.

Turns out, having a boyfriend who makes it his goal to help you relax and rest the second you walk through the door was the perfect remedy for maintaining stress-levels.

Luke has spent the past month making sure Lenny's is running smoothly since Emmett isn't ready to come back just yet, but he still finds ways to help me manage everything—rotations, meals, getting enough sleep—all while making me feel like I'm being taken care of.

A feeling I'm not used to.

It took a week or two to actually let him help, even with things I don't ask for, but his reassurance that he's doing it for me because he wants to, not because he feels like he has to, has been healing in ways I didn't know I needed.

It's the last weekend in September, and the Lenny's crew is together to plan our annual Halloween Party that brings all of us together plus the other people in our lives.

Luke always invites his brothers; Drew invites her brother, his wife, and her childhood friend, Lacey, and her husband; Eddie and Mia invite the Cross My Heart guys and Eddie's three sisters, and we all dress in costumes that go with whatever theme we come up with.

"I think we should do superheroes," Eddie says, from behind the bar. Lenny's is dead for a Friday night, so we're all just helping ourselves—all of us having bartended here for more shifts than we could count.

"We did that three years ago," Mia answers, throwing her straw wrapper at her husband from across the bar. "What if we did iconic music videos?

"Like when Luke dressed up as Britney Spears from "Baby One More Time" with pink bows in his hair and everything," Drew laughs, two-and-a-half-month-old Lennon in her lap, half asleep. She takes after her dad with how much she just watches and observes everyone and everything around her—and usually gets bored and falls asleep which is what I'm sure her dad *wants* to do.

"Excuse me," Luke chimes in. "I took creative liberties and did pink *pom poms* in my hair that year." He leans to press a kiss to the top of my head before walking back behind the bar to help Eddie make another round of drinks for us.

"I still can't get used to that," Mia says to me, resting her chin in her hand as she turns to look at me.

"Luke's obnoxious amount of PDA?" I joke.

She shakes her head at me, flipping her blonde hair over her shoulder. "No, smart ass. That you actually *let* him. Seriously, I never thought I'd see you two together."

"As if you weren't one of the biggest advocates for it." I laugh, taking my last sip of my gin and tonic. "You've had a month to *get used to it*, girlie pop."

"We were all rooting for it. Just thought your stubborn ass would never let it happen," Mia quips as if she isn't one of the most stubborn people I know.

In all honesty, I thought it would take some time for me get used to it too, but we fell into our relationship so seamlessly, like it was always meant to happen.

We sometimes struggle with that balance of picking up where we left off and starting fresh, but we've been able to find a happy medium between the two—making up for lost time while also taking each other as we are now, not filling in the blanks with what we once knew.

When I told Mia and Drew everything that happened between Luke and me after leaving our *eventful* Sunday Dinner at the beginning of the month, they couldn't contain their excitement, not only for us but because of how we opened up to each other—and by *we*, I mean *me*.

I also had to physically hold them down from leaving Luke's—*my*—apartment that night because they were seconds away from finding Devin and holding her down while I beat the shit out of her for what she did to Luke. The three of us spent our whole Saturday Movie Night ignoring *Suicide Squad* playing in the background—Drew's pick because of her new obsession with Jared Leto after rediscovering the song "Dangerous Night" by Thirty Seconds to Mars—and talked about how Luke, of all people, is the last person who deserves something like that to happen.

Of course, no one ever deserves to be taken advantage of in the way Devin took advantage of Luke. It's wrong and hurtful, and I can't wait for the day that I see her again because I won't be the Annie she knows the second I get my hands on her.

But Luke is so open, so warm, so willing to see the best in anything around him and everyone he meets, and I don't ever want him to lose that part of himself.

"How's living together, like for real?" Drew asks, passing a sleeping Lennon to Emmett to hold.

"The same I guess. Just more sex," I answer, honestly, getting a chuckle from Mia and Eddie, and Drew blushes. Emmett even snorts out a laugh.

"Why did I think I'd get a real answer out of you?" Drew says, shaking her head at me like I'm one of her students who made a "your mom" joke, one you want to laugh at but have to be the serious one.

"It really is the same," I add with my own laughter. "I go to my placement; Luke comes here. He gets home and either makes dinner or picks something up. I come home; we eat; we go to bed."

"Like an old married couple," Eddie jokes.

"You would know," I quip, looking at both him and Mia.

"Okay, okay," Drew says, waving her hands to stop our antics. Luke sets down another White Claw for her and a new gin and tonic for me, leaning forward on his elbows on the bar across from me. "Let's table the theme discussion for now. We have to figure out what weekend works best for everyone.

It's our turn to host this year," she continues, looking at Emmett who gives her a nod, "and we have enough room for anyone who needs to stay the night."

"We can't do the first weekend because the band has a photoshoot for their upcoming album," Mia explains, "which means Mateo, Theo, and Silas wouldn't be able to do it either."

"The second weekend?" Drew asks all of us.

Luke and I look at each other. "Annie girl?" he prompts.

"Second works for us," I answer for the both of us, gaining some knowing looks from our friends, but they quickly recover. We all decide to brush over how Luke and I went from me not wanting him to know *any* of my business to him now being the first person who gets to know it.

"Us too," Eddie adds.

Drew claps her hands together. "Perfect. I'll let my brother and Lacey know, and you guys can let all your people know. The girls and I will try to come up with our theme tomorrow at Movie Night."

"What's the pick for tomorrow?" Luke asks me, knowing it's my turn to pick the movie.

"Well, we didn't get to really watch *Suicide Squad* last time, so I think we need a re-do."

"Oh!" Mia exclaims, causing all of us to flinch in surprise. "What if we do bad guys for our theme?"

"Like villains?" I ask to clarify, and she nods. I look around seeing smiles from everyone, and it looks like we have our theme.

"What are we dressing up as?" Luke asks me.

"Just because we're a couple does not mean we are doing couple costumes."

"But that's the best part," Luke whines, and I ignore the laughs of our friends at this silly exchange.

"No, thank you," I politely say with a smile, batting my

eyelashes for good measure, but the way Luke's eyes darken, he knows I'm being anything but polite.

"Brat," he mouths to me, our friends too busy talking about their potential costumes to notice us.

"Luke." Emmett's voice has both our heads turning. "I'll be back, starting in November."

Luke nods, but I don't miss the way his shoulders slightly sink. He still hasn't figured out what he wants to do now that he officially gave up his place at the firm.

I think Luke surprised all of us with how well he did here at Lenny's with Emmett gone. He took all the owner responsibilities in stride and kept the place running while training three new bartenders.

I've always known Luke was a capable leader. I watched it in high school when the guys chose him to be captain of the hockey team, and I've seen it with who he is as a person—he has an aura that people gravitate towards, a positivity and level-headedness that comes naturally to him.

I know he struggles with what he's giving up at his dad's firm, and I know it's easy for people to assume he gave it up because it was too hard or because he wasn't cut out for it.

But the guy made it through law school with flying colors.

He didn't choose Lenny's or a job as a bartender over being a lawyer because he had to.

He did it because he wanted to.

"The warehouse next door has been vacant since Cross My Heart stopped practicing there," Emmett adds, and it feels random.

After this past month, Emmett and Drew now own the whole building Lenny's is in, buying the last space from a business that just moved to a different location, and leasing it out to a flower shop. The warehouse is on one side of Lenny's, and they lease the other two spots to a pizza place that recently moved in next door and a bookstore at the end of the building that opened this past spring.

Emmett continues, slowly rocking side to side to keep Lennon asleep. "The couple who own the bookstore said it would be a good spot for a coffee shop."

Luke nods his head again, not quite understanding what Emmett is trying to say.

Mia, Eddie, and I watch as Drew and Emmett exchange a glance before Drew jumps in to clarify, "What my husband is *trying* to say is that Elsie and Sierra suggested we lease the space in the warehouse to someone who could create a spot where people can read their books or buy a coffee before walking around the bookstore," she tells Luke. "I'm not sure if owning a café is what you had in mind, but we'd give you full freedom to run it however you want. It would be yours."

At the word "yours", Luke's eyes brighten, and happiness bursts in my chest at this opportunity and what it could mean for him.

And how it means so much more that it would be something he can do with Drew and Emmett, next to a place that means so much to all of us.

"You want to give me the space? To run?" His voice has a slight tremble as his eyes dart back and forth between Drew and Emmett, a mixture of disbelief and confusion but bright with hope.

"We've seen how well you handled everything here. We figured you'd be the best person for the job," Emmett answers matter-of-factly, but we all know that Emmett doesn't mince words; he doesn't say much, but he means what he says.

"Again, what Emmett is trying to say is we know you're the best person for the job, but we want you to be happy." Drew reaches across the bar to where Luke is now standing, his mouth agape and eyes cloudy. She grabs his hand and squeezes. "We're already so proud of you, but we know you deserve something of your own to be proud of."

I feel pressure build behind my eyes watching Luke process Drew's words and seeing the smiles on my friends faces—Mia, Eddie, and even Emmett all watch as Luke lets go of Drew's hand to round the bar and wrap her in a hug.

"The place needs a lot of work, almost a total renovation, but we can help however you need," Drew says as Luke lets go of her to look to Emmett who doesn't do hugs often but holds Lennon in one arm as he wraps another around Luke.

I feel my heart expanding to the point of explosion at the moment, and I know this is exactly what Luke needed.

"I have my trust and my savings. I got this. I won't let you guys down," he tells Drew and Emmett, his voice heavy with emotion.

"We know you won't," Drew replies at the same time Emmett says, "You better not."

"Shots!" Mia shouts, and we all laugh. She rounds the bar herself, pulling the bottle of tequila off the shelf as Eddie grabs six shot glasses and the bottle of gin.

As Mia and Eddie prep the lime for the shots, Luke closes the distance between us, pulling me into his arms and holding me tight, so many words passing between us without even opening our mouths.

I know how much this means to him.

He knows how proud I am of him.

But as he lets me go, I take his face in my hands, looking deep into his ocean eyes, and I tell him anyway. "I'm so proud of you, bartender."

He raises a brow at me, and his lips curve, his smiling making butterflies—the good kind—take flight in my stomach. "Won't be able to call me that for much longer."

"Not when you're a fancy coffee shop owner," I answer, bringing my lips to his and kissing him softly, not caring that his PDA tendencies—which are just as bad as, if not worse than, his stalker ones—are rubbing off on me.

"You love me?" he asks against my lips.

"Of course, I love you," I say back, leaning back to see his grin.

"Say it again."

"No, I just said it."

"Please?" he playfully begs, his grin fading and his bottom lip jutting out.

I roll my eyes, but I give in like I always do because it's like saying "no" to a puppy. "I love you."

CHAPTER 30
LUKE

ANNIE HEADED over to Drew and Emmett's early to help set up for the party, so I didn't get to see her when I got home from my Saturday shift at Lenny's.

It's not a bad thing though because she wouldn't have let me leave the apartment if she saw my costume.

The night we decided that this year's Halloween party was going to be a villain theme, my mind started reeling with all the different costumes I could see Annie in, and all the different costumes I could wear to match her.

She shut down the coordinating costumes that night, and she didn't change her mind—even when I asked her almost every day for the following two weeks.

She also wouldn't tell me what she was dressing up as, knowing that I would find a way to make my costume match with hers.

Little did she know, I saw the purple suit jacket and green hair dye she hid in the closet of her old room—the room that went back to being a guest room after I moved all her stuff into my bedroom when she was gone at rotations. I knew she'd be too tired to argue when she got home.

All she said was how she was going to make a mess and not clean it up.

I told her I signed up to clean up her messes the second she let me be her boyfriend.

I put two and two together, knowing the girls watched *Suicide Squad* and only one of those characters is known for that purple and green color combo. I figured out my costume relatively quickly.

Going with the version of Harley Quinn that they use in the movie, I picked up blue and pink spray-on hair dye on the way home, spraying one on each side of my head.

I figured no one wants to see me in shorts that show my ass and fishnets, so I opted for a more gender-bent version, wearing respectable-length black shorts with the red and blue jacket I was able to find at a costume store, and my favorite part of the costume being the little change I made to the iconic "Daddy's Little Monster" t-shirt.

I know Annie will think I look ridiculous, but it's her fault for not thinking I was serious about us doing a couple's costume.

I'm getting Rosie ready in her Waluigi costume—Eddie and Mia dressing Daisy up as Wario—when my phone vibrates. Grabbing it from the front pocket of my jeans, I see it's a text from Annie to grab the cupcakes she put in the fridge, so I make sure I do before I head out the door with Rosie, ready to show Annie how fun couple costumes can be.

———

Because I had to work until 8 p.m., I'm one of the last to arrive. I walk through Drew and Emmett's front door, finding a dark kitchen and living room, the place lit up with colored lights to give the party a spookier vibe.

Drew and Emmett's place is perfect for a Halloween party,

already decked out in dark colors with gothic decorations. They added a few more themed ones for tonight, with everything from pumpkin-shaped plates to bat cut-outs on the walls and cloth ghosts hanging from the ceiling.

I say my hellos to everyone as I walk in, getting the whistles and laughs when they see my costume. I say hi to Drew's brother, Cal, and his wife, Emma, in matching Slytherin robes, before making my way into the living room and find Mateo, Mia's brother, and the other Cross My Heart guys, Theo and Silas, dressed up as Michael Myers, Freddy Krueger, and Hannibal Lector.

Lacey, Drew's friend, is dressed as Dr. Frankenstein and her husband, Tyler, is the monster, and Eddie's sisters, Lucia, Carmen, and Isa are dressed up as three villains from the Powerpuff Girls: Mojo Jojo, HIM, and Sedusa.

I love how everyone took the theme so seriously.

In the kitchen, I find my brothers, Caleb, Bennett, and Jack. Bennett and Jack are dressed all in black flowy capes and Scream masks pulled up on the top of their heads, and Caleb is dressed as Kylo Ren, his mask under his arm as he chats with Bennett and Jack.

"Nice costume, little brother!" I hear Bennett yell across the kitchen when he sees me, and I walk over to them, letting Rosie off her leash to say her own hellos and setting down the container of Annie's cupcakes.

She hasn't been stress-baking half as much as I thought she would've, but I partly blame myself for my own methods of relieving her stress.

"'Mommy's Little Monster', Luke. Really?" Caleb snarks, reading my shirt and shaking his head, but I see the amusement on his face.

"Cute, huh?" I say, my smile accentuated by the pink and blue makeup I found of Annie's around my eyes and her cherry lip gloss of hers on my lips.

"It is pretty fitting," Jack laughs, taking a sip of the drink he's holding. "I saw Annie's costume when we got here. It makes sense you're dressed as the obsessed one of the two."

Bennett and Caleb let out a chuckle, and I don't correct them.

Obsessed is an understatement when it comes to Annie.

Before I can say anything else, the voice I've been waiting to hear all day booms behind. "What the fuck are you wearing?"

I give Caleb, Bennett, and Jack a grin before turning around.

Annie's brown hair is pushed back like she ran her fingers back through it. It has a green tint over it, and her oversized purple suit jacket perfectly showcases the orange bralette, little black shorts, and fishnets she has on underneath.

I have to will my jaw to not drop to the floor.

Her brown eyes are framed with triangles of purple eyeshadow, her lips looking more red than usually, the lines of her mouth exaggerated to her cheeks.

"Damn, honey. Crazy looks good on you," I tease, leaning into The Joker's main characteristic, and I walk to where she's standing behind the couch in the living room.

"I wish I could say the same," she quips, but I watch her eyes roam, staring at my pink and blue hair and down to my chest where she echoes Caleb's sentiment, "'Mommy's Little Monster', Luke? What is wrong with you?"

"Do we really want to get into that tonight?" I ask her, taking her chin between my thumb and index finger, pulling her closer to me, needing to taste her cherry lips before the temptation overpowers me.

Her kiss is soft, and I wish we weren't in the middle of a party of a dozen people because my need for her never seems to go away.

"You guys are so hot!" I hear Mia yell across the living

room. Annie pulls her lips from mine, and I find Mia and Eddie dressed as Chucky and Chucky's Bride, always killing it with their couple's costumes and winning the contests we always have at these Halloween parties.

Drew and Emmett are with them, dressed as Team Rocket's Jessie and James with Lennon in a baby Mew costume.

"Hot enough to win this year?" Annie questions playfully, grabbing my hand to walk us over to our friends. "Did you bring the cupcakes?"

I nod not being able to tear my eyes away from her. I lean in to kiss her temple, letting go of her hand to throw my arm over her shoulder. "Did you make my favorite?"

She laughs. "I won't say they're *not* dark chocolate and peanut butter."

I lean down. "That's what I like to hear," I whisper into her ear, keeping that little shiver I feel going up her spine to myself.

We spent the first few hours of the party mingling and catching up with the people there who we don't see too often. We've gotten to know Cal, Emma, Lacey, and Tyler over the years, and if they're important people to Drew, then they're important people to us.

Same with Mateo, Theo, and Silas—Mateo being Mia's brother and Eddie's best friend for all of his adult life, Theo and Silas being the other half of Cross My Heart—we've gotten to know them well since they practiced next door to Lenny's for years.

In the warehouse that is mine.

Mine to turn into something.

Mine to be proud of.

Mine.

When Drew and Emmett asked me to turn the warehouse into a coffee shop that could bring more business to the building they own, I thought I was hallucinating because it was too good to be true.

I've loved running Lenny's, being the person that not only Drew and Emmett can rely on but the bartenders and patrons. It felt good to be needed, to be the one that people could lean on, the one in charge.

I know being a business owner isn't the same as a hotshot lawyer in society's eyes. I know people are going to think I'm crazy for taking this path rather than the one I initially planned, but I don't care.

And that feels so good to say.

I don't care because I'm doing what I want.

That's something I can be proud of.

I didn't feel an iota of pride when I got into law school or when I made it through three years of it. I felt nothing when I got the diploma that secured my license to practice law in the state of Wisconsin.

Both were huge accomplishments, but I couldn't convince myself that they were something to be proud of.

But this. Starting a business from the ground up, being the one in charge, making the vision I have for it a reality, that makes me feel proud of myself.

Before Drew puts Lennon to bed, we hold our costume contest. Everyone has to pick their "walk-up" song like they do in baseball games, and then we each show off our costumes to our songs, either individually or with the person or group we dressed up with.

We all gather in the kitchen, being able to see everyone walk down the small hallway that separates the living room from the kitchen. Caleb, opting out of the contest, is on music-duty, having everyone's song queued up

Cal and Emma go first in their Slytherin costumes, walking down to "Magic" by One Direction, followed by Jack and Bennett in their Scream costumes walking down to

"(Don't Fear) The Reaper" before each going down on a knee, pouring their drinks in their masks and chugging.

As we all predicted, Mateo walks down to a remix of the *Halloween* opening in his Michael Myers mask, and Theo and Silas each follow him.

Lucia, Carmen, and Isa strut to "bad guy" by Billie Elish, making sure it was the one featuring Justin Bieber. Seeing them reminds me of when Drew, Mia, and Annie were the Powerpuff Girls, four years ago—Annie looked cute in green.

Lacey and Tyler walk down to "Dr. Feelgood" by Mötley Crüe, surprising all of us when we thought they'd go with the obvious choice and pick "Monster Mash". Drew, Emmett, and Lennon don't surprise us though, going with the "Pokémon Theme Song". They've won our contest a few times over the years, after Drew finally convinced Emmett that wearing a hockey mask with his regular clothes and saying he's Jason from *Friday the 13th* didn't count as a costume, and Lennon gives them the leg up this year.

As last year's champions, Mia and Eddie get to go last, so next up is Annie and me. We argued over if we should go with the easy pop, "You Don't Own Me", the remake by SAYGRACE and G-Eazy, but Annie has a different idea—one she won't tell me as payback to my costume surprise.

"Last chance to tell me what you picked before I leave a handprint on your ass," I whisper in her ear while Caleb queues our song.

"Now who's crazy?" she teases.

"Watch it," I fire back, but I know she acts like a brat on purpose for this very reaction of mine; I pull her in by the hip and press a kiss to her lips, just as I hear the familiar, "And I was like, why you so obsessed with me?" coming from the speaker before the beat drops and "Obsessed" by Mariah Carey starts, making the whole room burst into hoots and hollers.

"You're going to get it when we get home, honey. Mark my words."

She looks up at me, her Joker makeup being more of a turn-on than it should be, batting her long lashes and pouting her lips. "Promise?"

And then she slaps me on the ass, prompting our walk down the makeshift runway, to our friends cheering and clapping. I grab her hand, pulling her in against me, ready to press another kiss to her lips that I know will keep our crowd cheering, but she leans back instead, bending back into a dip with one of her long legs lifted.

She pulls herself back up, leaning in close enough for me to think I can close my eyes and feel her lips on mine, only for her to pat my cheek twice and spin out my grasp.

Fuck waiting until we get home.

The car is as good a place as ever to remind her just how obsessed with her I am.

Mia and Eddie end the contest with "good 4 u" by Olivia Rodrigo, the perfect pick for the toxic dolls they dressed up as, but I barely pay attention to the two because I don't take my eyes off of Annie.

I scribble down Jack and Bennett's name on the piece of paper Lacey hands to all of us while Drew puts Lennon to bed, one of the rules being we can't vote for ourselves.

Annie knows I'm watching her—she always does—but she pretends she can't feel my gaze.

Lacey and Mia count the votes, and I barely hear that Annie and I are the winners because I'm throwing her over my shoulder and walking us out the front door as everyone claps and cheers.

"Hey!" she squeals, and I smack her ass, returning the favor, our friends' laughs drown out behind us as I open the front door and slam it closed behind me. "Couldn't wait 'til we got home?" she sasses as I walk us through the cool

October night, fishing for my keys in my back pocket, still holding her over my shoulder.

I unlock my car, walking around to the passenger seat, opening the door and setting her down. My car is parked on the street in front of Drew's house, the street quiet and dark aside from the street light just down the road.

The air is cold, but I'm not bothered by it—heat overwhelms my body at the sight of Annie in front of me. Her purple suit jacket is draped over her shoulders, her tits pushed up by her orange bra. My eyes roam down her perfect body, looking at the fishnets covering her legs that are just begging to be ripped open.

I lean down, pushing the passenger seat as far back as it can go, giving me room to bend down in front of her and putting me right where I need to be.

Looking up to find her red bottom lip caught between her teeth, I shut the car door and grab her legs, yanking down her shorts and putting her legs over my shoulder and up on the dash.

I don't waste any more time, ripping a hole in her fishnets and causing a gasp to escape from her lips.

I pull her matching orange panties to the side, diving in like a starved man, licking up and down her slit, groaning at her taste.

"Fuck," she breathes through clenched teeth, her hands coming to the back of my head as I suck her clit into my mouth, feeling the sting on my scalp as she fists my hair.

"You taste so good, sweet girl," I say against her sensitive skin, her hips slightly bucking when she feels my breath against it, and my mouth is back on her.

She starts to roll her hips, taking what she needs from me, using her grip in my hair to move me where she needs me, and it doesn't take long until she's coming on my tongue.

I don't give her time to recover before I reach under the seat, lowering it down so it's flat and flipping her over. She crawls further up the flattened seat until I have room to come up behind her, ripping her fishnets even more, exposing her ass to me.

I bring my open palm down on the skin, eliciting a little scream in surprise.

I rub my hand to soothe the skin before bringing my hand down again, wishing it wasn't so dark so I could see her ass pinken with the print of my hand.

"Are you going to fuck me, or not?" she complains over her shoulder, but I hear the need in her voice. I unzip my jeans enough to pull my cock out, already hard and begging to be inside of her.

"You're such a fucking brat," I grit as I line up with her entrance, pushing into her with one thrust, both of us groaning as I bottom out.

I give her no more than a second to adjust before I'm pounding into her, thankful for the tinted windows, and I feel her tighten around me, already so close, so I reach around her, finding her clit, giving her what she needs until she falls apart again

My name on her lips as she comes sends me over the edge, my own orgasm taking over.

It takes us a few moments to recover, and I gently pull out of her, tucking myself back into my jeans, and opening the car door, a rush of cold air cooling my skin.

I step out of the car, making sure to use my body to block the open doorway, even though we're the only ones outside.

"We're too old to sneak off to have sex in the car," Annie says, sitting up and adjusting her clothes.

"Where's your sense of adventure, Annie girl. You're never too old for car sex." I reach my hand out for her to grab, giving her a grin that I only wear with her.

She shakes her head but takes my hand, and I help her out of the car. Her lips threaten to smile as we walk back into the house. "Your cum is going to be leaking out of me for the rest of the night." And the dirty words shouldn't excite me the way they do.

I shrug my shoulders, an apology being the last thing on my mind.

When I don't say anything, she lets go of my hand, walking in front of me to get to the door first. "Looks like you'll have some cleaning up to do when we get home," she says over her shoulder, and now I'm hard all over again.

Just when I think I have the upper hand, she reminds me of who's in charge here.

I groan as I walk into the front door behind her, her ass swaying as she leads us back to the party.

The music is playing and drinks are flowing, and there are animated conversations all around the kitchen and living room. No one acknowledges our absence, aside from the slap on the back of the head I get from Emmett that makes Eddie howl with laughter and the knowing smirk I get from Mia— but I give her one in return when I glance down at the "drink" she's been sipping all night.

One that I noticed smelled a lot like orange juice and very little like tequila.

She narrows her eyes at me, and a shared understanding of keeping our mouths shut passes through us.

"Just in time for dessert," Drew announces as she makes our way over to us, the cupcakes I brought over on a big pumpkin plate.

"What did you make this time, Ann?" Eddie asks as he takes one.

I reach for one as she answers, "Oh, I didn't have time to make them from scratch, so I picked them up from a bakery on my way home from the zoo yesterday." I pull my hand back.

"You didn't make them?" I ask.

"I still got your favorite kind," she answers with a little chuckle, grabbing one for herself, peeling the paper, taking a bite before holding it out to me, but I shake my head. She looks at me confused. "What?"

"I don't want it," I reply like a toddler refusing to eat his vegetables.

This makes her roll her eyes, and I feel our friends watching us, their amusement palpable in the air. "What's wrong with them?" she challenges.

"They're not yours," I answer, but before she can tell me I'm being stupid or whatever is on the tip of her tongue, I add, "Plus, I just had dessert."

CHAPTER 31
ANNIE

THE DAYS ARE FLYING BY FASTER than I can keep track. One minute, Luke was eating me out in the passenger side of his car dressed as Harley Quinn—the next, it's the first Movie Night of November, and it's all a blur of how we got here.

There have been at least ten separate occasions over the several weeks where I've literally had to pinch myself to make sure I wasn't dreaming. Rotations are as stressful as everyone warns, and you never feel like you have your feet solid on the ground.

Right when I start to feel stable, it's time to switch and start all over again somewhere else—learning the layout of the hospital, meeting the new staff, and feeling like a fish out of water. Again.

But, they have also been exhilarating and exciting because every day brings new challenges and new things to learn.

Luke and I are also almost too good to be true. We fell into such a natural rhythm, even for as busy as we are, and we have such a good time together. Even if it's just dinner on the couch and watching TV, any time I have with him feels like a dream.

I thought there would be more growing pains, especially as we learn to balance our past and the present, but I think our history made it all that much easier.

Drew, Mia, and I have plans to watch *Iron Man*, the second movie in our mission to watch all the Marvel movies in chronological order—Drew's idea because it's something she did with Emmett when they first started dating.

And because it started getting harder and harder for us to pick a movie that wasn't from the *Twilight* franchise.

We're cuddled up on the couch in my living room, Daisy and Rosie asleep at our feet.

While we cue up the movie, I give Mia and Drew the update on the whole Devin situation, seeing as Luke reached out to Grant and took him up on his offer to get together. Luke asked if we could all double-date, so we're meeting both Grant and Devin at Lenny's tomorrow night.

"I'm glad you guys are confronting her. You both deserve to finally move on from that night," Drew says as she crosses her legs, sitting between Mia and me.

"I don't see it going well though," I reply. "Devin has never been the kind of person to admit when she was wrong."

"Maybe you should hit her truck with a baseball bat," Drew scoffs.

"Maybe you should hit *her* with one," Mia adds, and we all laugh much harder than we should.

With the popcorn popped, the candy nearby, and the movie starting, we drift into comfortable silence up until the montage of Tony Stark building his first suit while he's being held hostage.

"How are rotations going, Ann?" Mia asks as she opens up a Kit Kat, handing one stick to me, one to Drew, and keeping two for herself because it's her favorite candy.

"Good," I answer, breaking the stick of chocolate and bringing one half to my mouth. "I'm doing my small animal dentistry and oral surgery rotation, which is a big difference compared to my time at the zoo."

"Did you hear back about that program?" Drew asks in between eating all the chocolate off the Kit Kat like a psychopath, her eyes still glued on what she calls her favorite Marvel movie.

During my rotation at the zoo, I found that I could really picture myself there, working with the staff and all the different exotic animals.

I know it is early in the rotation year, and this year is all about getting as much experience as we can before we figure out what we want to focus on. Plus, I always thought I'd end up back at the animal shelter or someplace like it, working with the dogs, cats, bunnies, and birds.

But when the practicing veterinarian at the zoo told me more about the Animal Health Center program and the externship that they have for fourth-year vet students, I couldn't get it out of my head, even after I started my next rotation.

After talking with my advisor, I decided to apply. If I get in, my last month of my rotation year would be the externship, followed by a 3-year Zoological Medicine Residency, which trains veterinarians in the zoo and exotic animal medicine field.

"I'm supposed to hear by Monday," I tell Drew.

"And how are things going with Luke and all the renovations?" Mia asks both Drew and I. Since Drew and Emmett asked Luke to handle the coffee shop, Luke has dived into renovating the old warehouse.

Now that Emmett is back at Lenny's full-time, Luke went back to his bartending shifts. When he's not at Lenny's, he's next door at the warehouse, meeting with all kinds of construction companies, electricians, plumbers, and distributors for all the equipment he'll need.

"Pretty sure he's going to start sleeping there one of these days." I laugh, then reach into Drew's lap where she's holding the popcorn. Luke wants to open by the beginning of December, so he has just about a month to get it ready.

Safe to say, he's working around the clock, and there are so many moving pieces that all his open time is spent there. He's using money from his trust, putting his whole heart and soul into it.

"There are people over there 24/7," Drew adds. "He's always directing people on what he needs and where to go. He's not messing around."

I let out a little laugh to cover up the emotion beginning to clog my throat. The idea of running a coffee shop might be silly to some, but for Luke this is important. It's something his name is attached to, something he can build from the ground up, something for him to call his own. "Luke has never been capable of putting in anything less than 100%, especially when it's something he wants."

Drew and Mia share a look before they look back at me. "We know," they say at the same time, and I resist the urge to throw my popcorn at them, opting to turn back to the movie instead.

When the movie ends, Drew and Mia help me clean up the living room, and I box up some cookies and brownies I made last night after another stressful week for them.

The three of us group hug at the door and say our good-byes, them making me promise to text them when I find out about the AHC program on Monday, and me agreeing.

I was surprised they didn't make me promise the same about our night with Devin and Grant tomorrow—until I hear them talking as they walk down the hall about meeting each other at Lenny's at six tomorrow night which happens to be the same time Luke and I will be there.

I laugh to myself, shutting the door as I watch the two walk down the hallway, Daisy on her leash walking between them.

Luke told me he'd be at the warehouse late—him, Eddie, and a few of Luke's law school buddies that he still plays hockey with helping him paint the warehouse now that the drywall is up—so I head to the bathroom to get ready for bed.

I'm almost asleep when I hear the front door quietly open and close. There's some fumbling around, a sink turning on and off, and the sound of clothes hitting the floor before I feel the bed dip behind me and a strong arm loop around my waist, pulling me in close.

"Goodnight, Annie girl," I hear in my ear as I drift off to sleep.

CHAPTER 32

LUKE

"ARE you sure we have to do this?" Annie asks as we put our shoes on. We're headed to Lenny's to meet Grant and Devin for a drink, and I'm even having trouble finding the silver lining in how tonight will most likely go.

I haven't had much time to think about it, not since Annie and I decided that confronting Devin about what she did to us—to me—was something we owed to ourselves and our relationship.

It's not that I think we *need* this conversation with her for our relationship to work, but I don't want anything, especially something as shitty as what Devin did, hanging over our heads for the rest of our lives.

"I didn't think anything scared you." I know that seeing Devin and Grant is hard for Annie. It's going to remind her about what happened at Grant's party and the night before, but it's also bringing up everything else she endured during high school.

Since we've gotten back together, she's been more open about her experience.

I've learned more about what Devin and the other girls did to Annie in high school, and how the bullying has had a lasting effect on her. I wish she would have been more open with me about it when it happened, but I'm glad I can be here for her now.

For someone like Annie, letting me in after closing herself off for so long, takes a lot, and I'm so proud of her.

Annie is almost unrecognizable today compared to who she was back then, and I know she is proud of who she is now, proud that she doesn't let anyone determine her worth anymore, and she isn't bounding herself to the background like she used to.

But that doesn't mean that seeing people from high school doesn't bring up those memories and feelings.

I don't blame her for not wanting to go, but I also know that my Annie girl doesn't back down from a fight.

She crosses her arms, narrowing her eyes. "I'm not scared of Devin, dummy. I'm scared *for* her."

I lean down and press a kiss to her forehead, the lines there instantly softening. "That's my girl." I open the front door, gesturing for her to lead. She's trying to hide the smile on her face as she lets her arms fall down to her sides and starts to walk out the door.

As she does, I slap her ass as she walks out. "Let's go get 'em, honey."

When we get to Lenny's, Emmett is bartending with Ava, and the only people here on a Sunday night are three yahoos in a corner booth who look oddly familiar in their black sweatshirts with the hoods up, one with a baby strapped to their chest.

Annie and I look at each other, shaking our heads. I glance back at the bar where Emmett is looking over at them and doing the same. Next to him, Ava has a hand over her mouth, covering up a smile.

We walk over to the booth, both of us crossing our arms and looking down at our friends—who we can now see are also wearing sunglasses as if the sun didn't set almost two hours ago.

"You guys look so stupid," I say with a laugh.

"Shh! We're incognito," Mia whisper-yells, but this just makes me laugh louder.

"You don't think it's more suspicious that the only three people in here besides us are three idiots dressed in black and wearing sunglasses at night?" Annie asks, and she's fighting a smile.

"I told you two this was a stupid idea," Eddie complains, taking off his aviators and unzipping his sweatshirt, letting it fall off his shoulders, his sun and rain cloud tattoo he got when I got my rose looking darker than the rest of the tattoos on his arms.

"You didn't have to come," Drew retorts, but she makes no move to remove her "disguise".

"Yeah, let Ava go home. You can help Emmett behind the bar," Mia adds, blowing a kiss to her husband. He groans then walks over to the bar.

"Are they here?" Drew whispers over Lennon's head, and Annie and I both shake our heads.

"Do you guys have a plan?" Mia asks, her voice also in a whisper, even though we are *still* the only people here, even more so now that Ava is going home.

"This isn't a top-secret mission, you guys," Annie says, finally letting herself smile. "We'll suffer through the small talk, and I'll fake a smile through Devin's comments about how Luke and I are still together, and then I'll confront her about the video and how shitty it was that she did that to Luke when he was drunk."

"And I'll be there for moral support," I add, slinging my arm over Annie's shoulder and pulling her in so I can kiss her on the temple.

Before Mia and Drew can complain how boring that is or

whatever they're about to say, the door to Lenny's swings open, and Devin and Grant walk in.

I haven't seen Devin since high school, but the way she carries herself is the same. I watch as she looks around Lenny's, not even bothering to hide her distaste, and she looks out of place with her designer bag and high heels, even more so compared to Grant's long-sleeve t-shirt and worn jeans.

"Luke!" Grant booms, his dirty blonde hair shorter than when I saw it in the summer. I grab Annie's hand, walking us over to them and meeting them at a high-top table not too far from the bar and close enough to the booth where Drew, Mia, and Lennon are.

Out of the corner of my eye, I notice both Emmett and Eddie not even bothering to make themselves look busy, both of them standing behind the bar and keeping an eye on Annie who reluctantly sits down at the high-top table, not saying anything to either Devin or Grant.

When I glance at her, I notice she's watching Devin, who's still looking around the bar as if she could contract a deadly disease by spending too much time here.

"I'm glad we could get together," I lie, standing next to Annie's chair, squeezing her hand before letting go and gesturing to the bar. "You guys want a drink?"

"I got it," Grant says, looking at Annie and giving her a once-over that makes me clench my fists. "What can I get you, Annie?" he asks her.

"Gin and tonic," she answers, giving him a small smile that doesn't reach her eyes, but at least she's looking right at him.

"You got it," he replies before turning to me. "Come with me to the bar?"

I look at Annie with a raise of my brow. She gives me a small smile and a slight nod, telling me she's okay. Grant is asking what Devin wants to drink, both too busy to catch our exchange.

"Yeah, I'll go with you," I tell Grant, not necessarily wanting to leave Annie alone with Devin but knowing that she can handle herself.

We walk over to the bar and order two beers for us, a gin and tonic for Annie, and Grant orders a glass of red wine for Devin.

I turn to see Devin saying something to Annie, but I can't hear it over Grant trying—and failing—to make conversation with Emmett over the Metallica t-shirt he's wearing.

I watch as Devin wipes the chair across from Annie with her hand before sitting down, her face twisting in something that's meant to be a smile but has a menacing look to it.

Whatever Devin says, Annie doesn't wait long to reply, looking at Devin as she answers, and Devin's eyes slightly widen, her body leaning back just an inch before she covers up her surprise quickly.

"Luke?" I hear Grant say, and I have to turn my attention to him.

"Sorry, what were you saying?" I ask as Eddie sets down two beers and a glass of wine in front of us while Emmett makes Annie's drink.

"I was saying how I'm not surprised you and Annie are still together." I watch as Grant follows my prior gaze, looking directly at Annie and Devin. The two must have given up the small talk and are both looking at their phones, and I don't like how most of Grant's attention isn't on his own girlfriend.

"Yeah," I say, giving him a noncommittal answer. The guys on the hockey team always tried to give me shit about my commitment to Annie, especially when I didn't join in on their excitement for the girls they were hoping to meet in college, despite most of them having girlfriends. I never entertained it, so they eventually gave up.

Back then, I didn't care about anyone's opinion about my relationship with Annie except for Annie's. The same is true now.

Grant shakes his head. "I never got your thing for her in high school, but I see it now. Never thought I'd be jealous of you hitting *that*."

Emmett and Eddie both freeze, and I feel their eyes on me. Grant's eyes are still on Annie, and it's Grant's lucky day that he has to deal with me rather than her.

If Annie heard him say that, he would've met a similar fate to Ava's douche of an ex-boyfriend, probably worse.

I've never been outwardly possessive over Annie—it's not really the kind of guy I am. I feel protective over her, wanting to protect her, but I learned over the years that she doesn't need that from me.

But right now, I don't care. I feel a rush of adrenaline funnel through me. "Watch your fucking mouth," I bite, and Grant finally stops looking at Annie and faces me.

"Relax, dude. I meant it as a compliment."

"Look at her again, and she'll be the last thing you see."

Grant tries to laugh it off, looking at Emmett and Eddie as if they'll be any help to him right now, but when he sees the way the two are staring at him, the laugh quickly dries out.

"Whatever," he scoffs, grabbing his beer and Devin's wine and walking back over to the table.

"Get those fucks out of here," Eddie growls, not at all concerned about his volume.

"You have five minutes," Emmett adds.

"Don't worry," I reply, watching as Grant stands behind Devin's chair, Annie looking up at him and Devin. "Annie will have them out in three.

CHAPTER 33

ANNIE

SMALL TALK SHOULD BE USED as a torture tactic because there is literally nothing worse. Devin and I lasted 30 seconds without Grant and Luke as buffers before I was about to flip this fucking table.

Just like I knew she would, she eyed me up and down before she sat down and said how she couldn't believe Luke and I were still together. I told her how it was new, that we recently got back together, leaving out all the important details.

I think I caught her off-guard—not by my answer, but by the fact that I answered without staring at the floor or talking too softly. She covered it up quickly though before nodding her head, giving me a fake-ass smile, and going on her phone.

I did the same, not in any rush to make more small talk. I wanted to wait for Luke to come back with our drinks before I brought up why we wanted to get together, and when I finally feel his presence behind my chair as he sets down my gin and tonic on the table, it's game on.

"So, Devin," I start, "there is a reason we wanted to meet up with you guys tonight." My voice sounds foreign in my own ears, the high-pitch tone and niceties feel weird on my tongue.

"And what reason is that?" Devin drawls, taking a sip of her red wine.

"You see, when my friends and I ran into you at the grocery store not too long ago, you made a comment about how you showed me that video for my own good." Her eyes slightly widen when I mention seeing her at the store, and widen even more when I bring up the video.

I knew she would assume I didn't have the balls to confront her about either of these things, especially in front of Luke and Grant, and I planned on using that to my advantage tonight.

I can say a lot about Devin—considering she was my friend for eight years. I know her well enough to know exactly what to expect from her, and that those nasty qualities of hers I always saw but ignored until she threw them in my face haven't changed.

Devin doesn't say anything for a moment, her wine glass frozen a few inches from her lips as if my words paused her movements. I use her falter to continue. "The crazy thing about that video is," I grab Luke's hand and hold it in mine on the table, watching as Devin's eyes fall to our hands before she looks back up at me, "when I told Luke about it, he didn't remember it. He didn't even remember that you and Penelope were at Alek's house that night."

I watch as the realization hits her. She's not stupid. She has to know what she did was wrong. She was just too confident, too cocky, that no one would call her on her bullshit.

Grant's eyes are going back and forth between me and Devin, occasionally looking at Luke with a confused— worried?—expression. "What the hell are you guys talking about? What video?"

I look up at Grant and feign innocence all over my face. "Oh, Grant. Devin never told you?" I turn to Devin. "Do you want to tell him, or should I?" I give her a smile I hope she sees in her nightmares, one that she's probably seen in the mirror.

Devin finally sets her wine glass down, her body thawing. "I don't know what you're going on about. I didn't do anything wrong." Her voice is defiant, and I don't miss how she always gets defensive over her actions.

Especially since I haven't even accused her of anything yet.

"Is this the video of you and Luke?" Grant asks, and he throws me for a loop because I didn't think he'd know about it.

"You know about the video?" Luke asks, his body tightening, making his hand squeeze tightly around mine.

"Devin told me you two hooked when we got back together during move-in week, but she didn't tell me about any video. It's news to me it was *that* night." He looks at his girlfriend. "I didn't even know you two were there that night."

I can't help but throw my head back and laugh. Not only did Devin probably think she got away with all of this, but this is going even better than I could've imagined. Devin spun this web of lies so tight, and it's all about to unravel. I have to let go of Luke's hand to wipe the tears from my eyes.

"What's so funny, Vivian?" Devin asks through her teeth, and it makes me laugh even more. I ignore the use of my real name, knowing she's trying to get a rise out of me. Vivian would be cowering; Annie is about to make *her* cower.

"So, let me get this straight. You assault Luke when he is too drunk to consent. You record it, corner me at a party to show it to me, lie to me *and* your boyfriend that you and Luke hooked up, and you honestly think that you did nothing wrong?" When I say it all aloud, it takes all the power away from it. Something that took up so much room inside my head for so many years is now all out in the open.

"Assault?" Devin gasps. "I kissed him, so what? You're making it sound much worse than it was." I feel my nails dig into my palms with how tightly I have my fists clenched.

"We didn't kiss, Devin," Luke argues. "I was too drunk to even know my name, let alone what was happening to me. You took advantage of that."

Devin scoffs, and I see red. "Don't be so dramatic. You're not some victim, Luke," she says, and it's the equivalent of digging her own grave.

"How do you not see anything wrong with forcing yourself on someone like that?" Luke replies, his voice growing in volume. I am so proud of him for standing up for himself and saying his piece, but I am not letting him fight this battle alone.

"Listen closely, Devin," I say before she can spew some more problematic nonsense. "I didn't come here to start a fight, but if you keep it up with this bullshit, I will drag you out of here by your hair."

"No need," she spits. "We're leaving. Let's go, Grant."

She gets up from her chair and starts to head towards the door, but Grant stays put. "But, Devin—" he starts, sadness lining his features.

"Oh, shut up. You're really going to listen to these two tell these horrible lies about me?"

"That's it," I hear myself say, and I hop out of my chair, walking straight up to Devin. Her face twists into fear as she starts stepping backward. She's tripping over her heels the closer I get to her, and I can't help the pride blooming in my chest at the role reversal.

I'm not a bully. Never was, never will be.

But I am someone who spent years being scared of one, and I can't deny how good it feels to see the fear in her eyes.

It's a knowing fear because she's never been in the position she is now, where the person in front of her holds all the power. A fear I know all too well.

Her back meets the front door of Lenny's, and I close the distance between us. "I have spent way too many years letting someone as pathetic as you hold so much power over me. That ends today."

Her face is pale in the low light of Lenny's, the neon lights all over the walls making her face look almost translucent.

She opens her mouth as if she's going to say something, but she closes it quickly.

"You have two options, Devin," I continue. "You can apologize to Luke, leave, and pray I never see your face again." She starts to shake her head, proving she is stupider than I thought, but I'm not done. "Or, you can get your ass beat before doing all of the above. Your choice."

All of her weight is pressed back against the door, anything to put space between her and me, and I reach to either side of her to push open the door.

Luke and Grant have made their way to the doorway, the Lenny's crew all right behind them, just in time to watch Devin lose her balance with the door flung open, and she falls on the concrete, landing right on her ass.

She screams, and it resembles a little kid who didn't get their way. "I'm sorry, Luke! There, you happy, you crazy fucking bitch?" Grant rushes over to help her up.

"Sweetie, you haven't seen 'crazy' yet."

Grant pulls her by the arm. "It's time for us to go."

"And don't bother coming back," Luke adds from over my shoulder, and I look up to find him beaming at me, a huge grin on his face.

We watch Devin and Grant speed off, and I can't help but flip off their car as it pulls out of the parking lot, knowing I'll never see either of them again.

CHAPTER 34
LUKE

I RIDE the high of watching Annie scare the shit out of Devin for the next week. It's no secret that Annie's edge, her confidence, her boldness, has been a turn on for me since I walked into Lenny's over seven years ago, but it's something else entirely when I'm not on the other side of it.

It felt good to confront Devin, both for myself and for our relationship, but I know it meant a lot to Annie. It was like she could finally shut the door on that part of her life, finally gain the power back she lost after so many years of being a victim to Devin's bullying.

I think Annie's riding the high too, along with the fact that she got accepted into a program with the Milwaukee Zoo, one where she can do an externship for her last month of rotations next September, followed by a residency where she'll train in the zoo and exotic animal medicine field.

She found out the night after our drinks with Devin and Grant, and I don't think I'll ever get the smile on her face when she opened the email out of my head. She also had an email that the investigation with her old apartment was found inconclusive, so it's safe to say she made the right choice by sticking with me and not going back there.

I'm finishing up my shift at Lenny's, about to head into the mess that is the unnamed coffee shop next door, and today, I'm supposed to get all the correct permits from the city.

On top of that, I have to choose which distributor I will be going with for the coffee and equipment, and direct the shipment of furniture coming in today.

We are only a week into November, but that is one week closer to when I'm hoping to get this place opened.

I still have to figure out a name, wanting it to flow with the other business names here, especially Lenny's and the bookstore since this place is between the two, but I figured that would be the last of my never-ending things to do.

Drew mentioned that selling some baked goods would be a nice marketing element for the coffee shop, but I would feel weird to have anyone else baking, so I've been meaning to talk to Annie about how she could possibly fit into this dream of mine.

The universe knows she is the center of every dream I have.

"I'm headed next door!" I yell to Emmett as I round the bar and head to the front door. He responds with a grunt of acknowledgment as the door to Lenny's shuts behind me.

The November air is cool against my cheeks, my hair blowing back from the rush of wind that meets me. It's about a ten-step walk from door-to-door, but before I can grab my keys to unlock the coffee shop, my phone rings.

"Hi, Ben," I say as I hold my phone between my ear and my shoulder. "What's up?"

"Jack and I were wondering if you needed any more help with the café. We'll have a day or two after today's shift is over."

Bennett and Jack work in a 24-hour shift with 48 hours off rotation, and they've been using their days off to help me get this place into shape, along with Eddie, Emmett, and some of my law school/hockey buddies. Annie will come and study or catch up on her charting and reports for school to keep me company in the evenings or weekends, but she's too busy to do more than that.

Mia and Drew are excited to help with the decorating, which we'll be ready to do in a week or two if all the other stuff goes as planned, and Mia will be taking charge of the social media, one of the skills she honed when helping grow Eddie's band, Cross My Heart, as their photographer and social media manager.

"I'll take all the help I can get," I tell my brother once I'm inside. The place no longer looks like a warehouse—the new drywall is painted a soft blue; the furniture being delivered today will be a dark contrast. "I want to get the coffee bar built and in place now that the plumbing is done. You guys good to help with that?"

"You got it. See you Thursday."

"See you guys then."

My brothers have been super supportive through this whole process, helping when they can and making me feel like I didn't make a mistake not taking the position at Owens & Son's. I have yet to speak to my dad, but I'm not holding my breath when it comes to that.

If my dad can cut out Bennett, his biological son, from his life after he decided he didn't want to be a lawyer, I'm sure my dad can easily do the same for his bastard son.

The rest of the day flies by with dozens of people coming in and out of the coffee shop; contractors, electricians, and deliveries.

I was able to finalize the date of the soft opening, emailing Mia the official date so she can start putting together content for the social media pages we'll be launching next week. It's been dark a few hours by the time the last delivery comes, and I can finally take a second to look at today's progress.

The outside of the shop is lined with small circle tables

and chairs, the new windows opening up the space, making it look much bigger than it did before.

It still looks unfinished, but I was able to sweep the floors and clean up all the dust, dirt, and miscellaneous tools lying around from people coming in and out before the furniture delivery, and installing the coffee bar will make the place look much more finished by the end of the week.

With today's work being done, I check my watch to see if I'll make it home before Annie, so I lock the door behind me and head home.

———

Phone calls in the middle of the night are never a good thing.

I wake up to my phone buzzing on my nightstand, Annie's naked body pressed up against mine.

I'm usually a pretty heavy sleeper—I haven't had trouble sleeping through the night since all the renovations started and how tired I am by the time my head hits the pillow—but, for some reason, the quiet buzzing of my phone pulled me from my deep sleep.

It takes a second for my eyes to adjust to the darkness. I reach for my phone and see it's just past one in the morning, and I have two missed calls from Caleb.

My mind begins to spin with why he would be calling me in the middle of the night, but I don't have much time to think about it because a third call from him comes in.

"Caleb?" I whisper into the phone, my voice groggy. "What's wrong?"

"It's Bennett."

———

Last time I was in a hospital, it was when Lennon was born. It was a happy, exciting night that ended with meeting my niece and seeing two of my best friends become parents.

Tonight isn't that.

And I don't think I ever want to be in a hospital ever again.

Hospitals are meant to save lives, even bring new lives into the world. They're meant to fix people and make them better.

But tonight, it's where the ambulance brought my brother so the doctors could declare him dead.

I feel Annie's arms around me as the doctors tell me and Caleb what happened to Bennett when he and his crew were responding to a house fire. She keeps me grounded as I hear that Bennett went back in, against orders, because a mother thought her young daughter was still inside.

I listen to Caleb's muffled cries next to me as the doctor tells us that the house collapsed with Bennett still inside, slowly dying of asphyxiation, external trauma, and third-degree burns. Jack tried to run in after him, but he was held back by members of their crew.

There was nothing the doctors could do to save my brother after the fire was put out and he was found buried under the debris.

My own tears finally fall when I hear that the daughter was never inside, that her brother got her out.

My knees go weak, and I collapse onto the ground, Annie not being able to hold my weight up as I feel my whole world crumble around me.

Bennett.

The brother who taught me that life doesn't have to be so serious all the time, that there's always a bright side of things, that going through life worried and afraid is no way to live.

The boy who didn't look at me differently when he learned we didn't have the same dad, the teenager who became more of a parent than my own parents ever did, the man who taught me—who *showed* me—what kind of man I wanted to be.

He's gone.

And the last conversation I had with him was about a stupid coffee bar.

I feel a set of arms pull me up and help me walk over to the chairs that line the waiting room we're in. I don't have to open my eyes or see through my tears to know it's Emmett. It's his silence I recognize as he holds onto me before setting me down in a chair.

Annie sits down beside me, and I let my body fall onto hers, my head falling into her lap. I feel her fingers tenderly graze the side of my face, wiping my tears and pushing my hair out of my eyes as my fists clench around her sweatshirt.

The familiar voices around me drown out as I cry into her lap.

CHAPTER 35

ANNIE

WHY DO such bad things happen to the world's greatest people?

Why would the universe take away Bennett for doing his job?

Why would the universe take Bennett away from Luke?

It isn't fair.

It isn't right.

It's been two days since we rushed to the hospital in the middle of the night, a devastating contrast compared to the last time we did when Drew went into labor.

Luke hasn't gotten out of bed since we got home from the hospital.

Emmett and Eddie helped me get him home, and the whole Lenny's crew met us at the hospital after Luke got the call from Caleb that Bennett was being rushed to the hospital. It wasn't until we got there that we found out he died in the ambulance.

There's no playbook, no guidelines, no "right" way to deal with this.

No way for me to know how to deal with the grief overpowering Luke's ability to function, the hurt and pain I would do anything to take away, the overwhelming hole in my chest that must only be a fraction of the one in Luke's.

And the worst part about it all, life just moves on.

Luke's life just fell apart, but everything around us is business as usual.

I still have to go to my rotation this morning after a weekend of feeling completely useless, balancing wanting to help Luke through this but also giving him the space to grieve however he needs to.

I offered to help Caleb with anything he needed, specifically the funeral arrangements. I want to help alleviate as much of the responsibilities and know that Mr. and Mrs. Owens would be relying on Caleb to handle it all.

Luke's shifts at Lenny's need to be covered, and there are still meetings and appointments with all the contractors for the coffee shop, scheduled deliveries, and meetings that need to be taken care of.

Eddie, Mia, Emmett, and Drew are helping where they can —Luke deserves to not have to worry about anything but what he's going through right now—but life doesn't slow down, not even for a second, not even when Luke's whole world has been turned upside down.

I've never been the most patient, or the most nurturing. Maybe it's because of the parents I grew up with not giving a single fuck about me. Or, maybe it's because I convinced myself that asking for help or needing something made people think I was more trouble than I was worth, and I expect everyone to have that same mentality.

I don't know how to help Luke. I don't know how to be what he needs.

But I'm not stopping until I figure it out.

I check the time on the clock on the stove, and I have ten minutes before I have to leave this morning. Mia is on her way to stay with Luke while I'm gone, our friends are all more than willing to be here in case Luke needs it, and to help us out with Rosie too.

I just don't want him to be alone.

I feel pressure build behind my eyes, remembering how it felt to have Luke's fist balling into my sweatshirt, his head in my lap, his tears wetting the leggings I was wearing in that cold, empty hospital waiting room.

I prayed to all the different Gods that I don't believe in to let me take his place, let me deal with the pain because he didn't deserve it. I wished for the doctors to come back and tell us that it was a mistake; that Bennett was fine, that he was asking to see his brothers.

I hoped, with everything I am, that it was all just a really bad dream.

Luke always liked to joke that we all have had a pretty shitty hand dealt to us—between the shooting at Drew's school, to a drunk driver killing Emmett's sister, to Mia's boyfriend's suicide, to Eddie beating his abusive, alcoholic father half-to-death, to my parents wishing I was never born —and he didn't have it half as rough. He laughed at his own expense, making light of his own hardships, saying he was lucky to have friends as strong as us because he's had it pretty easy.

It was his way of trying to see the bright side of things, always reminding us that we might have felt alone when all those things happened to each of us, but that we weren't alone anymore.

For how fucked up it is to say those horrible things brought us all together. It's the only way to look at all those shitty things and not lose sight of how beautiful life can be.

But that didn't mean Luke deserved *this*. He didn't deserve for something horrific to happen to him, just so he can overcome it and come out stronger, or whatever other bullshit people say to you when something terrible happens.

I feel a tear escape down my cheek, quickly wiping it

away as I throw together some things for lunch and pack up my backpack. I don't have time to be sad and curse the universe, not when Luke needs the space to do it.

Luke may not have been able to be there for all of us when it felt like things would never get better—when we were trapped in the grief, the trauma, the loss—but we're all here for him now, especially me.

I hear a knock on my door before the jingling of keys and the door opening. I gave both Mia and Eddie, and Drew and Emmett, keys to our apartment when they offered to be here for Luke in case he needed something—or someone—when I was at my rotations.

"Knock, knock," Mia whispers, softly closing the door behind her. Rosie hasn't left the floor next to Luke's side of the bed since we got home, so it feels even quieter in the house with no excited golden retriever to meet her at the door. "How are you doing, Ann?" she asks me as I open the fridge, pulling out an energy drink because it's quicker than making an iced matcha, and I still need the caffeine to get through today.

"I'm okay," I answer half-heartedly. It's not a lie. I am okay, dealing with the loss of Bennett in my own way, devastated about what happened but most of those feelings are wrapped up in what I feel for Luke and how he's feeling.

Closing the fridge, I find Mia on the other side. Her blonde hair is pulled up in a ponytail, and she's dressed in a matching hoodie and sweatpants set. It's early, not even 7 a.m., but she was willing to be here until Emmett could come later.

"It's okay if you're not, you know," Mia says to me, her eyes on mine.

I sigh. "I'm fine. I'm functioning. I'm just—" I pause, shaking my head, the tears from before she got here threatening to come back. "He doesn't deserve this." It comes out as more of a whisper.

"I know," she replies, taking the energy drink out of my hand and setting it down on the counter next to us. She grabs my hand in hers. "It's unfair, and it sucks, and I wish shitty things like this wouldn't happen to the people I love." Her hands squeeze around mine. "But he will get through this."

Mia pulls me in for a hug, and I let my tears fall as her arms hold me tight—she's giving me the space to fall apart, just like she promised, just like she did that day when we saw Devin in the grocery store.

"I know you're going to want to be strong for him, Annie," she whispers into my hair, "and I know if it were Eddie, I would do the exact same." Her hands find my shoulder, pulling me back, so she can look me in the eyes. "But you can't be someone's strength when you're at your weakest. Remember, we are all here to help."

I shake my head slightly, turning to look at the clock behind me and seeing that I have to leave, or I'll be late to my rotation.

I feel myself wanting to tell her that I don't need all the help, or that I won't for much longer. I want to tell her that I got this. I can do this. I can manage both my and Luke's responsibilities, so he has time to process and heal.

But instead, I tell her, "I have to go." I throw my backpack over my shoulder, walking over to the door to put on my shoes. "I don't know if he'll get up at all today, but text me if he does."

Mia nods along as I fill her in on how he hasn't eaten or drank much, but I make sure he has both water and some sort of snack on his nightstand in case he does. "He's mostly been asleep the past 48 hours, but I don't know how much rest he's actually getting."

"Don't worry, I got him," Mia says, before I head out the door.

CHAPTER 36
LUKE

WHEN I WAKE UP, there's a minute when I feel like everything is normal.

It's a minute where everything is okay and how it's supposed to be.

Bennett is happy and healthy; he's doing what he loves; he's *alive*.

Then, it all comes rushing back—I remember that my brother is dead.

Maybe that's why I'm sleeping so much. Chasing that minute of blissful ignorance every chance I get, anything to make this pain that is wracking my body subside, even if it's just a moment.

For a moment, I can forget the look on Caleb's face when the doctor told us Bennett was dead. I can forget the sound of his muffled cries while he tried to hold back the tears, or the feeling of loss so tangible I had to look down to make sure I wasn't just shot through the chest.

But then it registers that it wasn't just a bad dream.

Something woke me up this morning, but I couldn't bring myself to care—maybe it was the door opening or closing, someone coming or going.

I don't care.

I don't want to get up to check—I don't even want to open my eyes because even that feels like a daunting task.

I lost Bennett forty-eight hours ago, and the pain worsens with every hour that goes by.

I don't know how people get through this. I don't know how people find the strength to overpower their grief—it's scary how tempting it is to let it win because at least I wouldn't feel like this anymore and maybe I'd see my brother again.

I need another minute. Another minute where this all goes away.

And that's the last thought I have before I drift back to sleep.

———

"Are you sure you're okay?" I ask Bennett. We're on our way to the end-of-season banquet with the rest of my hockey team and their families—most have their parents as their guests, but I have my brothers and Annie to support me. Caleb had to work, so he's meeting us there, and Annie had an after-school rehearsal for the spring musical, so she's already at the school waiting for us.

"Why wouldn't I be?" Bennett answers, glancing at me from the driver's seat. He's only five years older than me, and sometimes the age gap doesn't feel that big, but on days like today, it feels like there are way more years between us.

"Because Dad basically disowned you last night," I answer, the collar on my dress shirt feeling tighter the more I think about the fighting between the two of them last night. They were downstairs in my father's office, but I could hear the screaming from my bedroom upstairs.

Between my dad's insults to Bennett's intelligence, to calling him lazy and ungrateful, to belittling his choice to give up law school and become a firefighter, I could hear it all.

"You're already in your first year of law school, why not just finish?"

We pull into the parking lot of my high school; Bennett pulls into a spot and cuts the engine. "It's not what I want to do."

"But Dad said—"

"Luke." His voice makes the rest of my words get caught in my throat. Bennett turns to me, and the serious expression on his face looks weird on him. Bennett is always smiling, always laughing, always looking on the bright side.

He doesn't look like my brother right now.

"Being a lawyer, that's what Dad and Caleb want. Me? It sounds like the worst possible job in the world. I'm not about to waste any more time doing something I don't want to do. Life is too short."

"But," I start. I hear the words he's saying, but I can't make them make sense to me. I can't imagine being in Bennett's position, going against our father, giving up the path and privilege he was given with law school and the position waiting for him at the family's firm.

"But nothing," Bennett says before I can say more. "Life isn't about doing what everyone wants you to."

"Then what is it about?" I challenge, anger simmering under my skin. It's being directed at Bennett, but it's not him I'm mad at. I'm mad for him. Mad that he is the greatest brother—greatest person—in the world, yet our dad doesn't seem to see it.

Bennett exhales. "I don't know. But what I do know is, we all deserve to chase after the things we want and let go of anything—or anyone—who holds us back from that."

His words catch me off-guard, but I'm not sure what I was expecting him to say in the first place.

Do I even know what I want?

I know I want to go to college and play hockey, and I get to with my scholarship. I know I want Annie by my side, my brothers cheering me on. I want to prove to my dad that I'm a son he can be proud of, and I want to be happy.

A few moments pass, the silence stretching in the car. I see my friends and their parents walking into the cafeteria entrance, but I'm in no rush to join them. I look at my brother and find his blue eyes, identical to mine, and some of my frustration subsides. "Are you sure you're okay?" I ask my brother.

I watch as that serious expression of his fades, a wide grin taking its place. A grin that shows all his teeth, making the skin near his eyes crinkle, accentuating the shine in them.

"I'm more than okay," he answers. "I know being a firefighter isn't as cool as being a hotshot hockey player," he lightly punches me in the arm, trying to make me smile, "and if Dad doesn't want to support me, I don't need him in my life."

I want Bennett to do what he wants, but if Bennett doesn't follow Dad's path, who will?

I'm the only one left.

I have so many thoughts and emotions swirling around in my brain, and I don't know if I'll ever get them all straight. Bennett deserves to be happy, but what about my dad? Caleb? Who's going to fill Bennett's spot? Junior year is almost over, and I have yet to decide what I want to major in. The scholarship allows me to choose, and I can play hockey as long as I keep my grades up. I thought I'd have all of senior year to decide, but maybe if my dad's path for Bennett didn't work for him . . .

I don't finish the thought because my brother digs his elbow into my arm, bringing me back into the moment. "Someone's waiting for you," he says, a small note of teasing in the way he sing-songs it.

I glance out the window to see Annie waiting outside the cafeteria doors, her brown hair pulled back in a ponytail, the familiar red sundress she wears for any formal event making my breath catch as if I haven't seen her wear it a dozen times.

"Shut up," I mumble to my brother. Even though I've known Annie for most of my life, we've only been officially dating for almost three years, and Bennett still gets a kick out of teasing me about it.

I reach to open the passenger side door, not wanting Annie to keep waiting outside alone, but I freeze when I hear my brother ask, "What would you do if someone told you that you were making a mistake with Annie?" I turn to look at him, confused why he would even be asking that.

Annie isn't a mistake.

If anything, she's the only thing I've ever gotten right.

Bennett continues, "That being with her was the wrong choice, or that there was someone better out there for you? What would you do?"

"I'd tell them to fuck off," I answer quickly, my eyes going back to Annie. She's looking around for me, constantly stepping out of the way of the people still filing in now that the banquet starts in less than five minutes.

"Exactly," Bennett replies as he opens his door.

Realization hits me. His words about life and chasing after what we want no matter what others say sink in. It all makes sense; why he quit law school, why he doesn't care about the horrible things Dad said to him, why he is doing what he wants anyway.

I want to tell him that I get it, that I understand, that I'm not some naive 17-year-old who can't wrap my head around going against our father.

I want him to stay in the car, to say more, to tell me—no, teach me—how to be just like him.

I want to tell him that he's already taught me so much, and I need him to stick around forever so I never know what life is like without him.

I need to tell him I am so proud to be his brother.

But I can't.

Because one second he's there, and the next he's gone.

And I'm staring at my bedroom ceiling.

———

It's been a week since Bennett died.

And today is his funeral.

It's the first time I'll be leaving my apartment since we got home from the hospital.

The past seven days have been a blur, for more reasons than one.

I crave the moment of bliss when I wake up, but it's been harder and harder to fall asleep, let alone stay asleep. The nightmares started a few days ago, so I'm constantly trying to decide between the lesser of two evils—staying awake and living with the loss of my brother, or falling asleep and reliving the moment I found out he died.

Either way, it got me out of bed, the need to do something to distract myself from being too strong.

When Annie is gone at rotations during the day, Eddie, Emmett, Mia, or Drew are here. Mia scared the shit out of me when I walked out of the bedroom and found her on the couch. It was the first time I got out of bed since Eddie and Emmett carried me there.

We didn't say anything to each other—she didn't try to ask me how I was doing or tell me how everything was going to be okay. She just kept watching TV, even as I brushed my teeth and showered—Rosie never leaving my side.

Even when I went to my bedroom to get dressed and chugged the cold water that was on my nightstand. Even when I scarfed down the granola bar that was there next to my water bottle, and the rest of the box of them in the kitchen.

Not even when I opened the cabinet above my fridge, the bottle of whiskey looking like it could solve all of my problems.

Not even when I turned around to see if she was watching me, and our eyes met.

She didn't say anything as she patted the spot next to her on the couch with a knowing look on her face—free of judgment but full of concern—and I closed the cabinet and sat down next to her, empty-handed, Rosie laying at our feet.

Mia didn't say a word as I wiped the tears forming in my eyes—she just reached out and grabbed my arm, giving it a squeeze, reminding me that she was there.

Emmett stopped by at one point that day with some pre-made meals Drew made—our afternoon and evening together being the same as my morning with Mia—and Mia left shortly after he arrived. I quickly caught on to the fact that Annie probably didn't want me to be alone.

And rightfully so.

I don't want to know what I would've let myself do if I was alone when I woke up that Monday morning, but I'm grateful to Annie and my friends that I wasn't.

When Annie got home that night, Emmett left, but I couldn't bring myself to say anything to her. I felt like I should voice these feelings—say them out loud—but it felt too intimidating, too difficult, too impossible, to form the words.

But just like Mia and Emmett, Annie didn't push me. She just set down her things and walked over to the couch, pulling herself into my lap and held me tightly, somehow knowing exactly what I needed.

The next few days looked the same—I was able to get out of bed, and that in itself was a feat. Every day, it took all I had to push the comforter off and swing my legs over the edge. It took all my energy to push myself up and stand.

But it was slightly easier knowing that my friends and my Annie girl never expected more from me.

And I didn't expect more from myself.

Until today.

Because today is the day we bury my brother, and I will not be missing that.

I still can't fully wrap my head around the fact Bennett is gone, half-expecting to get a text or call from him, laughing and full of life like I'll always remember him, but the funeral makes it so real.

I've always prided myself on being able to always look at the bright side, something Bennett taught me, but I've been struggling to find it here. There's no bright side to the world losing someone like Bennett, no silver lining in his life ending right before he could live out his thirties, doing what he wanted, finding love, spending time with the people who cared about him most.

"Ready to go?" I hear Annie say from the kitchen.

"Almost," I croak out, my voice still sounding foreign in my ears after saying maybe a dozen words in the last seven days. I straighten my tie, giving myself a once-over in the bathroom mirror.

My face is pale, my cheekbones a little sunken in, and I look about as good as I feel, which is about as shitty as you can get. The dark circles under my eyes give away how little sleep I've gotten the past five days, and I just hope I can hold myself together long enough to get through the day.

"Drew, Emmett, Lennon, Mia, and Eddie will meet us there," Annie says, peeking her head into the bathroom. She doesn't say where "there" is, but we both know it's the gravesite where Bennett will be buried.

She helped Caleb plan the funeral—my parents weren't even willing to help. Losing Bennett wasn't a priority in their lives, not since their commitment to disown him all those years ago—and it was another way she lets me lean on her in this process. I plan on thanking her when I finally get myself to sit down and voice all these thoughts and feelings I'm having.

We're skipping what most people do at a ceremony—the welcomes, introductions, prayers, and readings—and keeping it small with the burial and a eulogy from Caleb and Bennett's best friend. Both Caleb and I agreed we didn't want to do an open casket, wanting to remember Bennett how we last saw him, not what he looked like in his last moments.

"The celebration of life afterward will be at Lenny's, but

we don't have to go if you don't want to. It'll be us, your brother, Jack, and the crew from the fire station."

"No," I say quickly, "I want to go. Bennett's life deserves a celebration."

Annie nods, and for the first time all week, I take a second to take her all in.

Her black dress wraps around her body, half of her hair pulled back in a little black bow, the shorter pieces in front framing her face.

She's beautiful, breathtakingly so, but she looks so tired.

I've barely seen her this week, only when she gets home on time from her rotations, but there have been two or three nights where she texts that she'll be home late. I figured it was to do her charting and typing up reports she didn't have time to do during the busy day.

"Hey, honey," I whisper, reaching out and grazing my thumb against her cheek. "Are you okay?"

She exhales. "I'm supposed to be the one asking *you* that."

"You look tired."

She shakes her head, and I drop my hand back down to my side. "It's been a busy week, but I'm fine. Are *you* okay?"

"No," I answer quickly, and she closes the space between us and wraps her arms around my waist. I rest my chin on the top of her head, inhaling her jasmine and rose scent.

"That's okay," she says against my chest. "I'll be okay for the both of us."

CHAPTER 37
LUKE

HATE IS A STRONG WORD. One I don't use often.

I hate soggy cereal and too much cream cheese on my bagel.

I hate when people take too long in self-checkout lines at the grocery store, and when people don't use their turn signal.

But that's about it.

Or at least I thought that was it.

After today, I can officially say that I hate my father.

I don't know what would have made me hate him more, him *not* coming to Bennett's funeral or him coming and leaving during Jack's eulogy for a phone call and not coming back until Caleb was finishing up his closing one.

Not to mention giving me nothing but three seconds of eye contact the whole time we've been here.

Was I naive to think that this would be a family reunion where my father tearfully shared his regrets about his relationship with his late son? No.

But I at least thought he'd give enough of a fuck to be present during his fucking burial.

Maybe it's the anger I have at the fact Bennett is gone and

my father hasn't expressed any interest in him since dropping out of law school—even when he fucking *died*—or maybe it's the pure rage I have about Bennett being gone in the first place.

Either way, when my father saunters over to join the small pockets of friends, family, and the crew from the fire station—his grayish, blonde hair styled neatly, his eyes free of any emotion, his suit pressed and proper, looking like he's going to some work event rather than his son's funeral—he has no time to prepare for when my fist meets his jaw.

"What the fuck is your problem?!" I yell to my dad, feeling two sets of arms—presumably Eddie and Emmett—grab me from behind.

My dad was knocked a few steps back, but didn't fall to the ground. His lip is bleeding as he cups his jaw with his hand, and he's staring at me, his face tightened with anger, but he doesn't say a word.

I can't ignore the satisfaction of seeing the blood drip onto his perfect suit.

"You don't even have the decency to decline a goddamn phone call at your son's funeral?" I shout, everyone's eyes on us.

My mom rushes up to my dad, putting on a show for everyone here, as if she cares if he's bleeding or not. We all know she won't bother to show that fake concern to me.

She couldn't even shed a tear when one of her sons was being lowered into the fucking ground—her black dress is a stark contrast to her bleach blonde hair, her overall appearance looking way too put together to convince anyone she's a grieving mother.

"Bennett deserved so much better than you! Both of you!" I scream at them, ripping my arms from Eddie and Emmett's grip, walking up to the both of them until I'm only a foot away. Even though I'm inches taller than them, they still look down on me, their faces filled with contempt.

A moment passes and neither of them say a word, they stare at me as if I'm not even worth the words, waiting for my outburst to be over.

I point my finger at them. "How dare you come here and act like you gave a shit about him. You couldn't even *pretend* to care about him long enough to make it look real!" I spit, and my face feels warm and wet, despite the cold November air. I point towards the parking lot, feeling a familiar presence come up to my side, her arms wrapping around my arm at my side. "Leave," I seethe at the both of them, "you don't deserve to be here."

I have to clench my fists as my dad's eyes move from mine to Annie's beside me, and neither he nor my mother makes a move to leave.

My father looks at Annie as if it's her job to deal with me, "Looks like my *son* here," he says the word "son" as if there should be air quotes around the word, "needs someone to remind him that this day is not about him." Annie's grip on my arm tightens, stopping me from throwing another punch.

"You heard Luke," she says to my dad, her voice as cold as ice. I turn to look at her, her cheeks pink from the cold air, making her red lips look even redder. Out of the corner of my eye, I see Emmett and Eddie step up behind us—mostly behind Annie—Drew and Mia at their sides. "It's time for you two to leave."

I watch as my dad's eyes slightly widen, something about Annie's words or her expression—or the two very big men standing behind her—have him taken aback. My mom looks up at my dad, confused why he isn't saying anything, and then looks back at Annie. I watch as the wheels in her head turn, ready to say something to her, most likely for taking my side, but I chime in before she can.

"I'd be very careful with what you're about to say, *Mom*." My turn to use the air quotes. Even if she's the biological parent out of the two, she's no better than her husband.

"Let's go," my dad says to my mom, his eyes meeting mine one more time before he turns and heads to the parking lot, my mom a few steps behind him.

I exhale a breath I didn't even know I was holding, wincing when I run my hand through my hair as I turn to Annie. My hand will have a slight bruise to it tomorrow, but I don't care.

"If you didn't do it, I would've," Annie says, the heels she's wearing makes it easy for her to lean up and press a kiss to my lips.

"Her punch would've hurt too," Mia says from behind her, "because I'm the one who taught her."

I laugh for the first time in days, and it feels good. So good that I can't stop. I laugh and laugh until Annie and our friends join in, until my stomach cramps, until there are tears running from my eyes, until I wish Bennett was next to me laughing too.

It fades, and I don't think anything was that funny to begin with. "I can't believe he's gone," I say, the tears coming down a little harder.

"Me either," a voice from behind me says, and I turn around to find Caleb walking up to me, Jack at his side. Both their eyes glistening, sad smiles on their faces. Caleb claps a hand on my shoulder. "I also can't believe you just punched Dad in the face."

I offer him a small smile, shrugging my shoulders.

"He had it coming," Jack adds, knowing all too well how my dad treated Bennett.

"A long time coming," my brother echoes, pulling me in for a hug, surrounded by Jack and my friends, as we cry together next to Bennett's headstone.

CHAPTER 38

ANNIE

I'M RUNNING out of steam.

What was it that Mia said? You can't be someone's strength when you're at your weakest?

Technically, you can. I just highly recommend against it.

It's been two weeks since Bennett's funeral, and Luke is doing the best he can, as well as you can after losing your brother and punching your dad in the face at a funeral.

He's been seeing a therapist, but the grief comes in waves. Some days, Luke seems okay, good even, but other days, he struggles to do anything but log in to his online therapy session or even get out of bed.

I knew this would happen, and I know it's normal.

The reality of Bennett being gone will never get easier, and it's a battle in itself to learn how to manage all the feelings that come with it, and I'm supporting Luke the best I can.

I just don't know how much longer I can do this.

Don't get me wrong. I will go to the ends of this fucking Earth to make sure Luke has what he needs during this difficult time. I will make sure he feels seen, valued, loved, and that he knows he is deserving of anything he needs to heal.

But I don't know how much longer I can balance rotations,

his Lenny's shifts, and preparing his coffee shop for the soft opening in two weeks.

Luckily, he only has three bartending shifts a week, but the still-unnamed coffee shop is set to have its soft opening the first week of December, and we are in the 10-day countdown.

I assured Luke that I would handle everything until he was ready to take it all on again. It took some convincing, but I wasn't going to take no for an answer.

I didn't want him to feel rushed to jump back into work before he was ready or feel overwhelmed with everything to do when he finally did.

Emmett doesn't know I'm taking Luke's shifts because I didn't add my name to the schedule, so he thinks Ava, Mickey, and Cyrus are. I'm hoping nobody thinks too much about it, and that I don't fuck up payroll too badly—the extra money from the shifts would be nice, but the tips are good enough.

I know Emmett would offer to take them if he knew—but they are small eight-to-midnight weekday shifts that I could do in my sleep, and it's not like I have a three-month baby to take care of when I get home like he does.

It just so happens that I'm not getting a ton of that sleep with how early I have to be at rotations the next morning.

I'm finishing up a shift at Lenny's now—these weeknight shifts usually just need one bartender because they aren't too busy—and I need to run next door to make sure a few decor pieces we ordered were delivered and put them inside.

I'm wiping down the bar, waiting for the last couple left to finish their drinks and leave so I can close for the night when my mind starts drifting from all the things I have to get done, all the things I have to do, to the memory that reminds me why I'm doing all of this in the first place.

———

"Who knew watching paint dry could be even more boring than they say," I quip to the boys as I finish some charting from my rotation this afternoon that I brought home with me. I'm at the coffee shop, keeping Luke, Bennett, and Jack company while they paint the new drywall that went up earlier this week.

"Keep talking, and we'll see how good this color looks when you're covered in it," Luke jokes as he runs the roller covered in the pastel blue color, Bennett and Jack chuckling as they work on the walls on either side of him.

"You know, all this watching is making me hungry," I add, not being able to get the scent of the pizza place a few doors down out of my head, my stomach growling just thinking about it.

Luke turns to me and tosses the roller into the tray of paint; a few splotches dot his face, making his eyes look even more blue.

"One pepperoni pizza, coming up," he announces as he walks over to the table I'm sitting at, leaning down to press a kiss to my lips. "What do you guys want?" Luke asks over his shoulder, Bennett and Jack tossing their paint brushes down on the plastic covering the floor and walking over to us.

"I'll come with you," Jack answers, before looking at Bennett.

"I'll keep Annie company," Bennett adds, sitting down at the table in front of me.

Bennett and I grew up side-by-side, but I wouldn't say we grew up together. Him and Jack were always around when I'd be at the Owens' house, but he was five, almost six, years older than us, so I wouldn't see him at school past fifth grade, and I was too shy to ever hold a conversation with anyone besides Luke.

"Lucky me," I say with a smile, closing my laptop and gathering up all my things to put in my backpack sitting at my feet.

Jack and Luke head over to the pizza place, and Bennett asks me about rotations. I tell him about how they work and what the day-to-day looks like. I ask him about being a firefighter and he fills me in on how it isn't much like the TV shows or movies, but he still loves it.

"I'm glad you and Luke decided to go your own paths, rather than your dad's."

"Me too," he says, his smile slowly fading, his face so similar to Luke's yet so different. "Can you promise me something?"

I'm caught off-guard by the seriousness of his tone, not sure what he could possibly need from me, but I find myself nodding.

"Promise me you'll take care of my brother?"

Emotion clogs my throat, and I don't know why. This conversation feels heavy and loaded, and I can't think of a reason for it.

Either way, I answer with my entire heart. "Of course."

Bennett gives me a small smile, reaching out and placing his hand on my arm. "No matter what?" he questions, giving my arm a small squeeze.

I want to tell him that being loved by Luke is something I will never again take for granted, that taking care of Luke feels like the most natural thing for me to do, that I will spend the rest of my life making sure Luke always has someone in his corner, forever reminding him of the phenomenal human being he is.

And, even though I don't say the words, I think Bennett hears them anyway when I promise, "No matter what."

Looking back, maybe Bennett somehow knew his fate or what the future held for him. Or, maybe he didn't, and he wanted to make sure Luke was loved as much as he deserved to be.

I don't think I'll ever know the true reason Bennett felt the need to talk to me that night, but it makes me hold my promise to him even closer to my heart.

"What the hell are you doing here?" I hear Drew's voice echo through the near-empty bar. I was too trapped in my thoughts to hear the front door open or register the rush of cool air from outside. Drew has on pajama pants under her black winter coat, this year's November being much colder than past years.

"How long have you been working shifts here?" Mia's

voice chimes in, her hands on her hips as she sports her own pajama pants under her pink puffer jacket. "You know either of us," she says gesturing between herself and Drew as they walk up to the bar, the couple who was here finally finishing their drinks and heading out, "would have taken Luke's shifts."

The memory of Bennett rushes back to the back of my mind, not at all forgotten but back to being tucked away where I can keep it safe.

I haven't seen either of my best friends, let alone Emmett and Eddie, since Bennett's funeral, this month being way too busy to have our usual happy hours or movie nights.

We also couldn't do this month's Sunday Dinner because that was the weekend we got the call about Bennett.

"It's no big deal," I answer, but the last word comes out as a yawn, one so big I have to cover my mouth with my hand.

"Does Luke know you're working his shifts?" Drew asks, her hands on her hips.

I shake my head and feel the tips of my ears heat, as if she caught me with my hands in my pants. "I don't need his permission," I defy.

"Duh, we know that," Mia retorts, rolling her eyes, reminding me of me. "But we know he doesn't expect you to. I mean, come on, Ann, I knew you were picking up the slack with No Name next door," she says referring to the coffee shop, "but that is already a lot with your rotations. This," she gestures around the bar with her arms, "is too much."

"I said I can handle it."

Drew lets out a groan in frustration, running a hand through her red wine hair, flipping it to one side. "We know that, Annie. We know you *can* handle it, but have you learned *nothing*?"

I raise an eyebrow at her, looking back and forth between her and Mia.

Drew rolls her eyes, and I guess my antics have rubbed off

on both my best friends. "When are you going to learn that you can ask for help?"

I shake my head. "That's not what this is. I know I can ask you guys for help, but—" I stop mid-sentence, my mind going blank, not being able to come up with an excuse.

"I will tattoo 'Annie, you are not a burden' on my forehead if that's what it takes for you not to run yourself into the ground to avoid asking us for help," Mia says, leaning against the bar and staring right in my eyes, her blonde hair in a messy bun and her brown eyes on full display. "And what did I say about being strong for someone when you're at your weakest?"

"I don't know what you're talking about," I rush out, and my two best friends try to hide the smiles on their faces, knowing that's what I say when I'm trying to avoid the question.

"Say it with us, Ann," Drew starts, "'I am not a burden.'"

"No, I'm not saying that."

"Say it," Mia reprimands, slapping her hands on the bar.

"No, this is stupid. I'm sorry I didn't ask you guys for help, I'll nev—"

"Say it!" they both exclaim, and this time it's my turn to roll my eyes.

I exhale. "I am not a burden."

"Again," Drew says, with a little nod of her head.

"I am not a burden."

"Louder," Mia adds.

"I am not a burden!"

Mia and Drew look at each other and smile, quickly rounding the bar, coming up to me, and pulling me into a group hug. Feeling their arms around me was everything I didn't know I needed, the comfort I didn't know I was longing for, the reminder that I don't have to do this all alone.

"Wait," I say, pulling away from the two. "Why were you guys looking for me at midnight anyway?"

"Oh, I called a 911, and you didn't respond in the group chat," Mia says matter-of-factly, as if it is a perfectly reasonable answer to my question.

I don't know exactly when "calling a 911" started for the three of us, maybe around the time Drew and Emmett got married, but it became our way of saying "I need you to drop everything and find me" and it can't wait. It could be an emergency, big or small, or just a moment where we need each other, for both good and bad things.

I just hope Mia will be sharing good news tonight because I don't know how much more bad news I can take.

"But we got caught up in finding you for the past half an hour, so after going to your place and finding Luke fast asleep *alone*, we knew there were only a few places you could be," Drew adds.

"We thought you were going to be next-door, but when the door was locked, we were going to go back to Emmett's office and grab the extra key. Instead, we found you here, rather than of one of the three bartenders who *actually* work here," Mia concludes.

I let out a dry chuckle before asking, "So what's the 911?" Both Drew and I look at Mia, Drew not knowing her reasoning for calling the 911 either.

"Oh, I'm pregnant."

A moment of silence passes before Drew and I look at each other and then back at Mia who's wearing a small smile, as if she didn't just drop a total bomb.

"WHAT?!" Drew and I exclaim, pulling Mia back into a hug.

"Mia, oh my god!" I exclaim, pulling back to hold her face between my hands. "I'm so happy for you!"

"Me too!" Drew adds, her eyes glistening. "How far along are you?"

"Twelve weeks, as of midnight tonight. Everyone always says to wait at least twelve weeks or whatever, but I couldn't wait more than that. We found out at the end of September. I wasn't sure if it would be the right time to tell you guys, and I know things have been crazy with everything going on—"

"No, I'm so glad you told us," I stop her before she can even think about apologizing for sharing such amazing news, a tear escaping down my cheek. I also can't hide my grin at the fact she had to tell us at twelve weeks *exactly*.

I needed this.

Not just this amazing news or seeing my best friends after two weeks of running on empty, but I needed the reminder that I can ask for help, and that I don't have to do it all alone.

And if I want to be there for Luke, I need to make sure I'm strong enough to be his strength right now.

CHAPTER 39
LUKE

I THINK I'm finally ready to go back to work.

Kind of.

Maybe.

I don't know.

I've had the thought more times than I can count since the day after Bennett's funeral three weeks ago, especially since the soft opening for the coffee shop I still have yet to name is supposed to be in 72 hours.

I'm not letting myself spiral about it today though. Instead, I'm in my car, driving to Lenny's, ready to tell Emmett I can take my shifts back from Ava, Mickey, or Cyrus —whoever has been taking them—and take a look at the progress the Lenny's crew has put in at the coffee shop.

I don't know how I'll thank them all for picking up my slack. The coffee shop was supposed to be mine, my project, my responsibility, my *something* to be proud of.

But I would also be delusional to think that I could do it all alone, especially now.

I turn into the parking lot at Lenny's, sending a quick text to Annie that I'll most likely be here when she gets home from her rotation.

I've dropped the ball on supporting her through this tough year, and it can't be easy for her to also be putting in some of her free time to tend to the coffee shop. I plan on digging myself out of this hole Bennett's death threw me into and making sure she knows how thankful I am for her.

I've been a shell since coming home from the hospital. Sometimes I feel like a version of myself, and other times feeling I don't even recognize myself.

Annie has been patient with me, and therapy has helped. More than I thought it would.

Dealing with the loss of a loved one is something so many people experience—and I thought, for some reason, there would be more answers to how you recover from it. I know it sounds silly, but I thought my therapist would give me ten steps to follow, and I'd be cured of my grief.

What I've actually learned is there is nothing special, no specific way to cope.

You just do it.

It sounds cliché, but I've found the only way is to just keep living, keeping up with the life around you that doesn't slow down, and putting one foot in front of the other.

I've always heard people say time heals, but it doesn't, not really.

And I know life will be good again, but it'll be in a different way.

A way without my brother.

I knew life could be cruel. I saw it with the people I love the most—and lately it's felt like life takes everything away but the pain.

Annie has helped too.

No.

She saved my life.

It might sound dramatic or silly, but I wouldn't be getting through this without her.

I would have been drunk or high off my ass—looking for

solace in alcohol, drugs, or sleeping pills, anything to help me forget—if I didn't have her to remind me that life goes on.

She's never once rushed me, never once told me what she thinks I needed to do, or made me feel like I was wrong in the way I chose to heal.

Instead, she let me lean on her completely, reminding me how strong she is.

When I have been a mess, a train wreck, she's been here to clean it up.

"I can do this," I say to myself. The thought of walking into Lenny's isn't feeling as scary as it did a week ago. "I can do this," I repeat a little louder, gripping my steering wheel until I feel a pain in my wrist.

I shake my head, my blonde hair whipping against my cheek, reminding me I am in desperate need of a haircut. I spot one of Annie's hair ties in one of the cup holders in my center console, deciding to use it to pull half of my hair back in a small bun, just to keep it out of my face.

Rubbing my sweaty palms on my jean-cladded thighs, I take in a deep breath and let out a long one, just like my therapist says I should do when I start to feel like the walls are closing in around me. Like the only place I can escape the pressure is in the darkness of my bedroom.

"I can do this," I whisper one more time before opening the driver's side door.

I step out, still not used to the crisp air.

I've left our apartment maybe twice since Bennett's funeral, but time has flown by and suddenly it's the first day of December. It feels like yesterday Caleb called me in the middle of the night.

I shake the thought away, needing to keep my head on straight if I want to do this. If I want to keep up with life around me, if I want to put one foot in front of the other—just like Bennett would want me to do.

Caleb didn't have a choice but to keep moving, having to

go back to work with my dad who carried on business as usual, no surprises there.

And that makes sense for Caleb.

He needed to throw himself back into work, get his mind off of it, like those sharks who need to keep moving or else they'll suffocate.

He calls at least once a week, just like he did before Bennett died, and the conversation is always the same—he asks how I'm doing, and I say I'm fine. I ask him how he's doing and he says he's okay. We both know we're lying to each other, but we both know saying anything else will hurt more.

Jack was given time off from work, deciding to take a leave of absence and spend time at his family's cabin in a small town a few hours north. He drove up there the night of the funeral, stopping at Lenny's for a beer and then packing up and leaving. He checks in with a text or two here and there, but he needs space.

I lost my brother; he lost his best friend.

I reach out to pull the door to Lenny's open. The sun is about to set, the late-afternoon sunset catching me off-guard for a moment before remembering the long summer nights are long gone.

"Luke," I hear when the door shuts behind me. A familiar gruff voice I'd recognize anywhere. Emmett's long dark hair is pulled back in its usual topknot, dressed in one of his hundreds of black hoodies with the sleeves pulled up to expose his tatted skin.

"Emmett," I echo, going to run a hand through my hair but remembering it's pulled back in a hair tie. "I'm ready to get back to work. I'm grateful to you and the other bartenders for taking my shifts, but I'm ready to come back."

Emmett doesn't say anything, just slightly narrows his eyes and crosses his arms.

A few booths and high top tables are occupied, only one

bartender needed for the week night shifts. My shifts were the night ones, Tuesdays through Thursdays, and I'm lucky Emmett hired our three bartenders at the end of the summer; otherwise, I don't know how we would've kept this place open with just the two of us.

"I haven't been covering your shifts," he grumbles.

"Okay," I answer, "I'll be sure to thank Ava and the guys when I see them."

"You have Annie to thank," he replies, and my mouth forms a small O-shape in surprise.

Annie been covering my shifts?

There's no way Emmett would've let her do that.

I wouldn't have let her do that.

If I knew.

I think back to a conversation I had with her a few days after the funeral, her offering to coordinate all the final inspections, deliveries, and contractors at the coffee shop during the weeks leading up to the opening.

I hate that it's all a blur.

I hate that the last four weeks have been a blur.

"No, I– I didn't—" I sputter out.

"She's been handling everything next door too, barely letting us help out beside that fucking coffee bar."

"What?" I exhale, and I feel like the wind was knocked out of me. "She didn't have to do that."

"No shit," he growls, but he seems madder at Annie than he does at me. "Drew told me she found her here one night last week, so I started taking your shifts. Also said that she's been next door with any free time she has, only letting the girls help with the social media shit and decorating. I swear, that girl needs her fucking rest during these rotations, not spreading herself so thin she'll snap in half."

I nod my head, processing his words.

Honestly, I couldn't tell you what Annie's been up to the

past month. I've just assumed she was busy with her rotations and sharing the responsibilities of the coffee shop with the rest of our friends.

We've barely spent time together, talked to one another; we haven't laughed or smiled together in weeks.

I haven't even thanked her, held her, *kissed* her.

Why the hell haven't I kissed her?

I look up to find Emmett looking at me, but it's not a look I'm used to. I thought he'd give me one of his looks that makes me feel like I've disappointed a father figure, which I very well deserve after letting Annie run herself into the ground, but I've never seen *this* look before.

There's a semblance of understanding, of sadness, and it makes my eyes water.

"Why don't you have a seat?" he says slowly, nodding his head to the chair in front of him at the bar, so I pull out the chair and take a seat. "I'm not going to ask how you're doing or if you're okay because we both know you'll lie and say you're fine," he starts.

I'm not used to him talking this much without Drew around.

When I don't say anything, he continues. "I know what it's like to lose a sibling, and I'm not telling you this to take away whatever you're feeling about Bennett. Me losing my sister isn't the same as you losing your brother; I know that. But, what I also know is how the emotions that come with losing someone you love are confusing and painful as fuck."

I nod my head, though my throat feels dry and pressure continues to build behind my eyes.

"There's the sadness and anger about it being them instead of you, about them not deserving what happened to them. There's the guilt that comes with that too, along with the guilt that comes with the time you need to grieve."

It's like he's taking all the thoughts I've had spinning

around in my head for weeks and laying them all out in front of me, making them feel manageable.

I've talked about all of this in therapy, but this feels more personal, more real, more raw. It's different coming from a friend who has been through it.

Emmett continues. "My therapist once told me to think of my grief about losing Lennon as a balloon inside a box with a button. The balloon will change in size depending on the day, sometimes hitting that button, and sometimes not. That button is my grief—sometimes it's being pressed over and over again, and the day feels impossible to get through. Sometimes, the balloon never touches it."

The visual hits me right in the chest, helping me understand this overwhelming grief that seems to have a chokehold on me. Picturing it this way doesn't make it go away, but it makes it less scary.

"And I'm not going to give you that bullshit of 'time heals all wounds' or whatever the saying is," Emmett adds, his tone of distaste over the expression making me laugh despite the seriousness of this conversation. "But you reach a point where thinking of them hurts a little less than it did before."

"I thought time healed every wound until I lost him," I say, swiping my fingers across my cheek where a tear ran loose. "It's like time just makes you forget, but I don't want to forget him."

Emmett nods his head. "Lennon died when I was 18, and I'm at the point where I've almost lived more of my life without her than with her, and I can't tell you that it gets easier." A sad smile forms on Emmett's face. "I do what I can to honor her. This place and my daughter are things I wish I could've shared with her, but I try to tell myself she's still here, just differently."

More words I didn't know I needed to hear.

"Bennett's birthday is December 14th, about two weeks

from today." It may seem like a random thought to share in the midst of this conversation, but Emmett seems to know exactly why I said it.

He gives me a smile I've only seen directed at Lenny or Drew. One that makes me smile too. "Looks like you have two weeks to finish the place up," he says, and I'm out of the chair and heading towards the door, pausing before pushing it open.

Turning around to look back at my friend. "Thanks, Emmett," I say, and he gives me a small nod.

Emmett's right. I have two weeks to pick up where Annie left off—and I need to see her tonight. *Really* see her. Not just feel her climb into bed with me when I don't even know what time it is.

I need to tell her that this place wouldn't be what it is without her—both because she reminded me that I deserved to make my own path, the whole reason this coffee shop is a reality to begin with, but also because she didn't let it fall apart when I was.

I pull my keys from my pocket, quickly finding the key to open up the door, my body going into shock when I turn on the lights and see all the progress I missed these past four weeks.

As I walk through the space, across the black and white tiled floor, I can see how much work and love my friends and Annie put into it.

The sky-blue walls are decorated with vibrant, mismatched art pieces and lush greenery, and the industrial lighting casts a gentle glow over the coffee bar. The equipment that's been in boxes for weeks is laid out across the bar next to all the stacks of different types of pastel-colored mugs and glassware.

I can almost smell the aroma of freshly brewed coffee mingling with the scent of baked goods; I can almost feel a warm, inviting ambiance; I can almost see the different people sitting at the tables lining the place, working, talking, sipping their coffee, reading the books they bought next door.

It's perfect.

It's mine.

And I couldn't have done it without my Annie girl.

CHAPTER 40
ANNIE

LUKE TEXTED me that he was going back into Lenny's today, and that he wouldn't be home when I arrived.

Seeing that gave me mixed feelings.

My mind had to focus on everything being thrown at me for this new rotation at the animal clinic I started at this week, but it kept going back to Luke.

I couldn't keep my thoughts straight, and even on my way home, I was reeling over how he's doing, how he's feeling, what's going through his head.

When Drew and Mia confronted me at Lenny's, it really made me take a step back and reevaluate my job as a supportive partner to Luke.

Luke has always been the one to tell me that everything was going to be okay, that we would figure it out, that things would be okay. I've relied so heavily on his positive outlook on life, his golden smile, the sparkle in his eyes—and I took so much of it for granted.

He was also my rock to lean on, the constant I knew would always be there, even when I tried to convince myself I didn't want it.

Now, it's my turn.

And I couldn't be his rock when I was burying myself alive.

After Emmett took Luke's three night shifts, and Mia and Drew took on No Name, the coffee shop, I could finally just *be* there for Luke. Maybe Luke doesn't need me to do everything for him, maybe he just needs *me*, especially now that he's going back to work.

I unlock the door to our apartment, and I'm greeted by Rosie.

When Luke is home, she's stuck to his side as if ready for him to lean on if he needs support. She's been the one who stayed with Luke since Bennett's funeral, promising me, Drew, Emmett, Mia, and Eddie that he was okay alone.

A small part of me hoped Luke would be home, not because I didn't want his first shift back at Lenny's to go well but because I just want to see him.

We've been living under the same roof, but it feels too much like when I had to move in after my apartment break-in, something that feels like a lifetime ago. There's too much space between us.

I miss him. He feels so far away, even though he's right here.

I don't push him to talk to me, but our conversations don't go far. I don't recognize him right now while he's living in this fog, but I'll wait forever for the Luke I know to make his way out of it.

It's Thursday, so I have a little extra energy because tomorrow is Friday and then it's the weekend—it makes sense in my head—and I won't be able to wind down knowing that Luke isn't home, so I decide to do what I do best and stress-bake.

I haven't had as much time to do it as I had planned when rotations started, but that doesn't mean I'm less stressed than I thought I'd be.

I kick off my shoes and drop my backpack on one of the

chairs at the kitchen counter, and then head into our bedroom to change out of my scrubs and into something cozy.

I wash my hands when I'm back in the kitchen, trying to focus on the smile I hope blooms on Luke's face when he sees I've made his favorite dessert, rather than worrying about how he's holding up right now.

I start by putting a pot over the stove to melt some dark chocolate for my cupcake batter.

Thanks to my gift from Luke, my cherry-red stand mixer, I make quick work of the rest of the batter, pouring it into the cupcake tray I put liners in while the mixer was going.

Just like the break-in at my old apartment, Luke buying me the stand mixer after my first day of my rotation year feels like a lifetime ago. It's only been just over two months, yet it feels like it could've been two years—two *lifetimes*.

I place the cupcakes in the oven, then quickly move onto washing the bowl to start on the peanut butter frosting, the recipe I know by heart, but I can't help but think about how the hell I ended up here in the first place. I'm making Luke cupcakes in *our* kitchen.

How did I ever think Luke wasn't it for me?

How did I convince myself that I wasn't the luckiest girl in the world for being the girl he loved? Or, how did I ignore that I was the stupidest person on the planet to let him go?

They say if you love someone, you let them go. If they come back, they were always yours. If they don't, they never were.

But Luke didn't have to come back to show me he was mine. I never really let him go in the first place.

While the cupcakes are cooling and the frosting is chilling, I take a quick shower—taking a page from Mia's book and blasting music to keep my mind from spinning—and pull on sweatpants and one of Luke's hoodies, anything to feel a little closer to him.

The bathroom door is closed, the mirror foggy from the

hot steam of the shower. I brush my damp hair, tucking it behind my ears, the music filling the room enough that I don't notice someone opening and shutting the front door behind them until I step out of the bathroom to catch Luke red-handed, a cupcake in his mouth.

"Hey, honey," he sheepishly says, talking around the cupcake in his mouth. His long hair is half pulled back in one of my hair ties, and I can't deny that I get why Drew likes how Emmett ties his back. His gray sweatshirt looks big on him, but there's color back in his face, a slight pink tinge to his cheek from the December air.

"Those weren't ready," I reply, trying to hide the smile on my face and the emotion clogging my throat, feeling like I'm seeing Luke for the first time in weeks.

"I couldn't help myself," he answers, wiping his mouth with the back of his hand and closing the distance between us. He wraps his arms around my waist, my arms instinctively going around his shoulders as he nuzzles his head into my neck.

"I miss you," he whispers against my skin, and my hold on him tightens.

"I'm right here," I answer, one of my hands going to the back of his head as I feel a hot tear drop from his cheek to my neck.

We stay like this for a few minutes, holding each other in the middle of the kitchen. I feel Luke's fist ball the fabric of his sweatshirt I'm wearing, pulling me in even closer. "Please don't ever leave me, Annie girl," he whispers, the words going straight to my heart, the heart that beats just for him. "I don't know if I could survive it."

I pull back against his tight embrace, just enough to hold his face in my hands, looking straight into his glistening baby blues. "You're never getting rid of me, sweetheart. Never." I lean in, pressing a soft kiss to his lips.

Wrapping my arms around his waist, I rest my head on his

chest. He rests his chin on the top of my head, exhaling before he says, "I don't know how I'd get through this without you. You've been taking care of everything, all on your own, on top of rotations. Seriously, Annie, I don't know what I did to deserve you."

"What you deserve is the space and time to heal. I'll do whatever I can to give that to you."

"I'm getting there," he says, letting out a sigh. "Maybe today is a fluke, but it's the first one I've felt like maybe things will be okay." I pull back slightly, just enough to look up at him. He continues, "I decided to push back the opening of the coffee shop. I want it to open on Bennet's birthday."

"December 14th."

Luke looks down at me and gives me a small smile. "Two weeks." He squeezes me a little tighter. "I can't thank you enough for preparing everything to open on the original date, but I needed more than just three days for *me* to be ready. Plus, it's one way I feel like I can honor him."

"I think it's a great idea," I reply, knowing how proud Bennett was of Luke for building this place from the ground up. Bennett will always be a part of it, not only because it'll open on his birthday or because he helped Luke with putting it together.

Bennett gave Luke the push he needed to find his own way. Without Bennett's blessing, or advice, or whatever you want to call it, Luke's path would've been the law firm, a path he never wanted but thought he needed to do.

"And I think I figured out a name," Luke adds, but he doesn't say more.

Instead, he lifts my chin and his lips find mine, drinking me in like I'm the only water source he'll ever need. He kisses me until I forget my own name, until I'm a mess in his arms, until he's begging me to bring him to bed.

So I do.

He kisses me as I fall apart in his arms, him following

close behind me, and the world around us fades. It's just us, in the darkness of our bedroom, the security of each other's arms.

Luke tells me stories of him and Bennett until I can't keep my eyes open, his fingers drawing mindless circles on my bare skin.

I fall asleep to the sound of his voice, the touch of his lips against my forehead, and the feeling that everything will be okay.

We'll figure it out.

Together.

CHAPTER 41

LUKE

"WHY WON'T you tell me the name?" Annie asks as she walks in front of me. I have my hands over her eyes as we make our way through the parking lot, headed to the soft opening of the coffee shop.

"If it's *my* desserts and baked goods that will be sold here, I feel like I should have a say in the name," she adds, and she has no idea how right she is.

Annie didn't even let me finish asking her if she'd handle the bakery side of things at the coffee shop before she said yes, promising she'd make the time she could during rotations.

This soft opening of the coffee shop is just the Lenny's crew, the grand opening being the day we'll be joined by other friends and family, minus Jack who decided he would be spending a few more weeks up north at his family's cabin and Bennett who is here in spirit.

Mia has been gaining traction on the shop's social media accounts, gaining a following and some excitement for the grand opening. We're so close to having it open to the public.

It's Sunday morning and the first snow of December, and I like to think the beautiful day is thanks to my brother.

Lately, the days have felt easier, lighter, *brighter*, than they have in weeks, and I'm trying my best to keep putting one foot in front of the other.

Life won't ever be the same without Bennett—things like the opening of the coffee shop, his birthday, the holidays, and all the other celebrations to come will look different without him, but I know he wouldn't want me to stop living, even if I can't always ignore the guilt of going on without him.

My talk with Emmett, opening up to Annie, continuing therapy—all of it has helped me realize that Bennett was always right.

Life is too short.

It's too short to not chase after the things you want and letting go of whatever holds you back from that.

I won't ever let go of Bennett, not for as long as I live, but I'm working every day to let go of this guilt I have of living when he doesn't get the same chance.

I like to think it's what he would've wanted for me.

"You've waited this long, you can wait two more minutes," I reply, pressing a kiss to the top of Annie's head, the snowflakes in her brown hair wetting my lips.

After my talk with Emmett, my mind was all over the place, my feelings started to make more sense, but I couldn't get what he said about honoring his sister in his everyday life out of my head. I also couldn't get the thought of Annie out of my head.

When I ran out of Lenny's to my car, the air felt clearer, the moon shined brighter, the pavement under my sneakers felt more stable.

When I got home, it felt *normal*, like I was coming home from work, on any *normal* day, to find Annie in the shower after a night of stress-baking—the dark chocolate cupcakes cooling on our kitchen counter, the smell of the peanut butter frosting still lingering in the air.

For the first time in weeks, I felt like my senses were

awakened, that I wasn't just living in black and white anymore.

It didn't feel like I was underwater, that my limbs were fighting the pressure trying to drown me. I felt like I was finally able to swim.

"The guests of honor!" Drew yells, holding bundled-up Lennon on her hip, one of Emmett's arm around them, the other holding something behind his back, something I asked him to bring for me as a surprise for Annie.

Mia and Eddie are finishing up taping a big red banner, Eddie pulling a pair of scissors from his back pocket for me to cut as our official opening, and I can't believe we actually did it, that *I* actually did it.

The place is done, ready to open for business, and it's mine.

Not my dad's, not what I think he wanted or what would have made him proud—it's mine.

I walk Annie and me up to the door, all of our friends knowing the name of the coffee shop, and the reasoning behind it, Annie being the only one still in the dark.

"I haven't had a chance to say congratulations," I say to Eddie and Mia. Annie told me a few days ago that Mia was pregnant, but I kept to myself that I've had a strong feeling since Halloween.

"Thanks, man," Eddie says, from where he's standing behind Mia, his arms wrapped around her. I give Mia a little wink, gaining a smile and shake of the head from her, both of us keeping the fact that I already knew a secret for the two of us.

"Are we going to get this show on the road or what?" Annie says, my hands still over her eyes.

"So impatient, Annie girl," I tease, warranting chuckles from our friends, even Emmett.

"I'll show you impatient when I break your fingers," she says through her teeth, but the sentiment is quickly forgotten when I uncover her eyes and she sees the fresh vinyl on the door with the name of my—*our*—coffee shop.

In all honesty, anything that's mine is already hers.

She brings her hand to cover her mouth, the Hey Honey Coffee and Co. logo, beautifully designed by Mia, was the perfect final touch to the coffee shop. The bold letters are surrounded by a wreath of roses with little bees flying around them. Under the logo, the words in vinyl go straight to my chest. "Est. December 14"—Bennett's birthday.

It took me a long time to figure out who I was when I wasn't out there trying to impress the father who never cared much about my success to begin with, especially if it didn't benefit him. It took me an even longer time to realize that I didn't need him to be proud of me for me to be proud of myself.

Since high school, since giving up the hockey scholarship, I haven't made many decisions that were for me and my future.

Today changes that. Today marks the day where I am proud of myself, and how I got here, with the people who support me at my side—those who got in the way nowhere to be seen.

"What did I say about calling me 'honey'?" Annie asks, but the emotion in her voice is impossible for her to hide.

"What can I say? You're just too sweet," I reply, echoing my words from months ago, the words even truer now than they were then.

I knew naming this place after Annie was what I wanted to do because I wouldn't be the person I am today without her.

Without her and my brothers, I don't know where I would be.

I put my hands on her shoulders, turning her around to face me, and I will never get over how absolutely breathtaking she is. Her long brown waves, her big brown eyes, her cherry red lips—all mine.

"Thank you for loving me, Annie girl. I don't know how I got so lucky to be loved by someone like you. Growing up with you, watching you blossom into the beautiful person you are today, getting to live life with you, I truly am the luckiest man alive."

I place my hands on either side of her face, drowning in those eyes, watching them glisten as she listens to my words.

"You have been here for me through the hardest time in my life, and I plan on spending the rest of my life showing you how thankful I am for you. Life doesn't always give us second chances, so there's no way I'm letting you go this time. You're it for me, Annie girl. You're the fire that burns inside me, my better half, the reason I wanted to become a man like my brother, one that would make you proud."

I reach out to Emmett, his hand coming out from behind his back, revealing a bouquet of roses, one for all twenty years I have loved Annie. I hold them to her, a small gasp escaping her lips. "I have loved you since the moment I saw you, the love only growing as you let me be a part of your life. I couldn't have done this without you, honey."

A tear slips down her cheek, and I wipe it away with my thumb. She's wearing a small smile on her face, one that makes the smile on mine grow even wider. "I love you more," she says. The emotion in her voice makes my heart feel heavy —I don't think I'll ever get used to hearing her say she loves me, not after waiting for so many years to hear it. "More than you'll ever know," she adds.

"Is that so?" I hum, never backing away from one of Annie's challenges. "I guess you'll just have to show me then."

She rolls her eyes, but her arms wrap around my neck. "You wish," she teases before her lips crash into mine, and it feels like coming home.

EPILOGUE: NINE MONTHS LATER

ANNIE

I CAN'T BELIEVE I'm in my last month of vet school rotations.

Today marked my very last *first* week of a new rotation, and the beginning of my externship at the Milwaukee Zoo as part of their Animal Health Center program. After this month, I'll start my three-year Zoological Medicine Residency, working with the zoo and all the exotic animals.

It's been a busy year—and it's not slowing down anytime soon—but I love it and never felt so confident in where I am, what I'm doing, and where I'm going. I'm grateful to have the world's best partner supporting me through it, even more grateful to have finally learned to *let* him.

I'm on my way now to meet Luke at Hey Honey's to help him close for the night before we head over to Lenny's to meet our friends for a few drinks.

I've barely heard from Drew or Mia all week, so I'm excited to have some time to catch up with them. It's weird to hear so little from them, but I chalked it up to them both having their hands full lately.

My two best friends are *both* moms now, and it freaks me out if I think about it too much. Lennon is just over a year old—the girl already being such a sassy extrovert, so different from both her parents and keeping them both on their toes—and Mia gave birth to freaking *twins* a few weeks ago.

It fills my heart in ways I can't explain to see our little Lenny's family growing more and more with Lennon, Nadia, and Naomi, and I can't wait for Luke and me to add to the mix one day.

But for right now, we have Hey Honey's as our addition to the family.

Business has been great for the coffee shop, and I love that it's right next door to Lenny's—the two of us and our friends now having another place to spend time together.

Another place that's ours.

And even after nine months, I can't believe he named the place after his stupid nickname for me.

Luke is the only person in the world who uses the word "sweet" to describe me, even if I'm still convinced he just says it to get a rise out of me, and I think it actually just proves that he's insane.

And even though I tell Luke everything now, after keeping him in the dark for seven years, I'm going to keep to myself that I never really hated the nickname to begin with.

It was all hands on deck for the Lenny's crew the first month the shop was open. We figured it would be easy because we all worked so many bartending shifts at Lenny's, but we realized *very* quickly that Emmett, Eddie, and I were *not* meant to be baristas.

There was a learning curve for Luke too, but he was able to staff the place by January, hiring Ava as his manager—the coffee shop hours working better for her than the bar's—so he could take on more managerial duties.

Hey Honey's has also brought in a lot of customers to all the businesses in the building, and I'm so incredibly proud of Luke. He's worked his ass off since the grand opening on

Bennett's birthday, and I know having something that's *his* means so much to him.

Not going to lie, it was a little rocky at first because he put *so* much into it, trying to distract himself from dealing with the loss of his brother. His grief was unpredictable, and I didn't want him to bury it.

It took some time, but he eventually found a healthy balance.

I think Luke sees everything he's putting into Hey Honey's as fulfilling a promise he made to himself—and Bennett. Luke is doing what *he* wants to do while living by the lessons Bennett taught him.

It was really a lesson we all needed because life truly is too short to not chase after the things we want or hold on to things that try to hold us back.

Especially when that thing holding you back is yourself.

Luke works so hard to make Hey Honey's into something not only he can be proud of but something he knows Bennett would be proud of too.

When I pull into the parking lot, I notice Luke already turned the lights off. The coffee shop closes at eight on weeknights, which isn't for a few more minutes, so I'm not sure why it already looks like he shut everything down for the night.

It isn't until I climb out of my car and walk up to the door, looking through the rose wreath vinyl on the glass, that I see he hasn't closed just yet.

He's waiting for me.

I pull the door open about to ask what the hell is going on, but I can't.

My mouth goes dry when I see the shop lit up with candles, the welcoming scent of coffee still lingering in the air from another busy day.

I look down to the floor to see a path lined with rose petals.

A path that leads me to the coffee bar where Luke is standing.

He's in his work attire, jeans and a white t-shirt with his black apron strapped around his waist, a black Sharpie still tucked behind his ear.

He looks like he does after every shift on any normal day.

"Hey, honey," he says with a grin, so calm and nonchalant. It's a stark contrast to how fast my heart is starting to beat. The bright smile on his face lights up the room almost as much as the candles, and it makes my knees go weak, the same way it always has.

I know he wants me to walk down this path he set out for me with the rose petals, but I can't get my feet to move. It's fitting that, even in a moment like this, I don't do what he wants me to. It just so happens that I *can't* right now.

I'm too busy spiraling over what the hell is happening.

"Cat got your tongue?" he asks, closing the distance between us.

He takes a hand out of his pocket to place his index finger under my chin, closing my mouth, which I didn't even realize was open.

This isn't actually happening.

He isn't *actually* about to do what I think he's going to.

Right?

No, he wouldn't choose a random Friday night when I'm just coming to help him close before we get drinks with our friends. I'm still in my stupid scrubs from the day, my hair braided back in two French braids I'm sure are seconds away from falling out.

This is not happening tonight.

He places a small kiss on my lips, but I notice he keeps his other hand in the pocket of his apron.

I want to ask him what all of this means, but all thoughts cease when he opens his mouth.

"Well, while I've got you quiet," he starts, smirking. I

should give him back my usual sass, but I couldn't even if I wanted to.

No words are coming to mind.

"Annie girl," he whispers, bringing me back to focus on him. "There's something I've wanted to ask you from the moment I saw you."

There's a slight blush to his cheeks, his blonde hair looking more golden in the candlelight. He keeps his eyes on mine as he slowly drops down to one knee, and my hands go to cover my mouth. My eyes start to prickle as I see him pull his hand out of his apron, and the first tear falls when I see the little blue box.

"It probably wouldn't have meant much at the time, seeing as though we were only six, but it's true. I've always known you were it for me, Annie girl, and I plan on spending the rest of my life proving it to you." In disbelief, a small laugh escapes from me and another tear trails down my cheek —and I let it, no longer afraid of letting them fall.

He really is going to do this right now.

This is happening.

"You're the anchor that keeps me grounded, the moon in my sky. I want nothing more than to be yours forever." I watch as he opens the small box in his hands, pulling out a ring I can't even take a moment to look at because he's already slipping it on my finger as he asks, "Will you marry me?"

This helps me find my voice, "You can't even wait for my answer?" The sentiment makes his eyes sparkle even more. He knows my answer, knows that he's it for me too. After all we've been through, all our history and what we've overcome, we're inevitable in the very best way.

I look down at where Luke holds my hand, and I'm rendered speechless again.

"Luke," I manage to say.

"Just like the one I gave you, all those years ago," Luke

says. I still feel his eyes on me. "When you let me be your boyfriend. The first time," he adds, making me let out another small laugh.

The ring he chose has a band made to look like a vine, with its leaves formed by small diamonds, with the largest forming a rose.

"It's perfect," I whisper as I meet his gaze.

I have more to say to him—I want to tell him how much I love him, how much I can't wait to be his wife, how grateful I am that we made it here.

I want to tell him how proud of us I am, so proud that we finally made it—we did it.

But I don't have to.

He knows—he always does.

EXTENDED EPILOGUE: THREE YEARS AND THREE MONTHS LATER

LUKE

SHE DID IT.

After a crazy rotation year, a three-year externship at the zoo, and passing the North American Veterinary Licensure Examination and the Wisconsin Statutes and Rules Examination, she fucking did it.

Annie is officially a licensed veterinarian, specializing in exotic animals.

She did it, just like I know she could, and I'm so proud of her.

It's been just over three months since her graduation, and she wakes up every day excited to go to the Milwaukee Zoo and work with the animals in her care.

She's worked her ass off, and it feels like it's been forever since she's slowed down. I've made it my mission for this week following Christmas to take some much-needed rest.

Especially because our baby boy is due in less than two months.

I've watched my best friends become parents over the last four years—Emmett and Drew now having a four-year old Lennon and two-year old Knox, and Mia and Eddie with their three-year old twin girls, Nadia and Naomi. Our Lenny's crew has just gotten bigger and bigger, and I'm Annie and I are finally adding to the mix.

Jackson Bennett Owens will be here to wreak havoc with the second generation of the crew in no time.

We're headed over to Mia and Eddie's house for our Christmas Day tradition of holiday movies in our pajamas, and it's safe to say that the tradition looks much different than it did the first time we did it.

Now, we have two dogs and four kids with a fifth on the way that make the day so much more magical—and chaotic.

Annie also isn't the only one pregnant.

When Annie and I announced the pregnancy to our friends, it turned out, Mia and Drew were *both* also pregnant, but neither one wanted to say anything to steal Annie's thunder.

We didn't find out until a few weeks later that Drew was pregnant, Mia saying she was too when Drew and Emmett told us all.

Our three girls have three more boys on the way.

Just like our Sunday dinners, we switch off on who hosts the holidays every year—not that it really matters since Mia and Eddie's house is down the street from Drew and Emmett's, and Drew told me the one across from them just went up for sale.

I'm getting Rosie on her leash while Annie's finishing getting ready in the bathroom, and I take a second to look at the apartment we've shared over these last years.

I think we've officially outgrown it.

"No."

I turn to see Annie coming out of the bathroom, her brown hair is twisted back in a clip, her brown eyes and cherry lips on full display.

She crosses her arms, but it's not as intimidating as it used to be. Not when she has to rest her forearms on her swollen belly.

I'll never forget the day Annie came home and told me she was pregnant. We weren't actively trying because of how busy she was with her externship—we haven't even gotten officially married yet because things are *just* now starting to slow down.

She got home from work before me that day, and I came home to her holding a little red bag.

"I have a gift for you," she blurted out right as I walked in the door. She looked nervous, tucking her hair behind her ears as she watched me shut the door and walk towards her.

Seeing Annie nervous barely happens, not since I found her behind the bar at Lenny's over a decade ago.

I stopped just a foot from where she was standing in the middle of the living room, no doubt having been pacing since the moment she got home.

She was still in her scrubs, and I could see the tops of her ears were bright red.

"Okay," I slowly said, trying to fight the smile threatening to overcome my lips. Annie is usually so in control of her feelings, and it's taken years for her to be less and less protective over them. While, for the most part, I've always been able to see through the defenses, I like that she doesn't try to hide her emotions from me anymore.

"Here," she said, pushing the bag into my chest. "No, wait. This is stupid," she quickly added, taking the bag back.

I didn't move a muscle, not wanting to scare her in the moment of what I can only assume was vulnerability. These types of moments come more often now, but I still have to tread carefully.

I didn't know what she had for me or if there was something she needed to tell me, but I know my Annie girl. There are times I can push her and times I can't.

This was a time I knew I couldn't.

She groaned. "Whatever. Just take it," she managed to get out through her teeth, pushing the bag back into my chest. When she held it there for a few seconds, I decided it was safe to grab.

I felt her eyes on me as I took out the few pieces of tissue paper, pulling out a black t-shirt.

"Thanks, honey," I said, wanting her to know that I am grateful for any gift she ever wants to give me—I can never have too many T-shirts.

"You didn't even read what it says," she snapped, but I snuck a glance at her face to find her blushing, her lips pouted.

I put the gift bag and tissue paper on the coffee table next to us, using both hands to unfold the shirt, and held it out in front of me.

I read the white bubble letters aloud. "'I heart hot moms'?"

Realization hit me when I said the word "moms", and I dropped the shirt to the floor.

I stepped towards her, closing all space between us. "Are you serious?" I said in disbelief, a huge grin taking up most of my face.

I felt my eyes begin to water as Annie nodded her head. A small smile formed on her lips, and her teeth sank into her bottom lip. I wrapped my arms around her, pulling her into me and lifting her feet off the ground. Her legs immediately wrapped around my waist as I spun us around.

"We're going to be parents, Annie girl!" I exclaimed. Her laugh filled the room, and it was music to my ears.

I finally set her down, but I couldn't let go of her. My hands stayed on her hips as she reached into the pocket of her scrubs, pulling out two positive pregnancy tests.

"I found out today when I was showing one of the first-year vet students interning at the zoo how to do an ultrasound. She was a little nervous about using the ultrasound on one of the pregnant animals, so I let her try on me. Safe to say, it was a learning moment for the both of us when we saw the little black oval in my uterus."

We had a doctor's appointment the following week and found out Annie was six weeks pregnant and the hottest mom out there.

Today, in honor of our Christmas Day tradition, she's wearing her pair of green silk pajamas she got for the both of us. They're adorned with red and white stockings and candy canes, but I opted for a different look—the same look I wore last year. "You're not wearing that," she reprimands. "You scared the shit out of Nadia and Naomi last year, and Lennon already got Emmett to admit to her that Santa wasn't real."

"Come on, Annie girl. Where's your Christmas cheer?" I reply through the fake white beard I'm wearing, trying to make my voice lower and more Santa-like. "I'll even let you sit on my lap," I add with a wink.

"Ew. No one likes a creepy Santa. Take it off. We have to go," she says, but I can see her fighting a smile and can almost hear the laugh she's holding in. "Now," she adds, turning to walk to the kitchen to finish packing up the containers of brownies we're bringing over.

Annie now prepares *three* different types of brownies for these sorts of occasions—one batch with frosting, one with powdered sugar, and one with rainbow sprinkles for Lennon, Knox, and the twins.

"Fine," I concede, heading to our bedroom. I quickly pull off my Santa costume and throw on the pajamas that Annie got for us.

"Happy?" I ask when I meet her back out by the kitchen, buttoning up the long-sleeved green top that matches hers. Before she can answer me, I add, "Because I'm not."

"Oh, so now you hate matching with me?" she teases. "Where's that attitude every year during Halloween?"

She's facing the counter, putting the cover on the last container of brownies. I lace my arms around her, my hands resting on her bump. I pull her back into my chest, the scent of jasmine and rose washing over me, still somehow making my head spin.

She leans her head back against me, and I press a kiss to her hair. "Ready to go?"

I feel her nod, but neither one of us moves.

With Annie in my arms, I could stay right here forever.

I glance at the clock and see it's almost eight. We really do need to leave—we let the kids stay up later than usual after our Christmas Eve dinner last night at Drew and Emmett's, but children four and under aren't known to sleep, especially on Christmas morning—but I don't want to let go.

I slowly slide my hands from her belly, but I stop when I feel a little kick against my palm.

"Looks like someone else is ready to go, too," Annie laughs, her hands coming to rest over mine, giving them a squeeze.

Will it always feel like this?

Like I can never get enough of her?

I hope so.

LENNY'S BARTENDERS: FAMILY TREE

Drew and Emmett (*Giving Me Butterflies*)
Lennon Katherine Ryan
Knox Theodore Ryan
Beau Daniel Ryan
Lydia Genevieve Ryan

Mia and Eddie (*Crash & Burn*)
Nadia Tyler Ramirez
Naomi Taryn Ramirez
Ryker James Ramirez

Annie and Luke (*Back to You*)
Jackson Bennett Owens
Journee Brooklyn Owens

ACKNOWLEDGMENTS

We did it.

We made it to the end of the Lenny's Bartenders series.

It is such a bittersweet feeling to say that the series has come to an end. This is the series that made me an author; these are the characters who healed me in ways I never thought possible; these are the books that brought me to this one-of-a-kind community of authors and readers.

I don't know if I'll ever truly say goodbye to Lenny's crew because I just can't imagine their story ending here.

Thank you to my wonderful alpha readers, beta readers, and ARC readers. I have each and every one of you to thank for helping me make Luke and Annie's story what it is.

Thank you to my editor, Ellie (@byelliesedits), for all the time and effort you put into this story.

Thank you to all my readers who make my author dream a reality—this series is all because of your love and support. I am so incredibly grateful.

Thank you to my real-life found family who inspired these books and the Lenny's crew. This group of friends is inspired by you all—you've all shown me the true meaning of "friends who became family."

An extra special thank you to my Elle-Bell, who was with me for every step of the way for this book. I've said it once, and I'll say it over and over again—I never want to know what it's like to write a book that you aren't a part of. Thank you for loving these characters and this Lenny's Bartenders world; it wouldn't be what it is without you.

And last but not least, thank you to my wonderful partner in life, Max. I wish I could put into words how much you mean to me. So much of you and the love you've shown me inspired Emmett, Eddie, and Luke, and you are the reason it is so easy to write about love. I'm so lucky to be loved by someone like you.

WHAT'S NEXT?

The Lenny's Bartenders series is officially complete! So…
what comes next?

Read *From the Ashes*, book one of the
Hey Honey's Baristas series, now!

Rumi Matthews isn't just responsible for herself anymore. She has a daughter to worry about. And she refuses to let her daughter grow up in the same kind of house she did. Rumi will do whatever it takes to make that happen—even if that means fleeing in the middle of the night.

Jack Hasting has avoided his responsibilities long enough; it's time to go back to work. As a firefighter, it's his duty is to protect the lives around him. It's the one thing he couldn't do for his best friend, and the one thing he refuses to ever let happen again.

ABOUT THE AUTHOR

Katy is the indie author based in Milwaukee. Her favorite trope is forced proximity, and she is a firm believer that found families are the best families.

Lover of all things romance, pop punk, tattoos, anime, rainy days, matcha, her husband, and her daughter, Katy's purpose for writing is to remind readers that you are deserving of the love you read about.

When she's not writing, you can find her reading, or adding to her never-ending TBR.

instagram.com/authorkatymichele

tiktok.com/@authorkatymichele

threads.com/@authorkatymichele

goodreads.com/katymichele

amazon.com/author/katymichele

ALSO BY KATY MICHELE

Lenny's Bartenders

Giving Me Butterflies (Drew & Emmett)

Crash & Burn (Mia & Eddie)

Back to You (Annie & Luke)

Hey Honey's Baristas

From the Ashes (Rumi & Jack)

Call You Mine (Ava & Anderson)